THE GORE

Also by Joseph Citro

The Vermont Ghost Guide, 2000

Guardian Angels, 1999

Green Mountains, Dark Tales, 1999

Shadow Child, 1998

Passing Strange, 1996

Green Mountain Ghosts, 1994

Deus-X, 1994

Dark Twilight, 1991

Vermont Lifer (writer/editor), 1986

Hardscrabble Books—Fiction of New England

Sarah Orne Jewett (Sarah Way Sherman, ed.), *The Country of the Pointed Firs and Other Stories*

Lisa MacFarlane, ed., *This World Is Not Conclusion: Faith in Nineteenth-Century New England Fiction*

Anne Whitney Pierce, *Rain Line*

Kit Reed, *J. Eden*

Rowland E. Robinson (David Budbill, ed.), *Danvis Tales: Selected Stories*

Roxana Robinson, *Summer Light*

Rebecca Rule, *The Best Revenge: Short Stories*

R. D. Skillings, *Where the Time Goes*

Lynn Stegner, *Pipers at the Gates of Dawn: A Triptych*

Theodore Weesner, *Novemberfest*

W. D. Wetherell, *The Wisest Man in America*

Edith Wharton (Barbara A. White, ed.), *Wharton's New England: Seven Stories and* Ethan Frome

Thomas Williams, *The Hair of Harold Roux*

THE GORE

A NOVEL BY

Joseph A. Citro

University Press of New England

HANOVER AND LONDON

Published by University Press of New England, Hanover, NH 03755

© 2000 by Joseph A. Citro

Originally published in 1990 as *The Unseen* by Warner Books, Inc., New York

Printed in the United States of America

5 4 3 2 1

LIBRARY OF CONGRESS CATALOGING-IN-PUBLICATION DATA

Citro, Joseph A.

The gore : a novel / by Joseph A. Citro

p.   cm. — (Hardscrabble books)

ISBN 1–58465–053–2 (alk. paper)

1. Vermont—Fiction. I. Title. II. Series.

PS3553.I865 G67 2000

813'.54—dc21   00–009306

Contents

The Northeast Kingdom is a flint country. Sprawling for upwards of two thousand square miles south of the Canadian border, it's a mosaic of gnarled mountains, carpeted by forest, laced by streams that flow over the bedrock granite, the forests interrupted here and there by hardscrabble farms that milk the thin topsoil, and cold: no one who does not live there knows how cold.

The Kingdom has people to match its climate; they are a mixture of old Yankee stock and the descendants of French Canadians who migrated from Quebec over the last 100 years. Many are sunk in a desperate rural poverty; the bulk are country people with a distinctive life-style. Hardworking and harddrinking, dedicated to hunting and fishing, legally and illegally, they work at logging or farming or hold menial jobs in the handful of factories in the region. The land is austerely beautiful and holds a powerful appeal, even as it flays the fat from the lives of the people.

HAMILTON E. DAVIS

Of Rocks and Other Hard Places

Vanguard Press, August 1983

PART ONE

Seeing Things

Don't ever take a fence down until
you know the reason it was put up.

G. K. CHESTERTON

1

Lunker

The worry started the moment Claude "Lunker" Lavigne entered the bar.

Not wanting to stare, Roger Newton polished the countertop with a damp, sour-smelling cloth. Now and again he peeked over the frame of his eyeglasses, watching the big man.

Lavigne was bone-white, his blue work shirt dark with sweat, his eyes glazed. He lumbered like a tired plow horse through the maze of chairs and round-top tables, mindlessly bumping one, then another, making his way to a seat in the corner. When Lavigne sat, gripping the table's edge, Roger could see from way across the room that the big man's hands were shaking.

Roger knew Lavigne slightly, but only from the bar. Because of his size—well over six feet—and his bulk—an easy three hundred pounds—he had been nicknamed "Lunker" by coworkers at the power company. Yet in spite of his size, Lavigne was always soft-spoken and polite. A big, peaceful man, a gentle giant who reminded Roger of Hoss Cartwright from the old "Bonanza" TV show.

Lavigne rubbed his rheumy eyes, pressed the sweat from his forehead, ran his hands through greasy black hair. He closed his eyes and massaged his temples as if he were suffering from a disabling headache.

3

Roger glanced at the old railroad clock on the wall; it was three-fifteen.

I'll bet he's been laid off, thought Roger. Lots of people were getting the ax these days and as bartender, Roger was often the first to know it. *If not, and if he orders his usual Bud Light, he'll be drinking on the job and that could get him fired!* But it wasn't for Roger to judge. If he started judging his patrons he'd quickly put himself out of business.

Tossing aside the bar rag, Roger asked, "What can I get you?"

Lavigne didn't answer. He just looked straight ahead, his white-knuckled hands clenching the table's edge.

"Mr. Lavigne, can I get you something?"

Lavigne looked up. His eyes were red, glassy.

"I probably shouldn't." His voice shook as much as his hands. "But gimme a shot. A big one."

Stepping to a triple row of bottles that partially concealed the bar's mirror, Roger called over his shoulder, "What's your poison?"

Silence.

Roger shrugged, thinking his question had sounded dumb. He waited another moment for a reply before taking a nearly empty fifth of Canadian Club and pouring a double measure. There was almost another shot left in the bottle; Roger tipped it in. The guy looked like he could use it.

He brought the glass, nearly half full, over to Lavigne. Beside it the chaser, Lavigne's traditional Bud Light.

When Lavigne grabbed the glass he looked like a race car driver grabbing the stick shift. The amber liquid vanished in a gulp.

"Another?" Roger asked.

Lavigne nodded, reached into his pants pocket for a wad of bills, and threw them on the table.

Roger hesitated, spoke softly. "Is . . . is there something wrong, Mr. Lavigne?"

The man looked up. Then his eyes scanned the barroom as if making sure they were alone. He cleared his throat. "Somethin' damned funny," he said, reaching for the beer glass. It seemed as if he didn't want to say more.

Roger returned to the bar, empty glass in hand. Should he pressure Lavigne for more information? It had been Roger's recurring question ever since he'd become a bar owner: When does one say something? When does one mind his own business?

"Bad day at work, Mr. Lavigne?"

Right away Roger felt he was being too nosy. These Northcountry Vermonters were a private lot, closemouthed. Stereotypically taciturn. Thinking he'd better back off, he put the rye and chaser before the man, then turned away.

"Hold on a minute there, Roger." Lavigne handed him a ten-dollar bill. "Have one with me, why don't you?" There was an imploring quality in Lavigne's eyes. The bill vibrated in his hand as Roger took it.

"I will. Thanks."

After carrying the money to the cash register, Roger counted out the change—a five and a single—then poured himself a weak one, just strong enough to color the water. He hurried back to the table and sat across from his only customer.

This time Lavigne sipped the liquor, licked his lips. Belched.

"I seen somethin' in the woods today."

Lavigne's eyes fastened on Roger's, as if he thought he had told the whole story.

Roger was interested. He hadn't totally rid himself of his reporter's curiosity.

"What were you doing in the woods? I thought you worked for the power company . . . ?"

Lavigne cleared his throat. "Checkin' the lines. Part of my job. Twice a year I walk the path across the mountain. Inspect the wire, give the pylons an eyeballin'. Look for damage. Gotta make sure the brush ain't gettin' too thick or the punks ain't shootin' off any insulators. . .

"I was way the hell up in the boonies. Had to leave my truck more'n a mile from the road, 'cause of them ledges. The rest I done on foot, prob'ly two, three miles. Maybe more. Nothin' out there, you know, nothin' but trees and rocks and wind."

Roger nodded attentively as Lavigne continued. "Was pretty

early when I got there. The dew's risin' leavin' thick little swirls of fog everywhere you look. First thing I notice is, well, it's real quiet. No jays squawkin', no squirrels chitterin'. Nothin'. It give me a kinda funny feelin', know what I mean?"

Roger nodded again. He really didn't know, he wasn't a woodsman or hunter, but he knew better than to interrupt.

"Well, sir, there's a place up the gore—kind of knoll that goes up, then dips down, then goes up again. That's where you're in for some real heavy duty climbin'. That's where I seen it."

"What did you see?" For a minute Roger felt like he was about to be had, as if Lavigne were setting him up for the punch line of a joke. More than once Roger had been made the butt of good-natured jests. It was almost a rite of initiation, the locals' way of accepting him into their community.

But Lavigne didn't seem to be joking; he wasn't the joking type. Although he had calmed a bit, his hands were still trembling. His red-rimmed eyes made him look as if he might start crying at any moment.

What could have frightened the big man so much? What could leave him so pale and shaken?

Almost by reflex Roger thought that whatever it was might make a hell of a story. Then he paused, reminded himself that he'd given up journalism. His job as a reporter for the *Burlington Banner* had ended almost two years ago when he'd decided to try something new. He'd poured all his savings, and the money he'd inherited when his father died, into a down payment on the Fife and Drum Pub here in Eureka, Vermont. As the new owner, the first thing he'd done was change its name to The Newsroom, a kind of homage to his past.

Lavigne cleared his throat, groped in the pocket of his blue shirt for a package of cigarettes. He took a Camel and lighted it, inhaling deeply. He blew a great cloud of blue-gray smoke into the air, then looked at nothingness.

"I'll be goddamned if I know what I seen," he said, shaking his head slowly as smoke curled from his nostrils.

" 'Course, I've heard all the stories about the gore. Anyone growin' up around here's bound to hear 'em. But I never paid them much heed . . ."

Again, Roger didn't interrupt. He leaned forward to show Lavigne how carefully he was listening. Clearly the man wanted to talk about it, but he needed to work up the nerve with alcohol and a lengthy preface. Roger had seen the pattern before, knew better than to rush him.

"Let me get you another shot. On the house."

Lavigne nodded stiffly.

When Roger returned, Lavigne was tapping the table with callused fingertips. The men sat face-to-face. Lavigne's eyes moved furtively side to side.

In the background the FM radio played soft country and western music. The railroad clock ticked rhythmically.

"Well, like I was sayin', I'm comin' up on that little knoll up there. Sun's out nice and clear. Oh, it's kinda foggy, I admit, but there's no mistakin' what happened. I know for certain I seen somethin' back there in the woods. It's just beyond the edge of where them powerline trails is cut back."

Roger sipped his drink, never taking his I eyes from Lavigne's puzzled gaze.

"Now, you 'member how quiet it is, so okay, maybe I'm, sorta edgy already. I mean, hell, I'm lookin' all around to see what's spookin' the birds. I'm figgerin' maybe there's some big game around, deer maybe, or a moose that's wandered down from Canada. I figger I'll take note, maybe come back durin' huntin' season. 'Course them powerlines is always overhunted durin' the season. But I'm thinkin', hey, maybe I'll come back a little early. . ."

Lavigne forced a chuckle that changed into a cough. He cleared his throat wetly. "All of a sudden I've got the funniest feelin', like I'm bein' watched. Can you picture that? Here I am, miles outside of nowhere, way out in the middle of the damn forest, and it feels like somethin's got an eye on me.

"So I starts lookin' back, eyeballin' the line of the forest on either side a me. I got real good eyesight, you know. Never wore glasses in my life. So I'm tellin' you, fog or no, if they's somethin' out there, I'll see it . . ."

"Umm-hmm . . ."

" 'Bout a hundred yards up ahead, an' over on the right, I see somethin' in between a bush and a big maple tree. It's a little furry thing, no more'n two foot tall. Black colored. I figger prob'ly it's a little black bear cub. That's what it looked like, anyways. A bear cub. But it's back in the shadows enough so I couldn't've got a real good look at it even if that bush hadn't been partially in the way.

"Well, there it sets, pretty as you please, until . . ."

Lavigne's eyes widened as he watched the scene replay in his memory. His face was white as a cloud.

". . . until . . ."

He took his empty glass in both hands, squeezed it as his knuckles paled again.

". . . all of a sudden the fuckin' thing starts to change right in front of my eyes. I seen it! First it looks like it's risin' up on its hind legs, and then . . . and then, why Christ, it starts to grow! No lie! The damned thing gets bigger and bigger until it's standin' right up on two legs. Swear to God. It's standin' up taller'n a man! And I watched it happen! I watched that fuckin' thing change shape!"

Lavigne looked down to where his hands held his glass.

He shook his head, blowing air through pursed lips.

"Then what happened?"

Their eyes met. Roger saw a film of moisture along Lavigne's lower eyelid. Momentarily the water would collect and tumble out as a tear. Not wanting to embarrass the man, Roger looked away.

"I got the fuck out of there. That's what happened. I turned tail an' run all the way down the hill to my truck. I didn't dare turn around, I was afraid that goddamn thing was comin' after me, gainin' on me. Christ, it scared the b'Jesus out a me. I'll tell ya one thing, mister, I don't never wanna see nothin' like that again."

2

Mr. Spooner

Harley Spooner tipped his cap to the driver and stepped off the Vermont Transit bus. For the first time in his seventy-nine years he set foot in what he referred to as that modern Sodom, Burlington, Vermont.

With both sneakered feet on the ground, Harley faced the University of Vermont campus. He stood at the northern end of the green, looking at all the stately brick buildings surrounding him. Gosh, there were so many of them; he had no idea where to go.

Confused, he thought of his friend Cooly. Too bad the old badger couldn't have come with him. A pity, yes, but there was only enough bus fare for one. Harley's $127-a-month Social Security check didn't go very far. And there was never anything extra.

Clutching the wrinkled brown grocery bag to his chest, Harley started across the center of the vast lawned area. He preferred the feel of grass under his feet to the concrete walkways nearby. Book-carrying students passed him occasionally, and that surprised him. He hadn't expected anyone would go to school in the middle of summer.

A girl with thick, curly blonde hair looked curiously at Harley. The young man beside her, his hair in a crew cut scarred by a funny gray streak, wore army trousers with camouflage patterns. Both youngsters stared unabashedly at the old man.

9

Harley looked back at them, blinking. What were they looking at, his clothes? He thought he'd dressed pretty nice for the occasion. His medium-size red flannel shirt hung like a loose skin on his tiny grizzled frame. Buttoned to the neck, it rippled in the afternoon breeze. At a height of five-three Harley had always found it difficult to buy clothes that fit. His baggy blue jeans, salvaged from a plastic bag of discarded clothing at the Eureka dump, had to be rolled several times at the cuff to keep him from tripping on them.

As the young couple stared, he clutched his paper sack more tightly, noticing how heavy it had become.

"What you got in the bag, Pops?" the boy asked. The blonde girl giggled.

They obviously were not Vermonters. In fact, a trace of a New York accent distorted the boy's speech. Harley didn't want to visit with this couple, but as long as he had their attention he might as well take advantage of it. "Got som'pin to show one a yer teachers."

At first they just looked puzzled, as if they hadn't heard a word he'd said. Then the young man's face brightened with understanding. "Who you looking for?"

Harley wasn't sure how much he should tell this young fella. He hadn't missed the hint of ridicule at the beginning of their conversation.

"Gotta fin' somebody knows som'pin about rock."

"Jeez," said the boy, scratching at his two-tone crew cut, "I don't really know who to suggest. I mean, I'm an English major. . . . You probably want Geology or something. Why don't you check with 'Information' at Waterman?" The boy said, pointing, "It's that big building over there."

"I'll jest do that, Major." Harley nodded his appreciation. "Thank you kindly."

The girl giggled again as Harley walked off toward the massive, three-story structure on the western side of the green.

The woman at the information booth, Rita Quince, needed to give her jaw a rest. She was trying to decide where to hide her wad of chewing gum when the strange old man entered the building.

Half watching him, she stuck her gum into the little cavity at the back of her telephone. Because she wasn't very busy, she decided it might be amusing to see what the old guy was up to. She figured, *he's probably some old bum from City Hall Park looking for bottles to cash in at five cents each.*

He had planted himself in the foyer, right in front of the double doors, mindlessly obstructing traffic while looking the place over. Students walked around him, taking second and third looks at the human oddity in their midst.

When the old man ignored the trash receptacle, Rita knew that he wasn't searching for bottles. In fact—a wave of nervousness splashed over her—now he was looking directly at her!

My God! What if he's crazy? she thought.

She groped at the telephone, retrieved her gum. Covering her lips, she pretended to clear her throat and popped the gum back into her mouth.

Rita thought of Jiminy Cricket as the wiry little man quick-stepped toward her window.

Now he looked more like a farmer than a street person. No wonder he seemed strange; not that many farmers came in here. Even the folks who worked at the agricultural college didn't *look* like farmers.

Rita searched for some information on the old man's baseball cap. Boston Red Sox was all she learned.

Standing in front of her, he placed his paper bag on the counter with a thunk.

"May I help you?" Rita asked, chewing noiselessly. She looked into the old man's sparkling eyes, checked the stubble of gray whiskers on his face, noted the sunken lips and prominent jaw, both suggesting the absence of teeth.

"Got some stone here I wancha to take a look at."

His Vermont accent was so thick that Rita could hardly understand what he was saying.

She watched silently as he emptied the bag. Three stones tumbled out on to the counter. One, a little bigger than a grapefruit, the other two the size of fists. With talon-gnarled hands the old man arranged the stones just so in front of her. He had to manipulate them at chest level, because he was very short.

"Whaddya think of *them*?" He spoke with great pride and finality, as if be had just stated an irrefutable truth, as if he expected her to be impressed with his dirty old stones.

Rita looked at them, then at the old man's twinkling eyes. His lips pressed together to emphasize his point. She didn't know what to say.

"Wh . . . What are these?"

"Why, I figgered you'd know. Tha's why I come down here to the college. Y'er 'infermation,' ain't ya?" His voice was high-pitched and crackly, like twigs breaking.

"Well, I'm just a receptionist. Maybe you should talk to one of the faculty . . ."

The old man looked puzzled. He ran the back of his hand under his vein-streaked nose and scratched. "Them's *sacred* stones," he insisted. "An' they's more where them come from, too. Lookit that writin' on 'um."

He pointed to the biggest rock. On it a carved design resembled a flowing "X" with three dots on either side.

"That's really something," she ventured tentatively. "I bet you want to talk to somebody over in Archaeology, or maybe Anthropology . . ."

But he wasn't to be put off. "I figger them markin's a secret code. See, this 'X' here stands for Exodus. Them first three spots mean chapter three. Them there means verse three . . ."

Rita had no idea what he was talking about. With a sudden inspiration she reached for the phone. "I'm going to call Dr. Potter over in Archaeology for you. He's a nice guy. He'll—"

Then she remembered the gum in her mouth, and her supervisor's warnings. Not seeing how else to dispose of it, she swallowed the gum as she dialed.

The old man fished a mangled black book out of his pocket. Rita could see from the faded gold lettering that it was a Bible. He had marked his place with a Social Security envelope.

"Right here it says"— he followed the text with his finger—" 'An' Moses said, I will now turn aside, and see this great sight, why the bush is not burnt.' "

"Is Dr. Potter in?" The gum felt lodged in her throat. She fought the urge to cough, tears came to her eyes. "Do you think he'd talk to a man who's over here? He's got some marked stones that he brought in. I think he wants somebody to take a look at them . . ."

Harley looked up. His affronted expression said that Rita had understood nothing, "I wanna *sell* 'em."

"He says he wants to sell 'em, uh, them. Huh?" Then to Harley, "She wants to know where you found them?"

"Right on my farm, by jeepers."

"In Vermont?"

"Well a'course. Right up Eureka."

She had no idea where Eureka was, tried to tell him so with a perplexed look.

"Up the Kingdom . . . !"

Totally confused, Rita cleared her throat, trying to dislodge the gum, then continued hoarsely, "He says he found them in Vermont. Maybe I could just send him over. Would that be all right? Okay, good. Thanks."

After hanging up the phone Rita gave him a map of the campus. She wrote "Dr. Potter," with an arrow pointing to the proper building.

"Well, thank you very much, missus," he said, tipped his baseball cap, and winked at her. He carefully returned the stones to the brown paper bag, took a last look around, and walked away.

Rita watched him leave the building. Checking to make sure that her supervisor wasn't around she coughed, shooting the wad of gum into her closed fist.

3

Rare Specimens

FRIDAY, AUGUST 19, 1988

Roger Newton looked across The Newsroom, enjoying a fleeting moment of great satisfaction. Tonight business was good. It was better than good! Five out of the seven tables full, two booths occupied, and three men, solitary drinkers, sitting at the bar.

If things continued like this he'd have nothing to worry about. The unpaid bills in his office upstairs didn't seem so menacing when the bar was filled with cigarette smoke, music, and the throb of good-natured conversation.

Around six o'clock, after the furniture factory's ten-hour shift let out, a few more people would drop in for a drink and maybe a sandwich. Roger would be ready. If the place caught on the way he hoped, The Newsroom would be known for serving the best hamburger in the Northeast Kingdom. Maybe, in time, he'd expand and add a dining room, a wine list.

Maybe.

Initially Roger's plan had been to offer a wide variety of draft beers, foreign and domestic. The idea of exotic choices would have appealed to Burlington customers; he'd hoped it would entice crowds of Eureka's drinkers to The Newsroom. However, he quickly learned he was not meeting the more provincial needs of the locals. They wanted only Bud, or maybe Bud Light. The most popular drinks, he discovered, were schnapps, and Seagram's Seven. Nonetheless, he was proud of his well-stocked bar.

Laura Drew, the waitress, moved easily among the tables. She was graceful and shapely. It was still difficult for Roger to believe that she had a twelve-year-old son. Why, she hardly looked more than twenty-five herself. He'd noticed that many Vermont women looked old for their years; this had become especially obvious since he'd moved from Burlington to Eureka. Perhaps it was their diets, perhaps the demand for premature marriage and children, perhaps the limited prospects offered by life in the Northeast Kingdom.

Laura was an exception in many ways, to many rules. She was beautiful, young for her years, and she seemed to want for nothing more than she had. Her employment as a cocktail waitress— barmaid, she called it—seemed fulfilling. She never complained, never requested more than the four dollars an hour plus tips that he paid her. And she always seemed appreciative of the work, demonstrating a loyalty to her employer that was rare, almost old-fashioned.

Of course Roger couldn't delude himself too much; he knew there was much more to Laura's loyalty than old-time country virtues. As he watched her, sidestepping a pat on the ass from Roland Dubois, returning a smile from Keenan Whittaker, putting another round of drinks on Clifton Bullis's table, he thought how lucky he was to have her as his employee. He was luckier, of course, that she was also his lover.

There was only one more thing that he hoped for: if she'd only make up her mind, agree to his proposal. They'd make a great team, he was sure. It had been Laura's idea to one day open some of the upstairs rooms for bed and breakfast, maybe even renovate the whole place as a country inn. Together, as husband and wife, they could make a go of it. If only she'd agree . . .

Laura's long black hair shone in the subdued barroom light, somehow suggesting her French Canadian heritage. Her skin, white as fresh Vermont cream, seemed radiant. Her smile was quick and sincere; it showed that she was having a good time, encouraged others to do the same.

Roger knew he owed more to Laura for the growing success of The Newsroom than to his own fledgling business expertise. With-

out her, he might have returned to Burlington long ago. Without
her he might have given up.

Moving back to the bar, she smiled at him. Small points of gold
glittered on her ear lobes. "Another couple of Molsons," she said.

Roger uncapped two green bottles and slid them across the bar
to her. On the jukebox a Waylon Jennings song, heavy with bass,
competed with the noise of the crowd. Roger counted heads; there
were seventeen customers in the place, seventeen, and it was only
five-thirty in the afternoon. *Not too bad*, he thought as he nodded
proudly. *Not too bad at all.*

He smiled as his eyes scanned the room. Then he thought of
Lunker Lavigne.

And the worry returned.

For the last couple of days he'd been keeping an eye out for Lavigne. It had upset Roger to see the big man so tied up, so puzzled,
so in need of alcohol. In retrospect, there was something about
Lavigne's frame of mind that seemed almost, well . . . dangerous.
It was as if he were teetering on the edge of losing control, as if any
minute he would explode with rage or tears or violence.

And it was hard to understand. What could do that to such a
man?

Roger wanted to see Lunker again, wanted to know that he was
all right. Each time the door opened he looked up hopefully, but
Lavigne never showed.

*What, exactly, could he have seen up there in the gore? What could
have frightened him so much?* The questions nagged at Roger, persistent and painful.

He recalled an incident many years ago involving his own father. It must have been around 1958, when Roger was no older than
Laura's boy.

Mr. Newton—Billy to his many friends at the garage—had taken
the family to Maine for a week's vacation. They were driving at
sunset over potato-crowded backroads somewhere inland from
Portland. Roger, in the backseat, noticed a scarecrow standing in
the field fifty to a hundred yards away, between the road and the
sunset.

"Jeez. Lookit that!"

"Nothin' but a scarecrow, lad," Billy Newton said, his corncob billowing streamers of smoke out the Plymouth's window. But he slowed down so all three could get a look at the motionless black form against the blood-red sky.

Suddenly Mr. Newton saw what Roger was trying to point out. The outstretched arms of the scarecrow began to move, slowly, slowly—almost rippling, like the leisurely flapping of a gull's wings.

"My Christ!" Mr. Newton blurted. His jaw dropped. A worried expression that Roger had never seen before knotted his father's brow.

Mr. Newton looked away, hands clenching the steering wheel. He tromped the accelerator, leaving the animated effigy in a storm of dry Maine dust.

Roger had never seen his father so strangely upset, so haunted by something which, to Roger, was completely trivial. "How could it move like that?" Billy Newton asked his wife over and over.

The episode was something that had fit nowhere into his father's concept of the sane world. It was, for Mr. Newton, a disturbing, unsettling image, a vision that posed no threat whatsoever to anything but the validity of his experience.

Later they learned what they'd mistaken for a scarecrow was the idiot son of a local farmer. The boy would stand for hours in the fields, pretending to be a scarecrow, trying to coax birds to fly down and perch on his arms.

A chorus of laughter exploded, jarring Roger from his reverie. It came from Keenan Whittaker's table. Someone had spilled a beer, and the three other drinkers applauded. The ovation spread among the other tables.

"Gimme a rag," said Laura. "We got an emergency."

She took a handful of napkins from the bar dispenser and headed for Whittaker's table. Roger took a sponge mop and followed her.

He watched Whittaker, a forty-year-old employee of the furniture factory in Canaan, deliberately tip over another beer. The frothy amber liquid flowed along the tabletop and mingled with the suds that Laura was already trying to clean up. Roger saw right away what the attraction was: as Laura leaned forward, soaking up the mess in a wad of napkins, her ample breasts were partially exposed by her low-cut jersey.

" 'Bout time you finally got us some decent entertainment in this place." Whittaker guffawed as he stared unabashedly.

Gently, Roger nudged Laura aside. "I'll get that," he said.

"Come on," Whittaker protested. "She's doin' a fine job. I'll bet she's good at everything."

Realizing what was going on, Laura retreated to the bar as Roger swabbed the floor with his mop. "If she's going to provide entertainment, I'm going to have to double her pay, not to mention adding a hazardous duty bonus if you jokers keep hanging around here."

Smiling, Roger looked over the top of his glasses at Keenan. He watched the indecision in the man's face: Should he laugh this off, or should he push?

In his peripheral vision Roger could see all eyes were on him. And something else: For a moment he thought he glimpsed a face watching from the side window. His impulse was to look and see but he didn't want to break eye contact with Whittaker.

Whittaker checked out the mop handle in Roger's hand. He looked the bar owner up and down, sizing him up. Then sipped the remaining beer from his mug.

The crisis had passed. "Let me get you another one, but hold on to it this time." Roger looked at the others at the table. "Never seen a man have such a time holding his liquor."

Returning to the bar he heard laughter behind him, Whittaker's the loudest.

He glanced at the window again, but saw nothing. Laura was looking at it too. Her face was pale, her expression troubled.

"What's the matter?" Roger asked.

"I thought I saw— Oh, it's nothing." She looked back at Whittaker's table and smiled. "Well done, but you should have let me—"

"Ah, they don't mean anything. They're just having fun."

"I know but ... well ... Okay, I guess I owe you one."

"And I plan to collect, too. If we ever have a moment free." He gave her a comic leer. Turning, he lighted the second half of the gas grill. At any moment he expected a rush of orders for hamburgers, peppersteaks, and hot dogs.

The phone rang. Laura put a shot of schnapps in front of a fat woman in curlers, completed her three-sixty pirouette, and scooped up the receiver before the second ring.

"It's for you, Rog. Somebody from Burlington. A Dr. Potter?"

Roger pressed the phone to his right ear, plugging his left with his fingertip to shut out the noise.

"Dr. Potter, as I live and breathe!" He actually said: Doctah Pottah, z'oi lee-uv 'n' bree-uth, trying his best to feign a Vermont accent.

"So, Roger," Potter asked, "how's life in the wilds?"

Roger always enjoyed the jovial sound of Potter's "New Joisey brogue." It was difficult to hear him though; there was static on the line, mixed with the faint electronic tones of a telephone system far too modern to be Eureka's.

"Can't complain. I used to spend my time in bars to escape the paper, now I spend all my time in a bar. But I guess that's progress of a sort. At least it cuts down on travel."

David Potter and Roger Newton had known each other for about three years, first meeting when Roger had consulted the archaeologist about a feature he was doing on Vermont's ancient Celtic structures. Their acquaintanceship grew after Roger moved to Eureka. While remodeling the pub, located downstairs in the eighteenth-century house that he'd purchased, Roger had discovered a secret door that led to a hidden chamber, a staircase, and a tunnel. He phoned Potter, boyishly excited with his discovery and proud that his house had once been a part of the Underground Railroad, the cooperative humanitarian network that helped runaway slaves escape the repression of the South for the freedom of Canada.

David and Roger had spent a week together at the house. They'd had great talks and laughed like children. The professor even assisted Roger with his remodeling efforts. Each man came away with a published article and a new friend.

"It's going well for you then? Is that what you're trying to tell me?" Potter's voice was clearer now.

"Business is booming . . . At least at the moment."

"Listen, I had a rare specimen in my office yesterday. An old fellow from up your way, Harley Spooner. Did you sic him on me by any chance?"

Harley Spooner? In Burlington? "Nope. You can't pin it on me. But I know him. Last of a vanishing breed. He's what the guidebooks refer to as 'local color.' Jeez, David, I can't imagine what he wanted all the way down there?"

"Well, he didn't come to experience the joys of higher education, I'll tell you that. He had some rocks with him. He wanted to sell them to me. Says they're sacred stones and he's convinced they're valuable. Know anything about it?"

"Not really. He only comes in here once in a blue moon. I think I've heard him mention them when he's in his cups. I never paid much attention . . ."

"Maybe you should have. He's got something there, no doubt about it. There's authentic Indian markings on them, I think. It might be that the old boy's got an important site on his property. I'd love to come up there and check it out, but I can't, no time. I'm going to send one of my graduate assistants up to have a look. Thought you might be interested in tagging along. Who knows, maybe there's a story in it. In any event, you can expect some company, if that's okay."

"Sure. When?"

"How about next Saturday, the twenty-seventh?"

"Sounds good. You want me to act as interpreter, is that the idea?"

"Maybe. Spooner is a little difficult to understand. Especially when he gets excited. But we got along fine. I actually came to like the old guy. Anyway, Les Winthrop will be checking in with you a week from tomorrow. Might need some help finding Mr. Spooner's place. That okay?"

"Translator *and* guide? My rates should double."

"You sure it's okay, Rog?"

"Sure, I like to do all I can to promote local tourism. It's good for business. I wish you could come, though."

"Thanks. I'd like that, too. But if this site amounts to anything I'll be up. Got an extra bed?"

"Sure, anytime you want it. And thanks for the scoop."

"Anything for a pal."

"Yeah, right."

When he hung up Laura's son Stacy was standing beside him. Stacy's friend Jarvis, Lunker Lavigne's boy, stood in the background, looking uneasy.

"Well look at this," Roger said to Laura, "we got a couple more customers. And they look like big spenders. What'll it be, boys?"

"Wanna see something?" said Stacy, smiling, his dark hair tumbling helter-skelter over his forehead.

"Yeah? Like what?"

"You got your pocket watch on ya?"

Roger fished around in the pocket of his chinos and pulled out the antique watch, a family treasure his father bad passed on to him for a graduation present.

"Lemme see it," said Stacy, grabbing the watch before Roger had a chance to think it over. The Lavigne boy, less timid now, stepped forward into the tight circle of three.

Stacy displayed the watch in his right hand, holding it at eye level between thumb and forefinger. As Roger looked on, somewhat uncertainly, the boy slowly took the watch into his left fist, closing his fingers around it. Then, with a deliberate sweeping gesture, his right hand produced a large red handkerchief from his back pocket.

By now a group of four people at a nearby table were watching the performance. Laura peeked over Jarvis Lavigne's shoulder as her son covered his fist—and the watch inside—with the handkerchief.

Then he held the handkerchief by its four corners, swinging it like a cloth-covered pendulum. The watch, invisible within, added weight to the bottom. With a theatrical flourish, and before Roger could stop him, the boy swung the watch around his head several times and smashed it, hard, against the bar.

Laura gasped. Roger felt the blood drain from his face. The whole room fell into silence.

Jarvis Lavigne giggled.

Stacy smiled, slowly opening the handkerchief. One by one he removed what at first appeared to be fragments of glass. When he popped one into his mouth, Roger realized it was rock candy.

"Want some?" said Stacy nonchalantly.

"I want my watch," said Roger with mock irritation.

"Oh yes, your *pocket* watch." Stacy made a big deal of reaching into his back pocket and pulling out the undamaged timepiece.

Several spectators applauded. Laura smiled. Stacy bowed awkwardly as Roger felt his face getting warmer.

"Not bad, Houdini. I think you fellas have earned yourselves a couple of drinks."

The two boys took seats at the bar while Laura set them up with two Cokes.

At a quarter to twelve Keenan Whittaker stumbled out of The Newsroom. His companions had abandoned him earlier, leaving Keenan to finish the remaining beer in the pitchers and glasses on the table.

He chuckled to himself, recalling his first days in the navy. The deck of the *Admiral Hancock* had rolled and bucked nearly as bad as the sidewalk under his feet.

And the feeling in his stomach, it was very close to seasickness. He swallowed rapidly, trying to control his urge to vomit.

Keenan gulped a deep lungful of the cool night air. Struggling to stand still, he looked up and down the deserted main street of Eureka. The buildings were dark, their windows lightless. The long black line of the road seemed to undulate like an enormous snake.

Walking to the bar was always easy, but going home was another story. Keenan knew the route so well he could probably walk it unconscious. In fact, he probably had done so more then once. Just follow the stone wall separating the cemetery from Burt Proctor's property, cross Sander's meadow, follow the path through the orchard, and home. He'd be there in fifteen minutes.

The thought of returning to the empty house always bothered him. Especially at night. It had been so much easier when Mom and Pop were alive. Now the only thing that made going home tolerable was to get drunk first.

"So I'm a drunk," he screamed at the moon, then stumbled backward a few steps, bumping against the stone wall.

"So what?" he whispered.

He thought of Laura Drew. In his memory he saw her big firm tits, like restrained pets, trying to break free of her low-cut yellow T-shirt. They moved and quivered in the red light of the glass-enclosed candle on the table.

One of these nights he hoped Laura would agree to come home with him. He'd be real good to her, make her feel real welcome.

He thought way back to that time, long ago, when they'd gone out together. It was the last week of high school. Boy, that was a great night! Maybe the best of his life. They'd driven all the way down to the St. Johnsbury drive-in to see *Doctor Zhivago*. Laura had cried. Actually cried. Keenan had never seen anything so beautiful.

That was three days before he'd left for the service.

Oh, he'd kissed Laura good night after the movie and the long drive home. To this day he recalled her moist eager lips and the sweet smell of candy on her breath. But despite the demands the navy would soon make on his courage and manhood, he hadn't dared to touch her breasts. He'd never touched her breasts.

And still, more than twenty years later, he considered how they might feel.

If he'd timed it better, if he hadn't had to go to sea, things might have turned out differently between them. Sure, they'd swapped letters for a while, but he had stopped answering when she told him about Hank.

But things continued to change. Now Hank was out of the picture. Laura was available again. And Keenan was . . . unattached. Things just might work out after all.

In a moment of awareness he discovered that he'd made it all the way to the end of the stone wall.

"Must be on automatic pilot," he said, and laughed through pursed lips, spraying beer-scented spit into the night air. Droplets rained down on his fingers and he rubbed them on the front of his T-shirt.

Sander's meadow wasn't really a meadow anymore. Where acres of hay had once grown, now a thickness of brambles, berry bushes, and scrub pine hid the orchard beyond. The trail through the underbrush was well worn. Getting lost would be impossible.

But it was dark in there.

Keenan patted his pockets, searching for his cigarettes. In reality, his urge was more to see the match light than to smoke. Besides, he was trying to quit. Good thing he'd left his Marlboros back at the bar.

Keenan squinted into the gloom of the meadow. He thought he heard something rustling in the puckers.

Taking a wary step forward, he felt himself sobering up with a tiny surge of adrenaline. There *was* something nearby. He could feel it, or smell it, or hear it, or something.

He couldn't tell how he knew, but he *knew* something was close to him.

He opened his eyes very wide as if that would let in more light and improve his vision.

A dark shape stepped out on to the moonlit path thirty feet in front of him. It was nearly invisible against the indistinct wall of bushes.

"Who zat?" He tried to shout, but words came out as a fractured whisper.

The intruder took a step closer. Before Keenan could speak again the form was rushing at him. *Too fast!*

He tried to turn and run, but a crippling blow connected with his kidney. He couldn't tell if he'd been punched or kicked. All he knew was that the night had turned to pain, and he was on his knees puking his guts up.

Then he felt fingers around his neck, pushing his face toward the ground.

"Stop! No! I'm sick," he cried. A new wave of vomit sloshed across his lips and splattered on to his T-shirt and the ground below.

Christ! I'm being attacked!

Disbelieving, he readied to defend himself. From his kneeling position Keenan tried to raise a protecting arm. A heavy foot kicked it aside.

Then he tried to stand. With one foot firmly on the ground, he doubled his fist to deliver a defensive attack.

It was no use. Diamond-hard blows stung him with the rapidity of machine-gun fire. He couldn't even get in a punch.

And suddenly he was lying face down. He couldn't remember toppling. Everything was fuzzy. Dark and fuzzy.

It was impossible to move. There was no way he could protect himself from the avalanche of blows that pulverized his neck and shoulders.

Hands tugged at him now, turning him over. His eyes were wet, sand clung to them and ground against his eyeballs as he tried to see his attacker.

A sharp blow from a hammer-fist closed his left eye, grinding sand against his cornea.

"Stop, please," he whimpered, trying at the same time to talk and spit sandy grains from his mouth. His stomach heaved again. Not vomit this time. Warm blood dribbled across his battered cheek.

In an instant of clarity he saw the dark, unrecognizable form above him. Its hands were clenched together, raised over its head.

Keenan Whittaker passed out before the last blow fell.

4

Dark Things Remembered

TUESDAY, AUGUST 23, 1988

The boy was upstairs in bed. Peggy stood at the sink finishing the last of the supper dishes. As she stacked them in the drainer they rattled together, sounding like old bones. The noise irritated him.

He took a long swallow, polishing off his bottle of Bud Light. On the kitchen table in front of him seven empties clustered around an ashtray like hoboes around a campfire. Worn out, their usefulness passed.

"Be careful, Claude. You don't want to be drinking too much, now." She smiled wanly at him in the harsh light of the bare 60-watt bulb above the table.

He could sense her hesitation. She knew damn well he didn't like her to lecture him.

"I'm all right, gal. Just need a little something to help me sleep."

She walked over to him, her steps as hesitant as her voice. Her hand rested tentatively on his shoulder.

"Maybe you're too worried about this. You know? Maybe it was—"

"Cripes, Peg, you didn't see that damned thing the way I did. You didn't have its eyes boring little holes into you."

"I know, Claude. But it's over with now. Why not let it go?"

" 'Cause I *can't* let it go! Don't you see, it's the not knowin' . . .

26

the not—Christ sake, Peg, everybody knows them old stories about the gore. Monsters an' haunts an' strange goin's on. Why, I can't tell nobody what I seen without gettin' crazy looks."

He felt himself shiver and he let his head rest against her arm. He breathed the fragrance of her: perfume and dish detergent. When he spoke it was almost a whisper. "Maybe I should take a gun. Maybe I should go back up there and shoot the cussed thing. Find out for certain."

"Maybe you should leave well enough alone."

They remained silent for a moment. Her lips touched the top of his head and she squeezed his shoulders. "I'm going up to bed now," she told him. "You come up when you're ready."

She turned out the light over the sink. Then he heard her slippers on the stairs as she climbed up to their bedroom. He was glad she was gone; there were things he couldn't tell her, things she couldn't understand. And he didn't want her to see the tears welling in his eyes.

When he heard the bedroom door close he took out the bottle. Canadian Club splashed along his palate and warmed his insides. Yet, somehow, he felt cold. *Why do I feel chilled,* he wondered? *It's August, for cryin' out loud. Why should I be cold?*

He tipped his head forward and massaged his watering eyes with the hams of his hands.

I'm sick, that's why. Sick, and getting sicker. All the beers, all the prescription painkillers, all the shots of alcohol . . . nothing touched the pneumatic pounding in his head. It felt like two powerful hands inside his skull, plucking the nerves behind his eyeballs.

It was as if his eyes were being punished for what they'd seen.

Christ, next thing you know they'll be tellin' me to see a friggin' shrink.

The house was dark now, the only light was the one above the table.

What could it have been?

How long could he keep this up? It wasn't like him to sit around doing nothing. But what could he do? It shamed him to admit, even to himself, that he was afraid.

He smacked the table with his palm. Slowly he lifted his bulk from the chair and stood up.

Nothin' gained by fussin' over it anymore.

He held very still, listening to be sure Peggy wasn't moving around upstairs. Then he walked over to his gun cabinet. The tiny brass key was in the lock, just where it always was. He turned it, pulled open the glass-fronted door and took out his double-barreled twelve gauge. It felt as if he were preparing for an early morning hunting trip.

Well, in a way that's exactly what he was doing.

He opened the drawer below the gun rack and automatically grabbed a handful of shells. Then he stopped. He forced a dry, ugly-sounding laugh.

" 'M only gonna need the one," he whispered.

Turning the shotgun around in his hands he looked down the barrels. The parallel openings were wide dark eyes staring back at him, metal irises surrounding cold deadly pupils. It was like . . .

. . . it was *just* like . . .

. . . that day in the gore . . .

. . . those inhuman eyes fixed on him, staring . . .

What in the name of Christ could it have been?

Gun in hand, he walked out into the humid warmth of the evening. The night around him, moonless and silent, made him think of the inside of a crypt. He shuddered at the thought.

It was so dark he had to grope his way to the truck, guided only by the reflection of the kitchen light in the shiny chrome bumper.

He opened the driver's door, put the gun and single shell behind the seat. They'd be there waiting when he left for work in the morning.

5

Old Scores

The only thing keeping Stacy Drew from total relaxation was the knowledge that soon he'd have to go home for supper. Sprawled on the top of the wide stone fence that surrounded the cemetery at the southern end of town, he yawned and stretched, his eyes half closed to the afternoon sun. This was a favorite spot; he and Jarvis spent many idle hours here. Over the course of the summer, he guessed, they'd probably put in more than a hundred hours right here on this rock wall.

The stores across the street stood in a short row like a fat picket fence: Merrick's Rexall, Ed's IGA, Rand's General Store and Post Office. Up the street, the last building before leaving Eureka, was Allen's Garage, right across from The Newsroom.

Stacy watched the IGA until Jarvis emerged, returning to the wall with two orange sodas. Jarvis moved slowly, as if he were very tired. He'd been moving slowly all day.

Even though Jarvis was almost two years older than Stacy, they were the best of friends. Some kids thought it was kind of queer to hang out with younger people, but the minor age difference meant nothing to Jarvis and Stacy. Jarvis never hid his devotion for the younger boy. Perhaps the reason for his loyalty was that it had never, not even once, occurred to Stacy to make fun of him.

Stacy's friend was the target of a lot of abuse, verbal and physical, especially while school was in session. Stacy knew how much Jarvis dreaded returning to school, how he counted his remaining days of freedom as if they were a stash of rare coins. He had only a month left.

The kids from Eureka weren't too bad; they'd known Jarvis before he'd started in school, before his trouble began. Then Eureka Elementary closed, making way for Union 43. Jarvis was forced to mingle with kids from other towns. And things got really crazy.

Stacy could never figure out why things got so bad. Part of the reason, he guessed, was that Jarvis Lavigne had been forced to stay back a year because of the operation. This made him the oldest kid in his class, always a target for ridicule. Another part of the problem was that the operation hadn't completely worked. Jarvis had scoliosis, curvature of the spine. The name of the condition had such a musical ring to it, at least in the ears of the school's more sadistic kids, that they started calling him "Scoli," and mocked his irregular posture.

Stacy, on the other hand, liked having his older friend in the same class; it gave them more time together. Staying back a year didn't seem like such a big deal. Anyone would do the same thing after spending so much time in the hospital. Stacy couldn't understand why kids dwelled on it. Or why they ridiculed his friend's deformity. Stacy didn't even notice it.

And all he saw now was the pain in Jarvis's stride as he lurched across the street.

Putting his hands on the fence, Jarvis jumped up beside Stacy. "I was just thinking about Roger, when you smashed his watch. That was pretty good!"

"It's getting better. But thanks."

"What do you call that trick, anyway?"

"French drop. It's just a simple sleight. But Roger's the best audience in the world. He's so easy to fool."

"Could you teach it to me?"

"Why? When'd you start getting interested in magic?"

"I dunno. I'd like to show it to my father, maybe it would cheer him up. Or maybe you could do it for him?" Jarvis pushed his plastic-framed glasses back on his nose, then vigorously scratched at his stylelessly short haircut.

"Sure. Whatever. What's the matter with him, anyway?"

"I dunno. He's down in the dumps all the time lately. I don't think I'm s'pos't to talk about it."

"Okay. But if you want to, you can. It's okay by me." Stacy tossed his head, flipping black locks away from his eyes.

The boys sat silently with their legs dangling over the side of the wall. Occasionally a car passed on the main street and they'd study it with interest.

"Look," said Stacy, pointing in the direction of the general store, "there's ol' Rotten Pants Benson. And he's comin' this way."

"Yeah . . . uh, I think maybe I should be gettin' home to supper. 'S gettin' late."

"Stick around a minute. He won't bother us."

"Yeah, but . . ."

Robbie Benson, a short tree stump of a boy, was in junior high school. Well known as a bully, he inspired fear in kids he'd never even bothered. He had, however, bothered Jarvis Lavigne on at least one occasion that Stacy remembered. Now, as Robbie approached, Jarvis was shaking. "Come on, Stace, let's go."

About two years ago Robbie had stuffed the back of his T-shirt with a football and announced, "Okay, now it's a fair fight, hunchback to hunchback." He'd then proceeded to beat the piss out of Jarvis Lavigne.

Mr. Lavigne, concerned about his son's pain and embarrassment, and more than a little angry about an unnecessary doctor bill, had approached Robbie's father for reimbursement and to deliver a stern lecture on parenting. Mr. Benson, a summertime construction worker who collected unemployment benefits in the winter, refused. "Your boy's gotta learn to take care of himself. Either that or learn to pay his own doctor bills."

The boys remembered with great satisfaction how Lunker Lavigne, normally a patient and tolerant man, suddenly found that he had exhausted his supply of both. With three quick, well-placed punches he'd left Mr. Benson deep in an afternoon nap. Since that

day Mr. Benson had avoided Mr. Lavigne, and Robbie had avoided
Jarvis. But it was common knowledge, Lunker Lavigne was on
both of the Bensons' shit lists.

"Hey Scoli, I hear your ol' man's in the hospital."

"Wha' d' ya mean?"

"What happened to him, anyways? He pick a fight with somebody who was ready for him?"

"Nothin's wrong with my dad—"

"Oh yeah? Well my ma works at the hospital in Island Pond, and
she says—"

"Cut it out, Robbie," Stacy said. "We're not bothering you."

A '72 Caddy, scaled with Bondo and patched with sheet metal,
pulled up in front of the wall. A female face, so fat it nearly filled the
driver's window, peered out at the boys. The window rolled down
with electric precision.

"Robert, I tol' you not to go wanderin' off. You git inna car this
minute."

"Maaa . . ."

"*Now*, Robert, 'fore all the air condish'nin' gits out."

The tanklike child threw the boys a final hate-filled glare. "Be
seein' ya, Lavigne."

When he got into the car his mother slapped him several times.
Stacy laughed and looked at Jarvis. But Jarvis wasn't laughing.

"I better get home," he said, his face knotted as tight as a fist. He
jumped on his bicycle and pedaled quickly away.

It was a little after ten P.M. when Hank Drew pulled up in his
darkened car. He turned out the headlights long before he slowed
to a silent stop across the street from The Newsroom.

From his usual vantage point, partly concealed by the bushes
but more by the darkness, he could watch the bar's patrons as they
left.

He could clearly see any individual's features in the light from
two fake gas carriage lamps on either side of the entrance. There

was Cliff Bullis, staggering out the door. If the roads to Bullis's place weren't deserted at this time of night, the drunken bum would be a real menace.

Molly Pratt, one of those fiftyish, cigarette-smoking, raspy-voiced redheads, left about fifteen minutes after Bullis. As usual, she left alone.

Hank didn't like Molly at all. But somehow the sight of her too-rouged wrinkles and her bright painted nails made him feel sad. He watched as tiny moth-shadows flickered around her head, and he felt lonely.

The loneliness spread, a dreadful prickly sensation along his spine. Sweat erupted on his forehead. In the closed car he could smell his own body odor.

It's a test, he reminded himself. This is going to take courage . . .

But courage hadn't been much of a problem lately. He thought of Keenan Whittaker's terrified face, his wild frightened eyes, his torn lips spewing vomit.

And he smiled at the memory.

Whittaker had been sniffing around the wrong places lately. More than one person had said so. And Whittaker was the first to get what he deserved. The first obstacle to be removed.

Hank laughed out loud in the darkened car, thinking what a joke it would be if Whittaker tried to go to the police.

But, of course, Whittaker was nothing but a warmup. The real obstacle, the real target, was still out there.

Hank massaged the revolver on the seat beside him, trying, to control his excitement.

"Always be sure of your target," his father had preached to him long ago. His instructors in the corps had said the same thing. And he was sure it was true. He was *positive*.

Oh, he'd give Laura a little while to confess her error, to come back on her own. But if she didn't . . . if the criminal forces drawing her away proved stronger than her weak feminine will . . . ?

Always be sure of your target . . .

Newton.

Newton was the target. Newton was the criminal here, the wrongdoer, the evil one. Newton had turned Laura's head, that's all. Simple as that.

But so what? Her head could be turned right again.

Hank blew a long hissing breath through his nostrils, thinking how the right and wrong of the situation was so obvious and clear. So very . . . uncluttered. And simple. But Christ, wasn't it just like a woman to complicate a clear-cut issue with a lot of emotional garbage?

Yes, Hank thought with a chuckle, everything can be set right again. But timing was important. Timing was everything. Hank was confident he'd know when it was time to strike.

In the meantime he'd wait. Wait and watch. Gathering evidence. Gathering strength.

He took his hand from the weapon, flexed a fist. Then he rubbed his right hand. The knuckles were still raw and sore, outlined with tiny pieces of dead skin, yet he smiled.

Covering the revolver with a copy of *Soldier of Fortune*, he settled back, stretching out as best he could in the driver's seat. He never took his eyes from the door, he never even blinked. There was no way, he told himself over and over, that he could miss Laura when she left the bar.

6

The Monsters Are Due

THURSDAY, AUGUST 25, 1988

Naked to the waist, Laura Drew brushed her hair until it shone. It fell, long and thick across her white shoulders.

How pleasant to be home early! She smiled, trying to communicate her contentment to Roger's reflection in her makeup mirror.

It stung her when he didn't smile back.

She watched him in the glass. He lay on top of the floral sheets, flipping through a copy of *Yankee* magazine. Obviously his eyes, and mind, were elsewhere.

Had she done something wrong?

Just like every Wednesday night, there'd been no action at The Newsroom. The place was empty by ten-thirty. It had been Laura's idea to take advantage of an early closing. By quarter to twelve they'd locked the door and were on their way to her trailer. Could Roger be upset about that?

She knew how much he worried about losing money, about not making a success of the bar business. More than anything else, Roger seemed to fear failure. Perhaps she shouldn't have encouraged him to close early. Perhaps it had just upset him.

Normally the sight of her trim hips or the thrust of her breasts as she pulled off a jersey would have excited him, but tonight he seemed a million miles away.

She stopped brushing as a sinking feeling dampened her good

mood. Perhaps Roger wasn't worried about the mounting bills, perhaps he wasn't contemplating failure. Maybe the thing Laura feared most was finally happening: Was Roger considering giving up? Going back to Burlington? Returning to the newspaper?

Laura always thought that something, sooner or later, would come between them. Her relationship with Roger was too good, too right. But at any time he might lose patience with her. Grow tired of her indecision, her hesitation . . .

Or maybe he was getting sick of her altogether?

Laura had no illusions. She knew she wasn't like the women he had known in the city. She'd lived in Eureka all her life, by any standards she was a small-town girl. How could she seriously expect to hold his interest? How could she compete with the sophisticated ladies who lived in Vermont's biggest city?

On those first nights when she'd brought Roger home, she tried not to act nervous. She hesitated, sure. But her hesitation had come from her Catholic upbringing. It had nothing to do with him. She thought he understood that.

And now the idea of marriage . . . even living together . . . It was flattering, yes. But still . . .

Now, with her husband gone—out of her life entirely, she hoped—there was no reason to hesitate, no reason at all to feel guilty. It was the Catholicism again, buried as deeply in her personality as willow roots in Vermont soil.

If she was impatient with her own indecision, why should she expect anything different from Roger?

She put down her hairbrush.

She was being foolish, second-guessing everything like some dumb starry-eyed kid.

I'm so selfish, she thought, *so preoccupied with myself. Anyone can see there's something painful going on in Roger's mind; he needs me. I should be trying to comfort him, not drawing away self-protectively and feeling sorry for myself . . .*

She stood up, moved toward the bed. What was that funny old phrase her mother used to use? "The world is too much with you," she whispered.

"I know." He put down the magazine, then hoisted himself up to a sitting position, three pillows at his back. "It's really silly, I know, but I haven't been able to get Lunker Lavigne out of my head. Not since I spoke to him last week. I can't figure how whatever it was he saw up there could have upset him so much."

Lunker Lavigne?

Laura sat on the bed, ran her hand gently over his unruly hair, smiled down at him. "It probably wasn't what he saw in the woods. He probably had other problems, his job, maybe even his marriage, things he didn't even mention to you. It's probably a lot of stuff, all together, all built up."

"I don't know. I mean, you didn't see him the way I did. Something had scared the shit out of him."

Laura kissed his forehead, her fingers kneaded the back of his neck. "I can talk to his wife about it, if you want. Peggy and I, we've known each other since we were kids . . ."

Roger didn't answer, just gazed into her eyes. She liked what she saw there. She was hopeful. Maybe tonight would be okay after all.

Laura continued stroking his scalp, conscious of her heavy breasts swaying with the motion of her arm. After a while she got up, slipped out of her jeans, and tiptoed naked to the bedroom door. She peeked out to be sure that Stacy wasn't around, then darted toward the bathroom.

In the next room Stacy Drew turned off the television. He'd seen that episode of "Twilight Zone" at least twice before, but he'd watched it anyway: "The Monsters are Due on Maple Street."

With the TV off his bedroom was dark. Through the thin paneled wall he could hear Mom and Roger whispering. The sound was like the faraway rustle of bushes. Then their bedsprings began to squeak. To Stacy it sounded like mechanical breathing growing faster and louder, the last rusty gasps of a dying robot.

He tried not to think about the sound, knowing all too well what it was. Instead, he worked to imagine himself as the captain of a spaceship traveling through an unexplored universe. He was reclining now, preparing to enter a state of suspended animation that would last until their touchdown on some far-off alien world. The creaking bedsprings blended with the whir of the trailer's air conditioner to make the sound of the rocket engine, propelling the space-trailer at speeds faster than light.

Stacy settled his head between the pillows — he always slept with two — and relaxed a bit.

Sometimes, when he was very near sleep like this, he missed his father. Hank Drew had always been good to him. Stacy had to admit that, even after all the stuff that happened. Dad took him fishing, played toss and catch, and promised to buy him a .22 on his twelfth birthday. Of course that would never happen now that Dad was gone.

The thin walls of the trailer had often reminded him that his father was not always as kind to Mom. During those times when Dad had come home drunk — after a long day on the roads, followed by a long evening at some bar — he would always make a lot of noise, even if Stacy and Mom were asleep. Stacy remembered hearing his father stumbling around, bumping into furniture, yelling at Mom. In the last days Dad had hit Mom. That Stacy remembered clearly. The firecracker-whack of his palm against Mom's cheek was loud, even through the trailer's walls. Then the shouting, the punching, the crying all reverberated in his mind. The sounds couldn't be shut out by the heavy pillows or the machine noises of his imaginary rocket ship.

Tomorrow we'll land on Ubros-IV, he thought. *There I'll lead an exploration crew in search of alien life forms. Tomorrow I'll set foot on a brand-new world, make new and important discoveries. Tomorrow . . .*

Dad's violence was not always directed at Mom, though. Stacy had received some of it himself. But somehow, at least that one time at school, it seemed okay. After all, wasn't it okay for a father to punish his son? Wasn't it normal?

It had been on a weekend two years ago. Stacy was in the fourth grade. He'd left his gerbil at school but had forgotten to feed it. Fearing the little animal would starve to death before Monday, he and Jarvis rode their bikes the eight miles to the school. No one was there to let them in, so, not knowing what else to do, they jimmied one of the basement windows and crawled inside. Someone—to this day he didn't know who—had spotted them and called the police.

When Stacy's father got there he was very angry, much more angry than Mr. Lavigne. More angry, in fact, than Stacy had ever seen him. The color draining from his face was replaced by a flaming red. He hit Stacy. And when the blow had landed, he hit him again. With each slap Dad seemed to get more and more angry. He was screaming, "What will people think? My kid breaking into the school! *My* kid!" And then he hit Stacy with his fist.

No one saw but Mom, yet after that things got worse and worse, until—

There was a sound in the room!

He heard a strange noise, something other than the rocket engine. A tapping sound, a persistent, quiet tattoo that whisked him from his near-dream and back to his bedroom. He lifted his head, poised like a rabbit, nerves on fire, trying to hear the sound more clearly.

. . . tap . . . tap . . . tap . . .

The window!

Was someone tapping at the window?

Stacy looked around, holding his breath. He could feel his heart pumping, hear blood throbbing in his ears.

Now there was no sound at all. The bedsprings were silent, the air conditioner had clicked off.

Maybe it was just a branch scraping on the glass.

. . . taptaptap . . .

Stacy sat all the way up. By gosh he'd look and see. Stretching from the foot of his bed he could reach the window curtain. His arm extended like the head of a snake. He grasped the material in his hand. Then stopped. Maybe he shouldn't pull it back; what could be out there?

Nothing, that's what. Their trailer was way off by itself near the end of Coleman Road. The only other place was Mr. Spooner's, much farther beyond. No one would be out there on foot. And he hadn't heard any car drive up.

So nothing could be out behind the trailer, nothing but wilderness, hundreds of acres of woodland . . . and the gore.

The thought of the gore had always frightened him. And it still did. The word itself suggested injury, pain, bloodshed. When they'd moved into the trailer back when he was five or six, he had even been afraid to go outside. Especially at night. The dark forest behind the place was surely full of creatures . . .

Tap!

. . . ghosts, and dark shapes . . .

. . . tap . . .

. . . that would hunt him and harm him.

. . . taptap . . .

When Mom found out what was frightening him, she'd explained: *A gore is just a piece of land, Stacy, like an acre, or a town, or a county. It's a surveyor's mistake, when he measures wrong and leaves a little triangle of land unaccounted for that doesn't belong to any town. That's all, it's nothing to be afraid of. It's just a funny word, that's all.*

Stacy pulled back the window curtain and jumped when he saw the face.

Laura slept soundly, her body moist with perspiration, her head on Roger's shoulder. He enjoyed listening to her breathing, envied her ability to fall asleep so quickly after making love.

In the dim glow of the nightlight, Roger looked down at his naked chest. The thick mat of hair was a tangled mixture of brown and white. *God, I'm getting gray,* he thought. He didn't need a mirror to watch himself growing old, all he had to do was look at his chest. Every night he seemed a little whiter, a little older. It was scary, but at least it was slow; he'd have time to get used to it.

What frightened Roger was when things happened fast.

He hated the way things happened to people, suddenly, randomly, without warning. More than anything else it was the senseless pattern of violence and destruction that had driven him from

the newspaper business. He hated suffering; his position as a reporter had forced him to look at it headlong, day after day, paycheck after paycheck.

Someone was always getting robbed, beaten, murdered. Unpredictably, at any dreaded moment, people were struck down with
devastating illness. Little kids were stolen from their parents, raped,
sometimes tortured or sacrificed. Terrorists turned vacations into
sanity-destroying nightmares . . .

And his job had been to tell everyone about it!

Christ, he didn't want to know about it *himself!*

He thought about what had happened to his father. Dead.
Crushed under the car he'd been working on. Something had happened: an accident. A death. It had been in the newspaper for all
to see.

Where was the human dignity in such a news story? His father
had been a private person; he wouldn't have wanted the details of
his death on public exhibition.

Nevertheless, there had been a lesson for Roger in that death.
Perhaps it was the most important lesson Billy Newton had ever
taught his son: You're going to die, so why not die doing something you like?

Billy had died working on a car. Cars had been his father's life-
long passion. In a sense, Mr. Newton had died satisfied. But what
satisfaction could there be in Roger's last newspaper assignment, a
story about two fifteen-year-old boys torture-killing an eight-year-
old girl?

Billy Newton had taught Roger to get out of the newspaper
business.

Roger's mind jumped to his father's animated scarecrow . . .
then to Lunker Lavigne. It was so obvious: Billy Newton had been
a lot like Mr. Lavigne.

And now something's happened to him!

Enough! Roger thought. *I'm making way too much of this.*

But he couldn't stop. He possessed an almost supernatural instinct for news. Quitting his job as a reporter hadn't turned it off.
Buying the bar hadn't turned it off. Sometimes it grabbed him,

jerked him around with all the mysterious force of a dowsing rod over a spring. When that happened there was no sleep, not even any rest, until his curiosity was satisfied.

Thankfully, before Roger had a chance to grow any more melancholic, Laura stirred beside him.

Her eyes fluttered open and she kissed his lips. Her fingers on his thigh felt solid, real. It was wonderful.

"Still thinking about Mr. Lavigne?" she whispered.

"Umm-hmm."

"Try to relax, sweetie," she said. "If you keep this up you're never going to get the newspaper reporter out of your system."

"They say it's a gift . . ."

"You think there's something important to all of this, don't you? Something that needs investigation?"

He gave a mirthless chuckle, more like an exhalation than a laugh. "I got a nose for news."

Her expression changed, brightened into a mischievous grin. "A nose for news, huh? What's this for, then?" Laura snuggled down beside him, reaching under the sheet.

Roger held her very close as she wriggled beneath the covers. He wanted to tell her how much he loved her, but all he could think about was Lunker Lavigne, the pale face, the hollow frightened eyes.

"What are you doing here?" Stacy asked through the one-inch opening at the bottom of the trailer's aluminum window.

The boy on the other side of the glass motioned for Stacy to open the window wider. He lowered his face, its features obscured by the darkness, and whispered through the opening. "I gotta talk to you, Stace. Come on, open up."

"This thing's jammed. I'll come around."

Stacy pulled on his dungarees and sweatshirt, slipped sockless feet into his sneakers and tiptoed through the dark trailer to the door farthest from his mother's room. He stepped outside into the warm August night.

All day he had been noticing how tired Jarvis Lavigne had looked. Tonight, however, Jarvis looked more than tired, he looked miserable; his eyes were puffy, his face was a tight mask.

White light from a sliver of moon shone through the leafy branches of the oak in front of the trailer. Shadows and pale swatches of light made camouflage patterns on the boys' faces.

"My father's dead," Jarvis announced. His voice was flat, unemotional, his eyes unblinking.

Stacy didn't know what to say. He felt his jaw drop. For a moment he thought how stupid he must look with his mouth hanging open. "Wh . . . what?" He stammered.

"Didn't you hear me? My dad, he sh . . . shh . . ?" Tears filled Jarvis's eyes, sparkling like jewels magically appearing in the moonlight. He ducked his head and turned away, slapping an open palm against the unyielding trunk of the oak tree. Frozen there, shoulder against the tree, the mound on his back jumped up and down with his quiet sobs.

Stacy walked up behind him, put his hand on his friend's back, carefully avoiding the hump. "I'm sorry, Jarvis. I'm sorry. What can I do? Can I do something to help you? Oh, Jarvis, what haa—"

Jarvis whirled around, met his friend face-to-face. He seemed to struggle for control; the tears were gone, the features angry.

"What happened?" He glared at Stacy. "He shot himself, that's what happened."

Stacy felt heat rising from his stomach. He felt light-headed.

"Wh . . . why?"

"Why? How should I know why." Jarvis leaned against the tree, taking a step to the side so Stacy could see only his profile. He stood quietly, staring off into the night sky. "He's been acting funny lately, that's all. Like somebody's after him. He's been keeping the doors locked and he's been lookin' out the windows all the time."

"*Was* somebody after him?"

Jarvis sank to the ground, sliding his back down the trunk of the tree until he was sitting on the lawn. Stacy hunkered down in front of him.

"I heard him talking to Mom a couple times. He was upset. His voice sounded funny. It was crackin' and stuff, like he was gonna start cryin'. I heard him tell her he'd seen something in the woods."

"Something in the woods? Like what?"

"Like I don't know. My dad wasn't afraid of much, I'll tell you that. 'Member what he did to Old Man Benson that time? I don't know what he coulda seen that would scare him like that. I mean, he was even in the war, you know . . ."

"Maybe he saw some guys committing a murder, or something. Maybe he was afraid they'd come after him."

Jarvis thought about it. "Naw. He'd've told. He's not a snitch or anything, but he'd've told the police about something like a murder. I think he saw something that freaked him, scared the piss out of him, like . . . like . . ."

Stacy's mind filled with wonder. "A UFO, do you think?"

". . . or something like that. Something he didn't believe, *couldn't* believe. A ghost, or a monster, or something—"

"Jesus!" Stacy was intrigued, in spite of the circumstances.

"But you gotta come with me, Stacy."

"Come with you? Where?"

"Up there. Up in the gore. I gotta know. I gotta find out what it was."

Stacy looked around at the dark mountains behind the trailer, the endless acres of black shadows that stood distant, remote, savage beneath the cold moon.

"To the gore? Tonight?"

"No, not tonight."

"When?"

"Monday. After the funeral."

"Just the two of us?"

"Sure, unless we can get Cooly to take us. Think he might?"

Stacy nodded. "Sure. Maybe."

Jarvis's face collapsed into a distressed portrait of agony. His head jutted forward under the pressure of his back. "But either way, please, Stace, please come with me. I gotta know what happened to him."

Stacy hesitated only a moment. "Okay. Sure. I'll come."

7

The First Expedition

SATURDAY, AUGUST 27, 1988

If there was one thing that Harley Spooner wanted to do, it was to swear.

As a younger man he had cussed a blue streak, had even taken the Lord's name in vain on more than one occasion. His current abstinence was not because he was a religious man—although he was that. He knew the good Lord wouldn't get too miffed over a few good-natured blasphemies. After all, swearing was man-talk, and the Lord Himself was a man.

Actually, it was Harley's wife, Wilma, who'd put a stop to his "godless language." In the fifty years they had been married she had nagged him to the point that all his expletives were forever deleted.

When Wilma died, just ten short years ago, Harley had realized he'd never be released from that one particular bit of her tyranny. He was clever enough, however, to find plenty of words to take the place of those he couldn't use. His conversation was littered with meaningless babble that, along with his heavy Vermont accent, made him especially difficult to understand.

"Jack-nab it all!"

Today, Saturday, Harley couldn't sit still; he was as jumpy as a hen in a room full of roosters. Ever since he'd returned from Burlington, just a little more than a week ago, he'd been impatient for the arrival of the man from the college—the man with the check-book.

Of course Harley didn't want to part with the sacred stones, not any more than he'd wanted to give up those parcels of land he'd been selling off, one at a time, to supplement his Social Security checks. But a man had to do what he had to.

When he'd inherited the farm from his father there were about seven hundred acres of Spooner land. Now, as near as he could figure, he was down to around a hundred. Maybe less, and things were beginning to get kinda crowded. Harley didn't mind, though; he could make do. His had been a lifetime of making do.

"By jingley, I'll be down to a three by six plot by the time I'm through," he liked to tell his friend Cooly Hawks. And Cooly'd smile, and nod, and puff on his old corncob pipe.

"Where is that danged old blow-hog, anyways?" Harley asked his empty rooms. He kicked open the screen door to his sway-back porch, and squinted out across the meadow toward Cooly's shack.

"Might's well be talkin' to myself as waitin' on that black-bottomed old butternut."

Harley was in a bind: He couldn't go over to Cooly's; what if that college fella came while he was gone? And he couldn't stay put; he was feeling too rambunctious.

Oh well, Cooly'd show up sooner or later. He always did.

Or maybe the boys would drop by—Jarvis and Stacy, two pretty nice young fellas. Neighbors' kids, but polite and interested as you please. Not like most kids nowadays . . .

"And not like them danged college kids, neither," Harley sputtered to himself. "Educated fools! Why, a man can learn more inside a cow barn then they learn up to that flap-jackin' college of theirs, from all them panty-waist, piss-ant perfessers."

By now Harley realized he was not only edgy, but also he was getting irritated. That Dr. Potter said straight out that he'd send a man up on Saturday the twenty-seventh. And this was Saturday the twenty-seventh, by gum—eight o'clock Saturday morning, to be exact. And still that fella hadn't showed.

"Nobody's word's worth bull twaddle no more: What's the fella expect me to do, wait around all day?"

Harley walked stiff-legged out into his yard and took a seat on the tailgate of his lifeless, grass-bound pickup. From his favorite spot he looked up at the sky.

The Newsroom opened at three o'clock sharp.

Within moments a line of people assembled at the bar. They ordered drafts, munched chips or pickled eggs, and talked about the death of Lunker Lavigne.

Roger paid close attention to all the scraps of conversation, fighting his urge to ask questions or venture opinions.

A red-faced man, with hair slightly redder, who, Roger knew, worked at the grain store, said, "Claude was a good enough fella. To tell you the godforsaken truth, I'd a never pegged him for a suicide. Can't believe it."

"Nope, it was suicide all right," protested another man. He was fat, sweating, with a face like chewed gum. Roger thought his name was Benson. "My wife says they found him with the shotgun in his hand. He was dead 'fore they got him to the operatin' room."

"Christ, I know it was suicide," said the red-faced man, "I just meant I'd never've called it."

"None would," agreed a dark, sullen man with a pointed beard.

"No sir," continued Red. "My brother-in-law worked with Lunker over the power company. Says he was down-to-earth, real reg'lar. Type of fella calls a spade a spade."

"Musta made good money," said the bearded man.

"The brother-in-law does all right. Brings home enough to put some away. Goes to Florida once a year."

"I bet it's got somethin' to do with that kid of his," ventured Benson.

"Scoli?"

The word riveted Roger's attention to the speaker. He saw Laura glaring from behind the stack of glasses she was arranging near the tap. Clearly the man had meant no offense. To him "Scoli"

was simply a nickname; the word scoliosis would have been meaningless. Roger shook his head sadly; again he was witnessing the
kind of ignorance from which cruelties are born.

Red jerked his head as if instructing the bearded man to continue.

"Well, he's always been a sickly lad. Cost more than his share of
doctor bills. Boy like that can put a man in the poorhouse, then
right straight into an early grave."

"Jarvis Lavigne's a good kid." Laura held the man fixed in an
arctic stare.

"So he is, miss," Red said soothingly. "We don't mean no dis-
respect."

Apparently word about the strange thing Lunker Lavigne had
seen in the woods hadn't found its way into local gossip. The Lavignes were a private bunch, real tight-lipped Vermonters. Roger
vowed to keep their secret. Asking questions about it, no matter
how indirectly, would only add fuel to a fire that was quickly getting out of control.

Laura walked away from the group, heels tapping loudly on the
wooden floor. Roger watched her place bowls of peanuts on each
of the empty tables, thumping them down a little harder than
necessary.

At twenty after three a woman entered The Newsroom. Roger,
like the three men at the bar, noticed her with undisguised interest.

"Oooo-weee! Hi, honey!" said Benson, but only loud enough
for his companions to hear.

It was obvious from the moment she walked in that she was not
from Eureka, probably not from anywhere in the Northeast Kingdom. She looked as out of place as a mouse in a pitcher of milk.

She should have been a blonde, but she wasn't. Her hair was
gray, almost white, metallic; it fell long and straight to her shoulders, appearing more the work of a silversmith than a hairdresser.
And she was tall, nearly six feet. A lesser woman might have dyed
her hair, dressed or walked in a manner designed to deemphasize
her exceptional height. This woman carried herself with a poise
and dignity that were positively regal.

She looked around the interior of the bar, removed her sunglasses and blinked at the dim surroundings. Tight Levi's tailored to fit like designer jeans tugged suggestively at her bottom, implying that she wore nothing underneath. A blue denim shirt, with sleeves neatly rolled, molded to the contour of her high bosom. It was unbuttoned just a little farther than a local girl would have dared. A primitive-looking chain of dark metal hung around her neck.

As she walked to the bar a hush fell over the room.

"Are you Roger Newton?" she asked.

"Yes I am." He almost said, yes ma'am.

"I'm Leslie Winthrop. Dr. Potter said I should check in with you."

Roger could feel Laura watching them. "So you're 'Les' Winthrop. Somehow I thought you'd be . . . well . . . different."

She laughed a low throaty laugh. It made Roger feel as if he'd said something witty.

Laura joined them at the bar, waiting to be introduced. Roger felt relief when she smiled warmly at the newcomer. He noted, as if for the first time, the contrasting plainness of Laura's K Mart blue jeans and simple pullover.

"This is Laura Drew. Leslie Winthrop. She's come from the university to look at Harley Spooner's rocks."

Laura smiled, then giggled. Leslie joined her. Roger looked confused—he didn't realize what he'd said. When he did, he felt a blush rising.

"So you're going to be the guide, is that it?" Laura asked Roger.

"Umm-hmm."

"Guide and translator, right, Leslie?" Laura continued.

"Actually, I speak the language pretty well," Leslie's voice was low, almost a whisper. "I spent my summers in Bennington when I was growing up."

"Down country," said Roger in his ineptly exaggerated Vermont accent.

Laura looked at once surprised and disappointed.

"Laura, would you mind taking over here while I run Leslie up to Spooner's?"

"Sure," she said flatly. She smiled at the other woman—did it look a bit forced?—and extended her hand. "Nice to meet you, Leslie. Why not stop back for a drink before you go?"

"Thanks. I'd like that."

Before Roger and Leslie got into the 1986 Mazda, Roger hesitated. "I forgot to tell Laura something. Be right back."

He dashed into the bar. Laura waited by the cash register as Red paid his tab. He was muttering about the vision of loveliness he had just seen.

"You don't mind, do you?" Roger whispered.

"You are planning to come back, right?"

"Well, sure."

"Then of course I don't mind, silly!"

She kissed him quickly on the lips, and he left.

The first thing they noticed was the mailbox. It was oversized and positioned too near the road. "SPOONER" was scrawled on its side in large, awkward, childlike letters.

At Roger's direction Leslie turned left, followed a pitted, washed-out driveway up a gentle hill toward the house. They bounced past rusted wrecks of cars and pickups, grass-bound and vine-covered, that looked as if they'd been there for decades.

The Spooner residence was a two-story affair with odd-size sheds, one attached to the next, extending like a telescope from the east wall. The sheds seemed to reach for, but never quite touch, the weathered barn that crouched nearby like a fallen dinosaur.

All the buildings appeared overworked. Their sinking roofs made them look tired, old, dying.

The place had once been the traditional New England white. What remained of the paint had scaled and scrolled and faded. Bare, unprimed clapboard showed through in many places, like darkened muscle below colorless skin. Triangles of slate roof, steeply inclined for effortless snow removal, sloped upward from the four walls, to join at the double chimney on top. Facing the oncoming car, red slate, carefully placed among the gray, spelled out what must have been the initials of the house's builder—C.L.S. No doubt an early Spooner.

It was clear from the house's size and design that it had once been the prize of its occupants. Now the complex of buildings was like a mammoth relic of a vanishing Vermont, a forgotten monument where ancient vehicles crawled to die, their rusted carcasses littering the unmowed lawn and grounds.

Two unpainted two-by-fours, like crutches on either side of the open front door, were all that prevented the sway-backed porch roof from collapsing on the two men who waited there. Pipe smoke shrouded their heads.

Leslie and Roger left the Mazda and approached the men. Harley Spooner and his guest stared from their ladder-back chairs. Apparently they were waiting for the visitors to speak first.

"How's it going?" Roger called, holding up a hand in greeting.

Harley nodded stiffly, looking suspiciously at the woman. Beside him his friend Cooly Hawks grinned amiably.

Cooly was somewhat of an anomaly in the village for many reasons. For one thing he was the only black man in town. For another, no one knew just how old he really was. Once, in Roger's presence, Stacy had asked, somewhat timidly, "Cooly, how old are you, anyways . . ."

"Older'n the dirt, Mister Stacy, older'n the dirt." Cooly had chuckled mightily and winked at Roger, then ruffled the boy's hair with a black, big-knuckled hand.

Cooly's father, it was said, had been born a slave in some unknown southern state. He had made his way north toward Canada via the Vermont branch of the Underground Railroad. His wife, the story went, had to stop to give birth. So, finding Vermont to be a considerably more hospitable environment than the South, the family decided to settle in Eureka. Cooly's father became a logger, and Cooly followed in his footsteps.

It was said that Cooly knew the woods better than any man alive, that he could predict the weather by the turning of the leaves or the sounds of the insects, and that the medicine he concocted from his woodland apothecary was more effective than the pills prescribed by any doctor. Cooly knew all the local fishing holes; even during the dog days, when summer's hellish heat made the fish as lazy as people, he could always go out with his bamboo rod and return an hour or two later with his limit of wild, firm, pink-fleshed brookies.

Although Cooly had lived all his life a free man, he nonetheless demonstrated an exaggerated humility, probably programmed into him by his parents. Some said he was more than commonly respectful of white people. But Roger was sure that Cooly would be equally respectful of all people, had there been more of a variety in Eureka, Vermont.

"Mr. Hawks," said Roger with a smile. "Good to see you again."

Cooly waved and beamed. His black tightly curled hair, cropped close to his scalp, was completely free of white. The skin of his face was deeply lined, as if time had clawed at him with vicious nails, unable to leave its mark anywhere else on the old man.

Cooly seemed about to say something when, without a word of greeting, Harley Spooner jumped up. His beady eyes squinted at Leslie, his neck jutted forward. "You from the college?"

She nodded.

"Well, s'about time we lit out then, ain't it? Most the day's already wasted."

Roger guessed that it must have appeared a strange procession: the tiny old man in the baseball cap, bent and stiff-legged, hobbling along with all the agility of a grasshopper; his black companion, similarly aged, who, though extremely bowlegged, walked more erect and more gracefully than the younger man scampering along behind. And last, the silver-haired woman, dressed informally, but looking elegant in spite of her backpack, walking many steps to the rear.

The four of them followed a narrow path—no more than a parting of the grass, really—up from behind Harley's house, past his spring—from which a black conduit delivered water to the kitchen —and into the woods.

After passing a pathless belt of softwood trees, they entered an overgrown pasture defined by a tumbling stone wall. Harley sat on the wall, flipped his legs from one side to the other. Cooly stepped over it, and Roger jumped it with ease, then turned to assist Leslie.

Forging ahead now, Harley left the others behind, but never went so fast as to get out of sight for long.

Cooly slowed his pace, allowing the younger folks a chance to catch up.

"Mister Spooner, he's feelin' a little bit put upon," Cooly confided to Roger.

"Is that why he's not talking?"

"Oh, he was doin' plenty of sputterin' 'fore you people showed up. He's an ornery ol' man, that Mister Spooner."

"Well, he's in an awful hurry," said Leslie.

"That's a fact, miss. For a man without nothin' much to do, he sure goes about it in a powerful rush."

"At least you take time for introductions," Leslie said, finally introducing herself and explaining the purpose of her visit.

"Well, miss, Mister Spooner, he don't sleep much. He was prob'ly up this mornin' before the sun, 'spectin' you to be there, all decked out and ready for a hike 'fore the cock crowed. I didn't show up myself till after two, and he had words for me. Thing is, I didn't even know I was gonna be comin' along."

Leslie laughed.

"'Course, you understan', miss, Mister Spooner don't mean nothin' by it. It's just his way. Like I always tell him, an old bluejay's gotta squawk."

"Oh, I know." She put her hand on Cooly's arm. "My grandfather was just the same way."

Roger was surprised at how easily Leslie and Cooly established a rapport. She conversed nonstop with the old man as they struggled over stones and logs, fending off swinging branches that grabbed for her face. She moved so skillfully in the woods that she looked less and less out of place with each step. In fact, she seemed right at home.

Skirting an abrupt outcropping, which turned into a towering

ledge, the trio followed Harley Spooner through a marshy depression. He led them rapidly up to firmer ground, the trail banked by
a small stream. On the other side of the water uninterrupted forest
rolled back, and back, as far as the eye could see.

"This here's the beginnin' of the gore. Berthelson's Gore, they
used to call it. All that area on yonder side of the brook. Over here,
this here's Mister Spooner's prop'ty."

"You ever spend much time up in the gore, Cooly?" Roger was
thinking about Lunker Lavigne again.

"Oh, you bet. Back in my loggin' days 'specially. They's nothin'
much up there but tree and rock. We went up for the trees. Left the
rock where they set."

"Tell me something, Cooly. You ever see anything strange up
there?"

Cooly stopped and looked at the younger man. He squinted,
combing his fingers through the wiry stubs of his hair. "Strange? I
ain't so sure I know what you mean, Mister Newton."

Roger didn't want to lead him; he knew it was better to keep
the question open-ended. "Anything . . . you know . . . out of the
ordinary?"

Cooly shook his head. "Nope. No sir. They ain't nothin' up
there, like I tol' you."

From thirty feet ahead Harley Spooner called back to them,
"What about that ol' hotel. Tell 'em 'bout that, why doncha,
Cooly?"

Roger was amazed that Harley was able to hear their discussion
from such a distance. He raised his eyebrows to say as much to
Cooly.

"Maybe the cat's got ol' Mister Spooner's tongue," said the black
man, "but they ain't nothin' wrong with his hearin'." He chuckled
good-naturedly deep in his throat.

"I didn't know there was a hotel up there," Roger said.

"Oh yessir, they surely was." Cooly fidgeted a bit. "But they ain't
nothin' to none of them old stories, I can tell you that firsthand.
Strangest thing I ever seen up there is moose. Moose'll come wanderin' down once in a while from Canady, and—"

"Come on, Mr. Hawks," said Leslie, coaxing with a disarming smile. "What's the story about the hotel?"

Cooly looked around, as if searching for a way out of the conversation. Leslie pressed him with her relentless smile. "Well, I s'pose some might think them stories is kinda strange. But strange or no, the fact is that hotel ain't there no more. Burnt down way back a long time ago. Prob'ly by now has sinked right down into the ground, an' disappeared. An' good riddance, too, I say. Nobody never had nothin' but bad luck with that ol' place."

"What do you mean?"

"Well, like I says, some fella from downcountry built her back in the eighteen eighties or so, I guess 'twas. Maybe before. Run it for about ten years, then shut her down. Place never really caught on. It's nothin' more'n a mess-an-ruin now. That is, if you can find anythin' left of her."

"Why did they build it way up there in the first place? Seems like an odd spot for a hotel." Leslie's royal blue eyes were wide with interest.

"Well, miss, best I can figger, back in them days folks used to like to go to hotels and stay put. They'd settle in, relax, enjoy the waters that was so pop'ler back then. Not no more. Nowadays all folks wanna do is hop from one place to the next. An' I think the fella built this place had more than tourists in mind."

Leslie smiled broadly. "You mean he rented rooms complete with roommate?"

Cooly looked embarrassed. Now Roger could see what the old man was trying to avoid. "Yes, miss. So the story goes. Them boys in the lumber camps got a little tired of sleepin' on wooden bunks, all alongside one another. Hotel owner knew enough to build it in the gore, not in no town. That way he didn't need to worry about no town laws."

"So what happened to the place?" Roger was back on the case. When he'd asked about strange things in the gore he wasn't thinking of abandoned hotels. He'd expected to hear about ghosts, monsters, hidden treasure and murder, not about loggers, businessmen, and nineteenth-century prostitutes. But as a reporter he had learned to listen for that unexpected bit of information, the seemingly innocuous fact that would often tie unrelated things together. Cooly's story had him hooked; he wanted to hear everything. Perhaps he *would* do a short piece for some Sunday supplement after all.

"Lots of things happened. Mostly the loggin' business changed, pretty much died out for a while. An' tourist folks was losin' interest in mineral springs, especially at places with the wrong kind of rep'tation. I 'spect even though the hotel weren't in no town they still got righteous words from lots of good folks all around 'em. But there were somethin' else . . ."

Leslie and Roger moved closer to the old man, one on each side as they walked. Roger noticed how Cooly had fallen silent, as if trying to remember the facts, or trying to decide how to present them. Or maybe he wanted to skirt them altogether.

"What else happened?" Leslie encouraged.

"As I recall, some folks come up missin'. Not all at once, in a bunch, but one now, one a little later. Got so the owner couldn't keep girls up there. They was either too scared to hire on, or too scared to stay put. Word got out. Jes' stories mostly, I s'pose. But who'd want to go vacationin' someplace where folks was disappearin'?"

"What happened to them?"

"I can't say, miss, I jes' don't know. I can't even say if it's a true fact. But the place did have what you call a rep'tation. But then she burnt down, an' most folks forgot all about her. That is, most folks but ol' Mister Spooner."

Cooly squinted his dark eyes in thought as the trio passed over a little rise. At last they had caught up with Harley. He was sitting on a big rock, puffing his pipe, his feet not quite touching the ground.

"Well, Judas Priest! I was beginnin' to think the bears had got ya. You folks wanna see them flap-jackin' stones, or doncha?"

8

Strange Rituals

AT THE SAME TIME . . .

On the other side of the river the Watcher stood among the trees, deep in the shadows of the forest. Absently he massaged his aching leg as he peered through the forked trunk of a poplar, watching the cluster of strangers at their ritual.

He knew that he could not be seen. Yet he felt a tightness, a sickness, as he observed the intruders. As Watcher it was his duty to warn the others. But for now he must wait, continue to observe. And remember all. It might not be safe to abandon his watch spot until he knew the outsiders would come no closer. The Watcher had to be certain they were not a threat.

He crouched low among the bushes, his hide-covered back exposed to the treetops and the sky.

He had seen the moonfaces before. And he had been curious each time he watched them, alone or in pairs, at those rare times when they ventured too far into the safeland. But these moonfaces were different. These were purposeful, not just random wanderers with their death guns and bright colors.

And—could this be?—all of them were not moonfaces!

There was something else among them, something the Watcher had never seen before—the Shadowman. Many times he had heard The Descendant speak of Shadowman, but he had never believed in him—not as anything more than an old story—not until this day.

Why should Shadowman bring these moonfaced intruders to this place?

What sort of ritual did he lead them in?

The Watcher tightened his hand on the weapon; the comfort of its presence helped him not to move. Now his only purpose was to watch, to remember, then go quickly and tell everything to The Descendant. He knew he need not try to understand what this strange ritual was about; that was for The Descendant to decide.

But still he wondered . . .

Never before had he seen the moonfaces behave so strangely.

Never had he seen them stop, kneel, bow to the earth.

The strangest one—the one whose hair was like moonlight on water—bowed the lowest. It seemed to kiss the earth, whisper to it. Then, from the sack on the strange one's back, it took unfamiliar objects.

Were they weapons?

The Watcher felt his stomach tighten again. It was the spirits warning him to be still. He tried to control his breathing, tried to control the amount of sound he made when he breathed out. He was as still as a rabbit.

It *was* a weapon!

From the sack the moonface took a short spear. It was strangely small, the Watcher thought, no longer than the distance from the hand to the elbow. But the point was big and flat, broad as two hands side by side, smooth as the bark of a birch tree. The shaft of the spear was no thicker than the wrist of a newborn.

The moonface put the spear upon the ground, then removed another weapon from the bag. This one was like a knife blade that had been twisted round and round, coiled like a vine around a tree limb. It extended from a handle that was put on wrong. The weapon looked like some strange backward ax, where the hammerstone was the handle and the handle was the blade. He could make no sense of it.

The moonface removed something else from the weapon bag. A small silver box no bigger than the palm of the Watcher's hand. It frightened him terribly when the moonface pulled a blade longer than his arm from the tiny box. It was a kind of magic, he was sure.

The bag contained more weapons; he could tell from the way it rested on the ground. These the leader surely kept as private. So they must be the best of the lot! But the frightening thing, the thing that made the Watcher want to stand and run, was that the leader gave the three weapons to the other three intruders.

Now each moonface was armed!

Perhaps there was going to be an attack. Perhaps he should go at once, tell The Descendant, warn the others.

But no! He was to watch, not understand. As yet there had been no sign of hostility. As yet they had not crossed the protecting stream.

The Watcher's confusion increased when the leader pushed the twisted metal knife into the ground and started to turn it slowly, so very slowly.

And the Shadowman looked on.

And the little moonface sat on a stone, with fire in his mouth.

And the one with ice in his eyes knelt before the leader . . . The Watcher knew something bad was happening. It would require the wisdom of The Descendant to understand just what it was, just how it would change their lives.

But still he watched.

In a while, before the sun had fallen another measure, the leader took all the weapons back, returned them to the bag, and gave it to someone else to carry.

Shadowman looked all around, as if to make sure they were alone, then led the group away.

The Watcher hoped he had not been seen. He waited, motionless, until the intruders were out of sight. There was danger, yes. But, at least this time, they had not crossed the river. They had not yet ventured into safeland.

But what were they planning? And when would they return?

Mindless of his throbbing leg, the Watcher ran to The Descendant. He was swift and silent as a breeze across a mountaintop.

9

Some Kind of Premonition

LATER . . .

"What Mr. Spooner has up there," said Leslie Winthrop, her voice clear and authoritative amid the murmur of Newsroom customers, "is an Indian site. It may be two or three thousand years old, it may be comparatively recent. I couldn't tell from the small amount of digging I did today."

Laura struggled to smile at the silver-haired woman as she placed three cups of freshly brewed coffee on the table. She sat down beside Roger. Again she looked at the clock; Roger and Leslie had been gone a little more than five hours!

"You should have brought Harley back for a drink," she said to Roger. For some reason her voice was weak, it cracked as she spoke.

Roger glanced at Leslie and they both laughed. Laura felt herself blushing; had she sounded that funny?

"I think Harley's seen enough of us for one day," Roger said, chuckling. "The old boy got a little peeved when Leslie tried to explain that his marked stones had no religious significance."

"Just the same, I don't think he realizes how important they really are." Leslie was speaking directly to Laura.

Laura pressed her lips into a smile as Leslie continued, "If I can get Mr. Spooner to agree, I think Dr. Potter will want to bring a team up here to excavate that area. We may have nothing more than a simple campsite, but, quite possibly, we've located a whole

Indian village! Of course I really couldn't determine its dimensions from the sampling I did today, but a systematic dig can establish fairly accurate benchmarks and boundaries. It might well be an important find. In fact, I'm sure it is. All the conditions would have been favorable for a permanent settlement."

Laura swallowed a mouthful of coffee, then, "What do you mean, favorable?"

"Indians customarily made their camps on sandy knolls overlooking streams; they took drainage into consideration, you see. Mr. Spooner's knoll slopes to the south. This allows the winter sun to give maximum light and warmth, while at the same time, protecting the people from wind and cold. This site also would have been well protected to the north by the heavy forests of the gore. Almost an ideal location."

Laura was impressed—this woman was really excited about the discovery. Surely science was her only interest. So why did Laura feel so intimidated? So threatened? "What kind of Indians lived there?" Laura asked. "Were they Abenaki?"

"Probably. But it's hard to tell for certain right now. Abenaki Indians populated this whole area for thousands of years. But Mr. Spooner's marked stones may have been left by peoples other than the ones who settled the site originally. The cross and dot symbol was used by various Algonquin affiliated tribes to signal good hunting, good fishing, or good water. Or sometimes they were positioned to establish some kind of boundary. In any event, they have nothing to do with sacred writings or Christian symbolism."

"Harley didn't appreciate learning that," Roger said with a laugh.

"I just hope he isn't so angry that he won't give us permission to excavate."

"My guess is that Cooly will be able to talk some sense into him."

"Better him than me, that's for sure," Leslie said, laughing. "Maybe Dr. Potter can come up with a few dollars to twist his arm a little."

This woman seems to relate so easily to Roger, Laura thought. Again she forced herself to participate in the conversation. "Did you find anything interesting besides the stones?"

"Maybe. I made a few test holes with an auger and brought up some wood ash, a few pieces of pottery, and some stained soil. There was definitely something there. I measured between the test holes; my guess is that the site is at least thirty square meters, probably bigger. It's well worth taking a closer, more careful look. That's all I can really tell you right now."

Laura wanted to hold her attention. "Will there be room for any amateurs on the dig?"

"I'll give you both glowing recommendations." Leslie smiled at the couple. "But it'll really be up to Dr. Potter."

"It'll be up to Harley Spooner," Roger corrected.

Leslie's smile reversed into a comic frown. "Of course! How could I forget?" She looked at her watch, clicked her fingernails on the tabletop, and abruptly stood up. "I guess I'd better hit the road."

"Heading back to Burlington?" Laura asked.

"That's right. I'd wanted to make the drive before dark, but it's way too late for that."

A long trip, Laura thought. Leslie must be tired after all that driving and climbing. "You're welcome to stay the night," she offered, her voice quavering again. "You could stay at my place. Drive back in the morning . . ."

Leslie smiled. "That's awfully nice of you. But I can't. I've got a date for brunch in the morning. Thanks for offering." *God, she's pretty,* Laura thought. *But her smile is warm and sincere. I'm not being fair to her.*

"I'll walk you to the car," said Roger, rising beside her.

After shaking Laura's hand, Leslie led Roger toward the door.

Laura couldn't help noticing that the target of all male eyes in the room was Leslie's behind.

Keenan Whittaker opened the door to The Newsroom and entered. He brushed past the couple, head down, carefully avoiding eye contact with Roger. Laura watched him about-face and look Leslie up and down.

Laura turned her back on the room and began washing beer mugs in tepid, frothy dishwater. After rinsing each, she took special

care to set it gently on the plastic drying mat. She fought the urge
to slam the glasses down.

The pressure of tears pushed at her eyes. Why? Where were all
these doubts coming from? She hated herself for continually ques-
tioning Roger's devotion.

Then again, normally his temptations weren't so immediate.
And so . . . tempting.

STOP IT! Christ! She was behaving like a stupid adolescent. Her
common sense assured her that everything was okay, yet she was
acting like a petulant child.

No, Roger wasn't to blame. He couldn't be faulted. She was the
one who was stalling.

As she stared down into the sudsy gray dishwater, the din of
The Newsroom's patrons faded, transforming into Roger's voice.
It was that morning in the trailer, so many weeks ago . . .

"Okay, okay," he had said, studying her from across the breakfast
bar. "I understand that you can't say 'yes' until you're actually di-
vorced. But for now why don't you at least move in with me?"

She dried her hands on the dishtowel, watching his soft sad eyes
as they suddenly hardened. His voice rose in anger, "Why do we
have to keep visiting each other as if we were a couple of high
school kids dating or something?"

She wanted to go to him, hug him, assure him that all she
needed was time. But somehow his anger held her in place—anger
that reminded her too much of Hank.

Then just as suddenly, the anger was gone. Roger spoke quietly,
"Don't you want me, Laura? Is that it? Why don't you just tell
me?"

Still she could not go to him. How she wanted to say yes, of
course I'll live with you—but she heard other words coming out.
"It just wouldn't look right, Roger. You know Hank. Suppose he
used that in court? Or suppose—"

Roger stared at her. Then without a word he pushed his coffee
cup away, stood up, and left the trailer, quietly closing the door
behind him.

He's leaving me, she thought. *And I can't stop him.*

No, she couldn't blame Roger. She was the one who was acting foolishly.

Laura put down the last of the mugs and dried her hands on a linen towel. Furtively she wiped the tears from her eyes, then turned again to face The Newsroom.

In the parking lot, standing beside the Mazda, Roger felt strangely conspicuous to be with such a beautiful woman. He couldn't help wondering how the bar's patrons were assessing the situation.

With his mind only half on their conversation, he heard himself readily agreeing when Leslie asked that he have a talk with Harley Spooner on behalf of archaeology in Vermont. "But there's no real hurry," she added. "The site's been in the earth for hundreds of years. And that's the safest place for it. A while longer isn't going to hurt."

Then they chuckled at Harley's temper and Roger remarked how strange and charmingly incongruous it seemed to hear Mr. Hawks, an elderly black man, speaking with such a pronounced Yankee accent.

"Well, he's a real Vermonter," Leslie said.

As they spoke quietly, Roger studied the reflection of a lone streetlight in the Mazda's shiny surface. He felt an urge, weak and inappropriate, to ask Leslie not to go. The feeling embarrassed him; for a moment he couldn't look at her. Was he experiencing some sort of false closeness, a prodding of loneliness the source of which he couldn't guess? Or was he having some kind of premonition? Was this another irrational newsman's instinct that something was wrong? And if so, what could it be?

Roger watched as she buckled herself into the driver's seat, smiled one last time, and drove away. Then he stood motionless in the street as the Mazda's taillights, like twin fireflies, vanished into the distance.

Strange, he thought, the way a beautiful woman can inspire odd, misplaced feelings. At the same time he knew those feelings, mysterious though they were, suggested no fragility in his relationship with Laura.

He walked back into The Newsroom in kind of a daze. Clarity of thought returned when he noticed Keenan Whittaker sitting at the bar talking with Laura.

Whittaker looked peculiar. His spine was poised in an awkward angle; his left arm was in a cast. When he turned his head Roger saw the sickish blue-red colors of a black eye.

The railroad clock reported that it was nine-fifteen. Country and western music throbbed from the jukebox as evening conversation hummed from the five occupied tables. A party of four, seated at a booth, erupted in raucous laughter.

Roger cleared the coffee cups from the table where he had been sitting with the women. From there he could overhear Whittaker's conversation with Laura.

"Who's the dish your boyfriend just left with?"

Laura looked up, made eye contact with Roger, then looked away. "She's up from Burlington. She's doing some research on Indians in this area."

"I'll tell you somethin', Laura, if I had you waitin' to home, I wouldn't go runnin' off with nobody else. What d'ya say? Want to give it a try?"

"I still haven't changed my mind, Keen. Roger's my man. That's the long and the short of it." She winked good-naturedly at Keenan and smiled at Roger.

"I figgered that's what you'd say, an' I respect you for it. But still, if you ever get to feelin' lonely . . ."

Roger cleared his throat. Walking around the bar, he placed the dirty coffee cups near the sink. A quick glance showed him that Whittaker's face was badly bruised. A conspicuous gap loomed in his lower row of teeth. Roger knew better than to pry, but curiosity burned at him. "How's it going, Keenan?"

"Could be better." Whittaker about-faced, and looked directly at Roger. Then he extended his hand. As the men shook, Whittaker eyed Roger's hand.

"Nice soft hands. Knuckles in good shape. I'm glad to see it."

Keenan grunted a half laugh and smiled weakly. Then he picked up his bottle of Bud and went off to sit by himself at a table in the corner.

Roger was puzzled. "What happened to him?"

"He won't say. Keen's pride only allows him to talk about the fights he wins."

"What's with the handshake?"

"Believe it or not, I think he was just congratulating you." She gave him a kiss on the cheek and winked playfully. "But it's nice to know I have an admirer, if I ever need one."

Roger smiled. "Hey, that's what I'm here for." He returned her wink with a quick, inconspicuous hug, not wanting to arouse catcalls from any of the customers. He could sense a tension lifted, feel how happy she was to be with him. Her smile told him that any threat she might have felt from Leslie Winthrop was now no problem at all.

"Love you," she whispered.

In that moment of closeness, Roger felt the best he had all day. He'd be glad when this night was over. Tired from his hike, he wanted to lie down with Laura, relax, and take it from there. Yet he had to reconcile himself to a painful fact: there would be many more drinks to pour and many more people to serve before he'd be able to rest.

In the corner Keenan Whittaker finished his Bud and hurriedly left.

Perhaps it wasn't the most direct route back to Burlington, but it was the easiest—just the reverse of the directions David Potter had written out for her. She'd take Route 114A to Island Pond, then south on 114 to St. Johnsbury, west to the Interstate, and home. It would total more than one hundred miles. She'd be on the road for nearly three hours, arriving home after midnight.

The roads in the Northeast Kingdom were a puzzle, especially the ones from Eureka to Island Pond. Poorly marked, poorly maintained, they often changed inexplicably from pavement to gravel and back again. A wrong turn could get a traveler lost for hours. Trying to correct a mistake in this unpopulated area, a driver could get so twisted around, so disoriented, that there would be no choice but to wait at the roadside until morning.

"Better not mess up," Leslie warned herself. Her voice sounded oddly loud in the darkened car. The lights from the dash shone on her polished fingernails as she clutched the wheel. She wondered why she was gripping it so tightly.

"You're nervous, that's why," she said aloud, but softer this time.

She thought of David Potter's jovial admonition when he gave her the assignment: "Be careful up there, Les. Don't get lost; we may never find you. That country is definitely the wildest part of the state. Acres and acres are absolutely uninhabited. You could blast a howitzer straight up into the air and not have to worry about its landing on somebody. Just think of it, vast areas of land, larger than New York City, and not a single living resident!" Then he'd dropped his voice, assuming a mock-sinister drone, "At least no one the census taker wanted to talk to." He had winked at her and smiled, but somehow, now, the warning made her feel uneasy.

Leslie yawned and turned on the radio; she was tired, achy. *I must be getting a little out of shape,* she thought. *A short hike like that shouldn't tire me out this much.*

She shook her head, disappointed in herself. *Well, it's back to my exercise campaign, ASAP.*

She stretched, first one arm, then the other, never removing both hands from the wheel.

A commentator on Vermont Public Radio was talking about Mary Wollstonecraft Shelley. "Perhaps," the commentator said, "Shelley's creation, the Frankenstein monster, was in fact a thinly disguised biography of her husband, Percy Bysshe . . ."

Leslie made a face, turned the dial until she found some light classical. *That's better*, she thought, feeling herself begin to relax.

Cautious that she might get too relaxed, fearing drowsiness, she picked up her cassette dictating machine from the seat beside her.

I'll dictate a few notes about the site, she decided.

Pushing the record button, she held the tiny machine in front of her mouth, "Saturday, August twenty-seventh, nineteen eighty-eight. Arrived in Eureka at about three-thirty P.M. and met with Mr. Newton at his . . . ahh . . . place of business. He took me to the property of Harley Spooner, who . . . OH, FUCK . . . !"

I must be tired, she thought, *I'm trying to dictate with the radio on!*
She placed the recorder back on the seat and switched the car radio off.

Ahead of her the two-lane blacktop cut through the forests of the Northeast Kingdom. The Mazda's white headlights illuminated the road, pushing heavy shadows back into the woodland. Driving on this narrow road, not yet ten miles out of Eureka, was almost like driving through a tunnel; in places the trees grew so close to the highway that their branches intertwined overhead.

She shook her head, trying to clear her vision. Was that something in the road ahead?

Leslie hit the brakes to avoid colliding with a fat porcupine waddling across the pavement. She screeched to a halt not ten feet in front of the plump little animal. The porcupine, apparently not intimidated by such violent, noisy activity, didn't even quicken its pace. It didn't so much as glance at the car, refusing to acknowledge that Leslie had just spared its life.

She watched it amble off into the bushes. "Independent little critter." She forced a laugh, shifted back into first and accelerated.

The Mazda wound around unexpected curves, hugging the road like a race car. Ahead, as the road straightened, she could see the moon in the distance, a cold sliver of white resting on the peaked horizon—a star on a Christmas tree.

To the right, on the shoulder of the highway, a man was walking toward the car. He moved awkwardly, a lurching shadow against the backdrop of the trees. A drunk, maybe? *He should know better than to dress in black like that,* Leslie thought.

Before the headlights washed over him he stepped off the road and back into the bushes, nearly out of sight.

Leslie swerved into the left lane, planning a long arc around the pedestrian, who waited at a safe distance for the car to pass.

Closer to the man, she slowed a bit, curious to get a look at him.

His featureless form was a knot of shadows among the twisted trees.

Suddenly he vaulted into her headlights!

So quickly did he spring from motionless statue to frenzied attacker that Leslie gasped involuntarily. She bit down on her lip, trying to control the car as the form sped at her, arms raised and waving, legs pumping frantically.

Maybe he's in trouble, she thought, *maybe he's trying to get me to stop.* But she knew that wasn't right. Cramping her wheel to the left to avoid smashing into him, she knew that the man was acting oddly.

He dodged just then, as if trying to force her to hit him.

He's crazy, she thought.

Stomping the brake, she slapped the wheel to the left. And she was out of control.

"My God!" she cried. She screamed as the Mazda fishtailed to the left. Its rear end caught up to, then passed the front. She was almost in a spin as the front tires dug into the soft shoulder. The rear end continued its uncontrollable arc, rubber screeching on the asphalt.

The brakes, aided by the friction of the sandy embankment, yanked the car to a stop. The stink of hot rubber and burning clutch filled the interior. As Leslie's body slammed into the steering wheel, the breath blasted from her lungs.

She was nearly unconscious, hugging the steering wheel like a drowning woman hugging a life ring.

She knew she was hurt.

Eyes half-open, thoughts confused and fuzzy, she saw the dark, lurching form approach from the side. He passed so close to the headlights that she couldn't get a good look at him; all she saw was his indistinct bulk in the foreground, his immense shadow projected against the roadside trees.

She cried out when she heard his finger grappling with the outside of the door, as if blindly searching for the handle.

Gotta lock it, she thought.

Pain. She couldn't move.

The door jerked open, sprung hinges screeching. A rank smell filled her burning lungs.

Then she felt a coarse hand at the back of her neck. Another hand tugged frantically at her seat belt. He was trying to pull her out of the car! She struggled with all her strength, but the straps across her hips and chest held her in place.

Failing to extricate her, the hand pulled brutally at her hair, yanked her away from the steering wheel. She felt the fingers tighten, collecting a fistful of hair. Pain ripped across her scalp. It felt as if the skin was tearing from her skull.

Then, with an irresistible force, the powerful hand smashed her screaming face into the windshield.

For a moment she felt a shattering impact; then, nothing at all.

10

Resisting the Demon

Bright light, as sharp as a scalpel. Claude Lavigne, mushroom-white, reeking of alcohol and formaldehyde, stretched out naked on the autopsy table. The side of his face as featureless as hamburger; his pale puffy gut, slit, folded back like a bloody jacket.

Hank Drew smiled at the memory.

In his rented room above the Island Pond Apothecary, he whipped off the tangled sheets. They'd confined him like a straitjacket. The sickish odor of his body and the stink of unlaundered bedclothes assaulted his nostrils. But these things were not important.

He thought of Keenan Whittaker, sprawled and bawling on the ground, his left arm twisted at a lunatic angle. Again he smiled.

They were weak men. They could not get beyond the first temptation—the alcohol.

Booze, Hank knew, was for lesser men, men who didn't know how to defend themselves, men who couldn't protect what was theirs.

Booze was a demon, an evil god demanding sacrifice.

Hank saw the picture very clearly; he was man enough to recognize what the booze had taken from him. And it could take more, too, but only if he let it. Only if he didn't resist.

Already it had taken his wife, his son . . .

At the time of the separation Hank had been a victim, watching passively as more and more of his life eroded and washed away. Like a weakling he'd waited for things to right themselves, for justice to magically return to his world entirely on its own.

He had cowered like a criminal in his cell-like room, counting the hours, expecting that any minute Laura would come back to him.

In those days every sound in the darkened room had distracted him, brought him to immediate attention. That passing car might be Laura arriving. The creaking board could be her footstep on the stairs.

And sometimes she'd almost come. Almost. He could feel her, sense her getting closer. Sometimes she'd nearly appeared to him, a hazy apparition shaping itself from the cigarette smoke in his dimly lit bedroom, or forming herself, like a dark contoured shadow, from his black pants and turtleneck draped carefully across the back of a high-back chair. Sometimes she'd materialize briefly in the car, a fragile outline on the passenger's seat, undulating, almost invisible, like heat rising from a sun-scorched highway.

Temptations? Reminders? There was always something holding her back, pulling her away.

And he knew what it was!

It was then that Hank realized he'd have to take control, eliminate the barriers separating him from his wife and son.

The booze had been nothing but a temporary setback; he had beaten it. Now he could beat anything.

Whittaker had been easy, a bit of litter tossed away. But there was another greater obstacle—Newton!

What Newton had done wasn't right. It wasn't right at all. In fact, it was . . . criminal.

The new Hank, the stronger Hank, wasn't one to sit back passively and wait for justice to come about. He was a man of action, a man of conviction and high ideals.

He knew what he had to do; the waiting was over.

Hank pitched forward, landed facedown on the rug in front of his bed.

It was necessary to be in the best shape. His mind would have to be as clear as his conscience. He'd have to be rested, alert, fine-tuned, and ready.

But how could he rest? He had so much energy! He was charged, hot, sparkling with electricity! If he was going to get any sleep tonight he'd have to tire himself out. He did a pushup, just the way he'd done it in the corps. Up, down. He did another, thrusting his weight away from the floor, clapping his hands, catching himself, and lowering his body to repeat the process.

. . . up . . . slap! . . . down . . .

It was just like making love, the same position, the same surge of exhilaration.

. . . slap! . . .

He'd have Laura back. He knew it. He'd given up the booze—she was right about that. He'd admit it to her. But *she'd* have to admit that he was right about the other things. He knew she'd come to apologize, beg his forgiveness. Plead with him to take her back.

. . . up . . . slap! . . .

And he'd be ready to forgive her.

Then he'd leave this rat hole, join them at the trailer, and everything would be just the way it had been. Before the demon came.

They'd be happy. They'd be a family. And the loneliness would be gone.

. . . slap . . . slap . . . slap . . .

11

Another Expedition

Long morning shadows spread like cloaks across the lush green grass on the hillside. Stacy Drew, dressed in a brown suit that had become a bit too snug, stood between his mother and Roger Newton at Claude Lavigne's burial.

On the other side of the open grave, Jarvis stood beside Mrs. Lavigne. The wind pulled at her light black coat; the tails flapped like the wings of a blackbird. Occasionally she would pat her eyes with a white handkerchief. Stacy had never before seen his friend's mother cry. Watching her felt like an intrusion.

He switched his attention to the priest, strained to hear what he was saying. The words, however consoling they might have been, were lost in a gust of summer wind.

Beside the priest, a cluster of big, blank-faced men from the power company stood strangely close together.

Stacy felt the weight of Roger's hand on his shoulder. It felt good. Yet, at the same time, he wanted to be free of it—he should be able to stand alone at such a time.

Still unable to hear the prayers even after the wind had subsided, he searched for other things to occupy his attention. He noted the pile of earth, concealed yet most conspicuous, under a layer of green all-weather carpeting. *It doesn't look at all like grass*, Stacy thought, *why do they bother?* Nearby, the coffin—closed now, as it had been at the funeral—was suspended on straps over the open grave. Stacy wondered how they would lower the heavy box into the hole.

This ordeal was new to him. He was finally experiencing a real death firsthand, yet experience brought no better understanding, and he felt no more at ease. Part of him actually wanted to see Mr. Lavigne's body. He pictured his friend's father lifeless and cold, then cast the image from his mind. His morbid curiosity shamed him. Still, there was something he had to know about death. He wanted, somehow, to come to terms with it. But it wasn't to be.

The whole ritual made him feel as if he were part of a parade, mindlessly marching behind the funeral director, comprehending nothing, yet terrified of making some behavioral mistake. He was fearful about breaking rules he had never learned.

On one level he knew what it was like to lose a father, but not in so irrevocable a way. Stacy would be able to see his dad again, at least once in a while. Even so, he couldn't forget the days right after Dad left: the empty place at the table; the strange stillness in the house, especially at night; the abandoned plans for fishing trips and summer vacations.

Could it be any worse for Jarvis?

From across the grave Stacy watched his friend. With glazed eyes, face pale as chalk, Jarvis approached the coffin. He deposited there a single red rose. Mrs. Lavigne followed, leaving another rose. She hesitated by the shiny box. From where he stood Stacy could see her shoulders quivering. Jarvis walked up, took her arm, tried to lead her to the sympathetic group who waited a respectful distance in the background.

Mrs. Lavigne allowed herself to be led, but she looked over her shoulder, and called in a shattered voice, "Claude!" Stacy guessed this would be the last time she would ever speak directly to her husband. Probably it was the first time he'd failed to reply.

"Come on, son. Let's be going," said Roger. Stacy liked the sound of the word: son. His mother reached for his hand, and Stacy let her take it. He wanted to say something to her, but there were no words. Death was silence; this he understood.

Before the Lavignes got into the funeral director's big black car

Jarvis looked at Stacy—directly into his eyes. Although his face was expressionless, Stacy understood what he wanted and nodded his agreement.

Yes, they would go together into the gore.

Somehow Jarvis's hollow expression communicated everything: It said that he didn't know why or how, but he knew that something out there had caused all of this. It was easy for Stacy to understand why Jarvis wanted to learn what that "something" had been. Stacy had no choice but to help him.

On the drive back to the trailer Stacy considered the risks. If he and Jarvis went into the gore, they risked seeing the same thing that had terrified Mr. Lavigne. What would happen then?

Could there be things so strange, so frightening, that death was preferable to knowing about them?

In all the horror and science fiction stories he'd ever read there was rarely anything that couldn't be fought, that couldn't be set right. Vampires could be killed, monsters could be repelled, aliens could be destroyed with substances as ordinary as seawater or the germs of a common cold. And suddenly there was a clear difference between stories and real life: Both could be terrifying, but only the former could invariably be resolved with the simple act of closing a book.

Stacy felt trapped in the middle of the station wagon's front seat. He wanted to go to his friend, lend what comfort he could. He couldn't wait to get home, to the telephone.

"I want to go over to Jarvis's," he said, neither to his mother nor to Roger.

The adults looked at each other, then at him. Roger started to say something, but Mom cut him off. "Give them a little time, hon. Mrs. Lavigne needs Jarvis right now. Wait an hour or so, then go and pay your respects."

Roger took Stacy's knee in his hand, squeezed it, shook it gently from side to side. "You're a good friend," he said.

Stacy tried to smile, he knew he should, but he couldn't. At the same time he felt helpless. What comfort could he give Jarvis? All he had to offer was his presence, and what good was that?

He knew one thing though: Before the day was over he and Jarvis would go into the woods.

And he knew something else—the woods had changed. Now, because of some magical, unexplainable transformation, it was a very different wilderness than the two boys had ever explored before.

"I don't know," said Cooly Hawks. He spat a great, foul mass of tobacco juice into Harley Spooner's yard. "I guess prob'y I got no objections to takin' you boys out for a little walk. But I ain't so sure it's such a good idea if yer parents don't know."

Stacy and Jarvis looked up at him eagerly. "Come on, Cooly, you've taken us hiking before," Stacy said. "You know the woods better'n anybody. You said so yourself."

"That I do," said the black man with an emphatic nod of the head. "But before we never had no partic'ler reason to go, we was jest out hikin', or goin' fishin', or somethin'. Now you boys wanna go out there lookin' for trouble. I can tell jes' by the sight of you."

Stacy and Jarvis looked at each other. Stacy could see the urgency in his friend's eyes. "Please, Cooly," Jarvis implored.

Cooly spat again and studied the ground. He kicked some dirt over the oily glob of chewing tobacco. "I might be a little more inclined to agree if I knew just what you fellas is up to."

Again the boys consulted each other's eyes. Stacy raised his eyebrows in a question. Jarvis replied with a series of quick affirmative nods.

"But please, Cooly, you gotta promise not to tell, okay?"

"Well, Mister Jarvis, there ain't a man here'bouts who can't trust ol' Cooly with a secret."

Jarvis Lavigne dropped his eyes. So did Stacy. They had offended the old man.

Jarvis spoke looking at the ground. "I want to see what it was that killed my father."

Cooly sighed. "That's pretty close to what I figgered." He sat down on Harley's decrepit steps. "Now, you come over here and set right down beside me, Mister Jarvis. You too, Mister Stacy."

The boys sat.

As the old man searched for words, his jaw locked tight, his dark eyes squinted as if in pain. "Boy, there ain't nothin' out there killed your father. I want you to understan' that. What your daddy done, well . . . it took a lot of gumption, and don't you never let nobody tell you it didn't."

Cooly paused, as if waiting for Jarvis to argue. Instead Jarvis just stared at his clasped hands.

Stacy might have said something, but he knew he wasn't part of this conversation. Now, it was between his friend and the old black man. Stacy could sense Cooly's discomfort, could almost feel Jarvis's torment.

"I knowed your daddy, boy. Maybe not so good as you knowed him, but I knowed him all the same." Cooly's mouth continued to move, but nothing came out. It was as if he were trying on words before speaking them. "Bet you an' I'd agree to one thing though: Your daddy, he was a darned good man, one a the best hereabouts. He was strong as a bear, an' brave as an Injun. An' what's more important, he was always fair an' honest. With everybody. I even done jobs for him time and again, an' you know why?"

Jarvis looked at him. Cooly's brown eyes were as gentle as a doe's. They coaxed a whispered response from the boy:

"No."

" 'Cause he'd always say, 'Cooly, you got any time to help me out with somethin'?' That's why."

Jarvis blinked, seeming not to understand.

"Lots of fellas would jes' say, 'Cooly, I gotta job fer ya.' Well, sir, I wouldn't work for none a them. And they never could figger out why. You see what I'm drivin' at, Mister Jarvis?"

"I . . . I'm not sure. I guess so . . ."

"Well, what I'm drivin' at is this: Your daddy weren't only fair an' honest, he was a good man. A *good* man. He . . . well, he understood things. He understood people. To be that kinda man, why, a fella's gotta understand hisself. What your daddy done, Mister

Jarvis, he done for some good reason. Maybe nobody but him an' the good Lord knows what that reason is . . . But a man like your daddy, he understands hisself. When be does somethin', why, you, an' me, an' everybody else can be sure of one thing: He has a darn good reason."

Jarvis nodded his head. He turned moist eyes away from the old man's.

Cooly continued, "I wisht I could explain this to ya better, son, but you listen up anyways, 'cause this is important. Some folks is gonna say what he done was wrong. Or that maybe he was weak to do it, maybe even a coward. But you don't listen to none of them folks; they don't know your daddy. None of 'em do. You and me, we knowed him better'n that. We know he was fair, we know he was honest, an' we know he weren't no coward."

For a long moment the three of them sat in silence. Cooly's eyes were moist, his lips moved soundlessly.

In the background Stacy could bear Harley Spooner banging around inside. He was singing in the kitchen. Now and then the sound of clattering pans or the porcelain chime of a dish hitting the table rang out.

Stacy saw that Jarvis was crying; tears rolled down his cheeks as silently as rain on a windowpane.

"But Cooly, I heard Dad and Ma talking. He said he saw something out there. I *heard* him. And I heard her ask him what he was so afraid of."

"An' what did he say he seen?"

"He wouldn't tell her. That's just it. I gotta know, Cooly. I gotta."

The old man took a knife from his pocket, opened it, and carved off a bit more tobacco. Knife and tobacco went to his mouth. Then he flipped the knife closed against his pant leg and returned it to his pocket.

"Yup, I s'pose you do . . ."

"If you won't take us . . . an' even if Stacy won't come . . . I'll have to go alone."

"Yes, son, I s'pose you will."

"Please, Cooly, will you help me out?"

"I don't s'pose you'd believe me if I told you that whatever your daddy done had nothin' to do with nothin' he seen up in them woods?"

"I'd believe ya, but I'd have to see for myself."

Cooly smiled a soft, sad smile. "I know you would, Mister Jarvis, 'cause yer jest like yer daddy. An' I believe it would be safer for the both of you fellas if you have a grown-up tag along to keep an eye on ya. I bet yer parents would agree with that, too. I guess they's no harm in me takin' you boys out for a little hike . . ."

Jarvis smiled broadly as he fingered his tears away. Stacy felt good seeing that smile; he was grateful to the old man.

"But you fellas gotta promise me one thing—if we don't find what you're lookin' for up there today, then you gotta quit pesterin' me. No more hikes. No more walks in the woods. No more lookin' fer trouble. I ain't gonna spend the rest of my life prospectin' for gold mines I know jest ain't there."

"We promise." Jarvis nodded his head vigorously. Stacy did the same.

"Now what do you say we go an' see if ol' Mister Spooner's got a little somethin' in there so's we can wet our whistles. Then we'll be on our way."

Harley Spooner didn't like the idea one gol' darn bit. Cooly shoulda checked with him first, that's what he shoulda done.

He stood on his swaybacked porch, watching the three of them plodding waist-deep through the green, blowing fields of timothy, heading in the direction of the gore. Cooly had that gnarly old walking stick of his resting on his shoulder like a hunting rifle.

Maybe the right and wrong of it wasn't too clear. There were those who'd say it wasn't right going off on a hike the very day the Lavigne boy's father was laid to rest. Some might argue that the woods up in the gore weren't safe for anyone, especially for a man in his eighties, and two little boys not even old enough to buy hunting licenses.

But Harley knew the real reason why what Cooly'd done was wrong: There were things in those woods, wild, dangerous, godless things. Things that in the old days grown men would huddle around the fire at logging camp trying to figure out, or sit alone in their tents, trying to forget.

There was nothing wrong with Harley's hearing, never had been. He'd definitely heard the boy say his father'd seen something in the woods. And pretty likely he had. Maybe Harley didn't know what—not exactly—but the news made him think twice about his offer to sell the sacred stones.

Those stones had been placed there for a reason. He was sure of it now. Maybe years of living safely on the edge of the gore had made him forget the stones' purpose. Maybe the need for extra cash had made him foolish. But those stones were put there—by Indians or angels or whoever—for a very good reason. They were put there as a kind of fence.

And now Harley realized the mistake had been his, not Cooly's. There was nobody to blame but himself. He never should have moved the stones in the first place, never should have carted them off to Burlington.

Thank the good Lord they were back in place now. And, by jiminy, that's where they were going to stay, come hell or high water.

He just hoped he hadn't been so stupid that he'd locked the barn door after the horse had already escaped.

After *something* had already escaped.

12

A Message from the Past

"Hello, Roger?"

"Yes?"

"Dave Potter, here."

"Dr. Potter! I was going to call you. I wanted to thank you for at least temporarily improving the scenery around here."

"Rog, listen, there's been an accident. Leslie's hurt. It's bad . . ."

"Hurt . . . ?"

"I'm surprised you haven't heard. She cracked up the car on the way back from your place."

"My God, David. I hadn't heard. Is she all right?"

"They don't know. She's . . . she's in a coma."

"Oh, shit. I'm sorry, David. Christ. What happened?"

"The police figured she fell asleep at the wheel, but I don't know. In any event, she went off the road, smashed her skull against the windshield."

"Oh no . . ."

"Roger. I want to come up there."

"Sure. Of course. Anything I can do . . . ?"

"The state police phoned me around midnight on Saturday to give me the news. It was my Mazda she was driving. And they found one of our dictating machines in the wreck. I picked it up yesterday at their office. It was smashed up pretty bad, but the tape was okay. I played it last night. It sounds as if she was dictating when she went off the road . . ."

"So she wasn't asleep at the wheel?"

"So it would seem."

"You tell the police?"

"No. I . . . ah . . . I want you to listen to it with me."

"Yeah. Sure, anything . . ."

"She said some queer stuff on the recording. Stuff that doesn't make any sense, if I'm hearing it right. She was dictating notes about your trip to the Indian site at Spooner's place . . ."

"What did she say?"

"I'd rather you listened to it. Is that okay?"

"Sure, glad to. When you coming?"

"I'll be there tonight. Under the circumstances . . ."

"Can you stay the night?"

"I'd like to. You got enough room?"

"Nothing but. I'll keep dinner warm for you."

"Where'll you be?"

"I'll wait for you at my house. The bar's closed Sunday and Monday. Even us godless types need our rest. You remember where I live?"

"Same place?"

"Same place."

"Great. I'll be there in three hours."

Harley Spooner walked in from the porch. It was cooler inside; that's why he kept the shades down and the drapes closed. As he passed the grandfather clock in the hall he jumped as the striking mechanism whined to life.

Four o'clock!

He picked up his pace and clattered across the linoleum floor to the kitchen so he could look out the back window. In the distance, across the sloping pastureland, a crude stone wall held the forest at bay. Harley looked at the shadow-filled pockets between the trees, hoping to see Cooly and the two boys.

He rested his elbow on the pump beside the sink, squinting into the distance. *Rag-ass old nigger,* he thought. *Stupid to bring them boys up there. Dang stupid!*

But Cooly wasn't stupid; Harley knew that. Perhaps Cooly was just humoring the boys, hoping a walk in the woods would help Jarvis Lavigne get his mind off his father. Too bad for the kid. Too young to lose a parent.

Harley thought the world of those two boys. He liked the way they'd come around to visit him. He liked the way they'd badger him with a hundred questions about this and another hundred more about that.

In a way—with the exception of Cooly, of course—those two boys were his only friends. They were the only people who visited him regularly, especially during the summer when school was out. And he expected he'd be seeing more of them in the future, now that . . .

Now that neither one of them had a daddy.

That chilling thought filled the old man with an icy tension. No fathers . . . and them so young.

Harley thought back on his own father. He had learned a good deal from that man—lessons he'd never forget, like the value of a man's word, that hard work keeps you healthy, and how to make do. Pa had also taught him the importance of staying home, and above all, never to be fussy.

And humor! Why, the old man'd had such a way of laughing! Harley remembered all the times he'd come in tired from shoveling in the barn. Pa would meet him at the kitchen door and he'd be sniffing the air like an old hound dog. "Why, you reek-a-Vermont, boy," he'd say, and he'd laugh and laugh and laugh.

Eureka, Vermont . . .

Ah, those had been fine times, and the lessons he'd learned had taken Harley a long way in life. A good long way.

"Too bad for them boys," Harley muttered.

If his own father had died, or run off, when Harley was their age, why, he wouldn't be half the man he was today. Harley knew he had something to pass along. It was his job—his and Cooly's maybe—to take care of those boys, to teach them everything he could in the time he had left.

Harley had always wanted a son of his own. By now, of course, he knew it wasn't to be. Wilma had blamed herself because the Spooner line had daughtered-out. But Harley never held it against her. No, she'd been a good wife, and, like he'd always told her, having a daughter was better than having no children at all.

But it had been years since he'd heard from that daughter of his. Last time had been at Wilma's funeral . . .

Why cripes, thought Harley, *I'm all wound up like a two-dollar pocket watch.* He tried to slow his breathing, which was coming in shallow, noisy gasps. The pain in the middle of his gut was like heartburn. It was the same pain he'd felt walking those people up to the sacred stones. He swallowed a mouthful of air, hoping to belch. *Blammed nuisance*, he thought, *pain in the butt*.

The burp came, rumbling up along his esophagus like a freight train in a tunnel. When it erupted into the quiet kitchen another chilling thought struck him: what if something's happened to Cooly and the boys? The woods weren't safe; Cooly knew that. *Oh, why'd he hafta go and drag them boys up into the gore?*

"Jim'ney, jim'ney, jim'ney," Harley sputtered, wrestling with his growing frustration. Somewhere, on a subtler level, another feeling mixed in—fear. If something happened to those three, why, Harley'd be all alone.

"*Stupid* ol' nigger." Harley bit down on his pipe stem so hard that it hurt his gum. The flash of pain burned some sense into him: Cooly wouldn't do anything to harm those boys. *No sir. He's probably paradin' them around in circles up there, just to tire 'em out. Then he'll bring 'em home and be done with it.*

Harley knew he could trust Cooly to do the right thing. Couldn't he?

Through a thin veil of pipe smoke, Harley Spooner looked out into the woods.

After taking two beers from the refrigerator, Roger Newton led Dr. David Potter into the den. He was amazed at how dramatically Potter had changed. Instead of the paunchy, balding man he had last seen, Potter looked trim, muscled, somehow taller. The soft-looking flesh of his face was now angular and tanned. A bright strip of white skin across the bridge of his nose betrayed that contacts had recently replaced Potter's horn-rimmed glasses. Roger was surprised to see that a strong jawline had been hidden under the unkempt, furry beard be remembered.

Dressed in razor-creased white slacks and a green three-button jersey, David Potter was a completely new man. Yet, in spite of his healthy appearance, he seemed somehow reserved, quiet, almost sullen. He didn't laugh as easily as Roger remembered. He hardly smiled.

"God, David, I'm sorry to hear about Leslie."

Potter turned away, began to inspect the titles on Roger's bookshelves. "It was a shock, that's for sure." He cleared his throat. "And I'm worried about her. She was doing so well . . . professionally I mean. Had a job offer in Ohio for next year . . ."

Roger nodded, letting his friend talk.

"If she ever comes out of this, who knows what shape she'll be in. Christ, she was smart, a real hard worker. She had a bright future ahead of her . . ."

"What are the doctors saying?"

" 'Wait and see.' What else can they say?"

Roger shook his head. "God's been throwing us some real sucker punches lately . . ."

Startled, Potter looked up, habitually peering over eyeglasses that were no longer there. "You mean there's more?"

The two men sat down in imitation leather easy chairs. Roger's was a recliner; he tipped back and made himself comfortable. Harpsichord music played in the background.

"Well, maybe yes, maybe no. A guy I know from town just committed suicide. And it's really been on my mind. His funeral was this morning."

"A friend of yours?"

Roger wanted to answer yes, but it wouldn't be true, not exactly. Yet he bad been feeling strangely close to Claude Lavigne lately.

"Not really a friend, no. He'd come into the bar now and then and I'd talk with him. I liked him. Nice man. His son and my girl-friend's boy are best friends."

"So what happened?"

Roger wasn't sure he should be talking about the Lavignes' tragedy. He didn't want to upset David anymore. "I don't know for sure." He took a pull from his bottle. "But I think I might be the only one he talked to about it. Wish I could make better sense of it."

"Are you going to continue to be cryptic?"

Roger chuckled. "I don't mean to be. I'm just thinking about it and trying to talk at the same time. I was never much good at doing two things at once."

The two men laughed uneasily. Then Roger continued. "He came into the bar one afternoon when I was there all alone. This was about a week before he shot himself. He was shaking and looked as if he'd seen a ghost. Then he proceeded to drink more in thirty minutes than he'd ever had in all the time I've known him. I could see he was upset so I tried to get him to talk a little."

"And did he?"

"Yeah. He told me he'd seen something weird out in the woods."

"Weird?"

"The way he told it, he'd seen some animal, or something, that suddenly got up on its hind legs and walked like a man."

David's eyes widened. "The *loup-garou*?" There was a thorn of sarcasm in his voice, but Roger could see he was interested.

"No. Not a werewolf. He said it looked more like a bear."

"Bears will rise up on their hind legs; that doesn't seem so off the wall."

"He was having a real hard time explaining it; he wasn't a verbal man. But apparently the thing didn't just stand up. He also said it seemed to change, to grow, to actually alter its shape."

Potter opened his eyes very wide, as if to say, I don't believe a word of it. Roger remembered that expression. It used to accompany a series of thoughtful puffs on his briar pipe. Now there was no pipe; apparently David had given up smoking as well. "A shape-shifter, huh?" The professor's chuckle sounded forced. "Maybe he'd been reading up on Indian lore. They have a lot of stories about shape-shifters."

Roger considered that, but it wasn't right. Somehow he wasn't able to communicate his sense of unease to David Potter. The unsettling quality of his meeting with Claude Lavigne was lost in retelling. One missing element, of course, was the big man's pale, frightened face. Another was his haunted eyes . . .

"I can't tell you what he saw, David. And Lunker Lavigne couldn't tell me, even when he tried. I remember his frustration in trying to make me understand why he was so scared."

"I know. It's difficult for anyone," said David, his voice trailing off in thought.

"I can't really believe he saw anything change shape, but I do believe he saw something, whatever it was, that shook him up so bad that it led to his suicide."

"Come on, Roger. Don't you think he had other things on his mind, other troubles, heavy-duty worries . . . ?"

"Probably. I guess we'll never know." Roger took a deep breath. "But I suspect whatever he saw was partly responsible. Maybe it pushed him over the edge. Lavigne was a hardworking, level-headed Vermonter. You know the type as well as I do. I can't help but ask: What could push a man like that to the point of taking his own life? What could he have seen that would so threaten the foundation of his world, his sense of what is and isn't real? What could have done that to him, David?"

"What could do it to you, Roger?"

Roger looked Dr. Potter directly in the eyes. Then shook his head in resignation. "I don't know. I've got no idea. But I have a sense about this thing. Somehow I know it's important. I think I'm going to investigate it . . ."

"Aha! Going back into journalism, are you?" Potter seemed to like the idea. With that one simple question he conveyed that he'd never approved of Roger's career change. Roger felt a tug of resentment.

"I probably won't do a story on it. But for my own mental health I'm going to check it out."

Potter sat quietly for a while. His eyes seemed transfixed on some invisible scene far in the distance. Roger could sense the nervousness in Potter's inactivity. He watched the agitation work its way to the surface: First Potter's fingers tapped soundlessly on the arm of the chair, then he blinked rapidly, wiped his eyes with his wrist.

In a moment he jumped up.

Reaching into the pocket of his jersey, he said, "Well, if you're in an investigative mood, I got something here you can practice on."

He tossed Roger a cassette tape.

Roger folded up his recliner, stood up, and took the cassette to his stereo system. After inserting it into the tape player, he flicked on the power and pushed the "play" button. The harpsichord vanished, replaced with an irritating expanse of tape hiss. It sounded like a far-off wind.

Both men stared at the illuminated level indicators, waiting for them to move, listening intently.

When it seemed as if the tape were empty of sound, a startling click intruded—the dictating machine turning on. The level indicators jumped up and down like a tiny green and red light show. Roger recognized the strains of Pachelbel's Canon.

He glanced at Potter and Potter glanced back, muttering, "Insipid piece of drivel."

Roger shrugged. He saw nothing wrong with Leslie's choice of music. Why was David acting this way?

The notes of the violins sounded as if they came from far away, nearly hidden behind the tape's persistent hissing.

Leslie Winthrop cleared her throat. Her low, sensual voice was almost alive through the loudspeakers. "Saturday, August twenty-seventh, nineteen eighty-eight. Arrived in Eureka at about three-thirty P.M. and met with Mr. Newton at his . . . ahh . . . place of business. He took me to the property of Harley Spooner, who . . . OH, FUCK!"

Alarmed, Roger looked at David Potter. David shook his head signaling: No, this isn't the problem. "Wait," he whispered. "I think she just realized the radio was on."

As if to prove him right, the music stopped. Now the tape hiss was accompanied by what might have been the indistinct sound of the car engine, or its tires on the road.

"She's left the recorder running," David said. "Listen."

The twin hum of engine and tape continued. Suddenly Leslie gasped. Breaks squealed. The men heard Leslie exhale.

"Independent little critter," she said, a sparkle of forced amusement in her voice.

The Mazda's engine sound grew. Roger heard first gear change to second. Then to third, and fourth. He could almost identify the low rumble of wheels on the road's surface.

A subtle change in the symphony of hums suggested that she had slowed down a bit.

"Listen. Here it comes," David whispered, holding up a professorial index finger.

They could hear a flurry of motion in the car: the sound of hands slapping the wheel, a foot stomping the break pedal.

"My God!" Leslie screamed, the terror in her voice as sharp as a razor. Tires screeched against the road.

"Aaaaahhhh."

The car's horn blasted, a dying wail, fixed forever in magnetic impulses. Then there were other sounds, chilling, but impossible to identify. Bumping, thrashing sounds.

Roger clearly sensed that the car was no longer in motion. Yet he could still hear the irregular throbbing of its engine, as if it were about to stall.

Leslie groaned. It sounded as if she were whispering something. Roger strained to hear. He turned up the volume of his amplifier, adjusted the treble to increase intelligibility.

Leslie was speaking, softly, as if there were not enough breath in her lungs to drive out the words. Much of what she said was completely lost. Other words, though faint, were almost recognizable. She sounded as if she were talking in a fevered sleep.

" . . . immm mmmmert. Hellll . . . help . . . mmmmeeee . . . "

Roger looked at David as the sounds continued, "Oooooo . . . Thasss . . . aaahhsss. Sooooommmmm. Aaaannn . . . "

And she was still. The engine stopped. There was only the sound of the hissing tape.

"Listen," Dr. Potter mouthed the word.

Roger heard a new sound, a scratching, like bushes scraping across the car.

They heard the sound of the car door opening.

Roger looked David in the eyes.

He felt himself blanch as Leslie's final sound was followed by the smash of one solid object against another. The windshield glass?

The car door slammed.

The tape recorder, silent. Only the hissing remained.

"My God," Roger said. He leaned against the edge of his desk, feeling empty and afraid. "Do you think it was Leslie who opened the door?"

David Potter slowly shook his head.

"You think someone else did?"

"I think so."

"And then what?"

"You tell me."

Roger felt sweat flowing from his pores. He was uncomfortably hot, his mouth dry as dust. "It sounded like someone opened the door. And then . . . deliberately . . . pushed her face into the windshield. That's what it sounded like, David."

"That's what it sounded like to me, too." David's jaw was clenched, his fists tight knots at his sides.

"But they left the tape recorder . . . ?"

"I guess so."

"Why would they leave the tape recorder?"

Potter shrugged, shook his head.

It was a struggle for Roger to continue. He really didn't want to think this thing through. "So somebody . . . my God, David, somebody did this to her?"

"It looks that way to me."

"Did you tell the police?"

"Not yet. I wanted you to hear this before I did anything."

"Who could have done it to her?"

"I have no idea. But maybe she tells us."

"What do you mean?"

"Put on that part where she's mumbling again. Just before the end."

Roger played that section of the tape several more times.

Both men struggled to make sense of the faint, indistinct nonsense syllables:

". . . immm mmmmert. Hellll . . . help . . . mmmmeeee. Oooooo . . . Thasss, aaahhsss. Sooooommmmm. Aaaannn . . ."

With repetition the sounds began to make a kind of sense. Roger couldn't be sure if he was hearing Leslie's actual words, or if he was doing some kind of aural Rorschach test, making recognizable patterns from meaningless utterances.

". . . I'mmm ert. Help me. Oh! Tha'sss oh man."

The first part was easy—"I'm hurt. Help me." Then a sigh of pain. And . . .

"That's oh man."

Roger listened to the faint words again and again. He was able to impose several designs on the sounds. Which was correct? What had the suffering woman really said?

Discouraged, he looked at Potter. "What do you make of it, David?"

"I think she said, *'That's no man.'*"

"And I thought she said, *'A snowman.'* Neither one makes much sense to me."

David Potter sat back down, his face colorless. He looked up at Roger with moist eyes. "You don't think so?"

Roger stared at his friend. What David had heard, or pieced together from Leslie's final words, *did* make sense. In fact, either interpretation made the entire situation frightening, brought to mind horrifying possibilities. Leslie Winthrop had been attacked! Apparently someone had tried to kill her, then left her for dead.

Roger asked, "Now are you ready to bring this to the police?"

David seemed to freeze. Then he buried his face in his hands. His muffled voice was soft. "I think I've got to. I wanted to be sure first, play the tape for you, get your opinion. But now, I guess I've

got no choice . . ." He looked up. "They may not believe what we
think we heard, but they'll know for sure whoever opened that car
door did . . . something to Leslie."

"I think they could determine that without understanding a
word that she said."

David looked miserable, lost. "I know. Maybe I was just stalling.
I guess I just wanted to put it off. I . . . I also wanted some backup."

"Backup? Why? What do you mean?"

Dr. Potter got out of his chair and paced silently around the
room. Finally he stopped at the stereo. He ejected the cassette, returned it to its case, and pocketed it.

"I guess I was putting it off because if I report it the police will
know it wasn't an accident. Then there'll be an investigation." He
walked to the window that faced the main street and looked down.

Roger walked over to him, put a hand on David's shoulder.
Together, in silence, they looked at the street below. A car passed,
followed by two kids on bikes. They watched Laura leaving Rand's
General Store, a brown grocery bag in her arms.

David turned his head away, hiding his face in the crook of his
arm. "But Christ, there's no way I can avoid being a suspect."

A suspect? Controlling his voice, Roger spoke soothingly, "What
are you talking about, David? What kind of suspect? You were in
Burlington when it happened . . ."

"Sure. I know. I don't think I've got anything to fear legally, but
. . . well . . . an investigation could make things awfully uncomfortable for Gwen and me."

Roger gave a start. *For Gwen and . . . ? What did David's wife have
to do with—?*

And then, suddenly, Roger knew where all this was coming
from: David Potter's trim new physique; the stylish mode of dress;
the forsaken horn-rimmed glasses . . . He tightened his grip on
David's quivering shoulder.

Not wanting to judge, not wanting to provoke, Roger phrased
his question carefully. "David, did you have a date for brunch with
Leslie on Sunday morning?"

David nodded. Then he slapped the window frame. "Oh, God,

Roger, everything's falling apart." His voice broke into a breathy whisper as be turned to face Roger. Tears flowed down his cheeks. He wiped at them with his fingertips. "Damn these contacts. I can't seem to get used to them."

"Stay here," Roger said. "I'll get us another couple of beers."

13

Things Unseen

AROUND FOUR O'CLOCK . . .

At about the same time that Harley Spooner was standing at his kitchen window wondering what had become of his three friends, Cooly Hawks stood beside the north branch of the Nulhegan River. Hands on hips, he looked on proudly as Stacy Drew pointed up into the branches of a tamarack.

"Cooly, what's that up there?"

The old man ambled over to the boy and looked up. A winsome smile split his face. "Just suppose you tell me what you make of it, boys."

Jarvis approached, joining Stacy and the old man as they gazed up into the thickness of light green, triangular-clustered leaves. There, tight to the trunk, slung over a stout branch, was a dark, lumpy object.

Stacy looked at Jarvis, who squinted at the shapeless thing. There was no clue in Jarvis's puzzled expression. Since Cooly wasn't talking, Stacy had to study the mysterious object without assistance. Black, somewhat oval in shape, it looked a little like a deflated football. It seemed crusty, dry, cracked like worn leather. Spines in symmetrical patterns protruded from the bottom. Their rusty color betrayed that they were metal spikes.

"They look like shoes," said Jarvis, uncertainty softening his voice.

"An' tha's just what they are!" The old man stared at the ancient boots above their heads. He raised his walnut walking stick and gently prodded the antique footwear.

"Let's take 'em down," said Stacy, looking around for a long stick of his own.

"No, sir," said Cooly. "You leave 'em right where they set."

"How come?" Stacy had found the perfect poking stick and was raising it like a flagpole.

" 'Cause they're a grave marker, that's why."

"A grave marker?"

"Yup. Years ago, when we was on a log drive, the whole surface of this river was choked-up with floatin' softwood every spring. A whole river of wood, far as the eye could see. 'Course, spiked boots or no, a careless step while runnin' them logs would always land a man in the drink. Happened to the best of us. We'd sometimes lose one, two men a year to the river. After we pulled him out we'd mark the spot it happened by hangin' his boots high up in a tree. I betcha them boots been up there for fifty, sixty years. Maybe more."

"Zat right!" said Jarvis, his eyes wide with fascination.

Stacy, too, took new, more reverent interest in the boots. He let the poking stick fall from his hands. "Do you know whose boots they were, Cooly?"

"I can't tell you that, Mister Stacy. But if you said the man's name, I bet I'd know him. I knew 'em all, hereabouts."

The old man moved away from the tree. The boys followed, glancing back over their shoulders at the strange monument. Cooly walked inland from the riverbank, stepping gingerly into a thickness of trees. His walking stick was more a prop than a cane; much of the time he just held it, never touching it to the ground.

Moving easily along a nearly treeless ridge, the old man raised his scratchy voice in song:

> "Oh, our bateaus are broke,
> And our boss, he's a joke,
> And the men they don't know what to do.
> But with peavey in hand

We set out over land
And we sure make one heck of a crew.
Oh, we sure make one heck of a crew."

There was a deep silence in the woods when Cooly stopped singing. The only sounds that Stacy could hear were the screeching of occasional bluejays and the soft rustling of the distant treetops, stroked constantly by an unfelt wind. It was like the sound of the forest breathing. He could smell the forest's breath, the hot, pungent odor that rose from thick brown layers of needles at their feet.

"Now you boys looky here. This here's something else I want you to see. Okay, now you tell me what kinda tree this is." Cooly leaned against its trunk, his hand darker than the bark beneath it, his face deep ebony leather.

"It just looks like a pine."

"Yup, I s'pose it does. But I want you boys to take a good look, and get to know this tree. This here's a hemlock. A lotta these got cleaned out a the woods durin' the last century, an' I'll tell ya why: It weren't no good for lumber. So they took to making roads out of it. Used hemlock to make a plank road between Waterbury and Stowe. Cripes, musta used two, three million board foot on that road.

"When I was workin' the woods we let 'em stand. For one thing you couldn't float 'em; they sink jes' like hardwood! For another thing, these hemlock are better'n any compass. You boys look right up there—all the way to the top."

The boys did as they were told. "You see that tippy-top twig? Way up the very top a the tree?"

The boys nodded. "Well, I can't tell you why, no more'n I can tell you why a compass always points north, but that tippy-top branch will always be pointin' to the east. You can count on it. If you boys is ever lost in the woods, you jest remember to find an ol' tree like this here. And don't forget what ol' Cooly tol' you about that top branch. It'll help you to find yer way home."

Stacy looked at Jarvis, trying to assess how much he was getting out of Cooly's instructions. Jarvis, Stacy knew, had his mind on

other things. In spite of Cooly's efforts, the boy hadn't smiled easily all day. His face was frozen in a near-grimace, a sturdy dam designed to hold back a flood of tears. Stacy could sense the forces
competing in his friend: the agony of his father's death warring
with the need to know what had caused it. There was an impatience in Jarvis; he wasn't getting what he needed from this walk in
the woods. Instruction in woods lore and rudimentary survival
skills were not what Jarvis was after. Even Cooly's well-intended
distractions couldn't get Jarvis's mind off his real need: answers.

"Cooly, let's walk a little further up into the gore," Jarvis suggested, as if encouraged by Stacy's thoughts.

"Well, if that's what you wanna do. I calc'late it's about four
o'clock now. Let's go on till about five, but no later, then we'll head
down. Your mommies'll skin ol' Cooly alive if I don't get you back
for suppertime."

The three walked among the trees, strolling randomly past fat
dark trunks, over fallen logs and around abrupt outcroppings that
jutted from the rich earth like thick granite teeth. The wilderness
was unbroken by discernible trails or roadways. Nothing but the
upward slope of the hill as Cooly's keen sense of direction guided
their route.

"Let's cut over that way so's we'll come out closer to town,"
Cooly suggested, pointing southwest with a twiglike finger. "We
can be workin' our way down as we go."

Jarvis lagged behind. Stacy looked back and saw his friend stumbling woodenly as the gap between them widened. Stacy felt tired
too; he waited for his friend to catch up. Amazed, he watched
Cooly. How could the old man forge ahead with no signs of
fatigue?

The boys followed Cooly through a little division in the woodland. It was like a combed part in a thick head of hair. Now there
was a path to follow. Stacy guessed that it might once have been a
logging road.

"Right again, Mister Stacy. That ol' road used to take us up to a
camp name a Hell's Hinges. 'Course there's nothin' left of it today."

No vehicle had passed along the nearly invisible road for many years. Now passage would be impossible. Fresh grass and mature bushes surrounded saplings big enough to discourage even a four-wheel drive machine. Erosion had bitten away much of the road. Fallen trees provided additional obstructions.

Cooly sat down on one of the fallen logs and began to fill his pipe. The boys sat beside him.

No one spoke. They listened to the wind in the treetops, the chattering squirrels. From the distance came a crashing sound.

"SSSShhhh," Cooly cautioned, squinting into the forest. He pinched out his match before touching it to the tobacco.

Jarvis snapped to attention. All three knew something big was moving through the underbrush. Moving rapidly.

From the north, from up the slope, the crashing continued. A heavy body moved, snapping dry bushes, brushing green ones out of its way. Farther off, from far up the bill, dogs yapped and howled.

"Get down," Cooly said. Stacy saw the old man's muscles tense, watched his dark eyes scanning the battered underbrush. Moving cautiously, Cooly squatted behind the log. The boys did the same.

Crouching in anxious silence for what seemed a very long time, the three listened as the crashing and yelping faded into oblivion. Cooly stood up first. He struck a match. This time he lighted his pipe.

Stacy looked at Cooly, waiting for an explanation. "What *was* that?" Jarvis said.

"Coyotes. Pack a dogs. I didn't get a look."

"No. I mean, what were they chasing?"

"Prob'ly a deer, my friend."

Jarvis eyed the woods, exploring every tree trunk, every stone, every pit of shadows. "You pretty sure it was just a deer, Cooly?"

"I ain't sure. But I'll say *prob'ly* that's what 'twas." Cooly had to fire up his pipe a second time. He dropped the match, pushed it into the ground with the tip of his boot. He worked it deeper and deeper into the earth, watching his toe with great interest.

"Cooly," Jarvis said slowly, "you ever seen anything strange in these woods?" He looked up at the black man, his hopeful eyes

distorted by thick glasses. Stacy could see that the question made
the old man uncomfortable.

"Well, Mister Jarvis, it just so happens that one time I did see
somethin' a bit peculiar up here . . ."

Jarvis sat back down beside Stacy. Cooly stood in front of the
boys, puffing his pipe, a teacher before a class of two.

"It was a time when I was up here huntin'. Must a been ten, fifteen years ago. All of a sudden I hear a whole lot of commotion in
the woods, just like today. I takes cover behind a tree and waits as
the thrashin' an' crashin' gets louder and louder. Somethin's comin'
closer to me.

"Pretty quick a big blackish brown animal reveals hisself 'bout
fifty yards from where I'm standin'. It's one big sonavagun, that I
seen right off quick. Well sir, I looks it up and down, tryin' to make
some kinda sense outta what I'm lookin' at. The animal had the size
an' shape of a deer, and, by golly, it run like a deer, too. But it ain't
jest exactly like any deer I ever see. There it was, standin' in a clear-
ing, pretty as you please, big rack a horns on his head. It's some
kinda buck, I thinks to myself.

"This ol' buck, he tosses his head, once, again. Then he dives
straight into the forest an' he's gone, just like that! I'll bet you boys
never seen one like that before. I know I never see its like, before or
since."

"So what's so weird about it?" said Jarvis.

"Two heads, that's what!" Cooly chuckled, smoke extruding
from the corners of his mouth.

"It *didn't* have two heads," Jarvis protested.

"I guess maybe it didn't. Not really. But it sure looked that way
to these ol' eyes. Then I figgered her out. It was *almost* as if he had
two heads—one attached proper-like to its neck, the other locked
in its antlers with ribbons of flesh and hide trailin' off like streamers
out behind it as it run.

"Y'see, sometimes, durin' ruttin' season two bucks will fight
over a doe, usin' their antlers as weapons. What I seen is what happens when their antlers get all tangled up and stuck together. The
strong one wins, the weak one not only loses his life, but his head

to boot! But you get to wonderin' what the winner's really won. He hasta drag the other carcass around with him, kickin' at it, an' thrashin' and scrapin' till the neck breaks off, leavin' him with jest the head. Then he gets to carry his prize around with him until a hunter, or maybe the dogs, bring him down. S'at a weird enough sight for you, Mister Jarvis?"

Jarvis looked sidelong at Stacy, then back at Cooly. "You think that deer is what my father saw, Cooly?"

It was clear to Stacy that the old man's attempt to get Jarvis's mind off his father had failed miserably.

Cooly looked at the ground again. His voice sounded far away. "I can't tell you what he seen. I s'pose to some that deer might a been a pretty upsettin' sight. I don't think it woulda bothered your daddy, though. Not really."

Stacy put his hand on his friend's shoulder. "Come on, Jarv. Let's go. We'll come up again when we'll have more time to look around."

"That's right, Mister Jarvis. Next time we'll bring some vittles. Make a day of it. How's that sound?"

Jarvis stood up. He nodded wearily. As he walked away looking exhausted, Stacy noticed he was limping.

"We'll just follow this road down a ways. It comes out right by the powerlines. Then we'll cut through the woods back to town. I'll have you boys home 'fore suppertime, you wait an' see."

Going downhill was easier. Jarvis walked ahead, letting the downward momentum carry him along. His neck jutted forward more than normally, emphasizing the curve of his spine.

Then Jarvis stopped. He seemed to be making a low growling sound. Stacy knew his friend was tired; his back must be aching something wicked. The idea of a seizure came to mind as the growling continued.

As Stacy hurried to join his friend he saw the real source of the noise.

An animal stood in their path, no more then twenty-five feet away. Possibly it was one of the animals that had been chasing the deer—one of the animals that had tasted blood.

Cooly grabbed Stacy's arm and yanked him back before he could make a move. "Stand still, Jarvis," Cooly whispered.

Head down, tail and ears erect, the animal leered menacingly. Long yellow teeth glared from its black jowls. Saliva glistened on the blood-matted fur around its muzzle. A low growl, like the hum of an engine, riveted the three to their spots.

Cooly inched very slowly ahead, his walking stick pressed invisibly against his side. In graceful slow motion he stepped in front of Jarvis, never moving his dark eyes from those of the animal.

"Coydogs," Cooly whispered.

Stacy had heard about coydogs. They were a hybrid of the wild eastern coyote and domestic farm dogs whose owners allowed them to roam free. Coydogs had the innate savagery of the coyote, but, like pet dogs, no strong instinctive fear of man. They were considered very dangerous. More so when they ran in packs, killing deer, sheep, other dogs. And there were stories about them attacking people . . .

Stories? The thing in their path was no story.

Cooly carefully maneuvered his walking stick to the front of him. "He's waitin' for his buddies b'fore he attacks. Now you boys do what I tell ya . . ."

Stacy tried to control his shaking. He reached into his pocket for his Swiss army knife.

"Hold still," Cooly instructed.

Stacy watched a dark stain spread down the leg of Jarvis's pants. He'd pissed himself. The thought of it drove home the reality of Stacy's own fear.

Cooly spoke over his shoulder. "That maple tree over there to the left. When I move on the dog, you boys run for that tree and climb it quick."

"But Cooly—"

"Goddamn it boy, you do what I tell you!"

Like a warrior with a battle-ax, the old black man raised the stick. "RUN!" he cried.

Stacy turned and bolted. The last thing he saw was Cooly charging the coydog, his stick held high.

Both boys reached the maple at the same time. Its thick branches were as easy to climb as a stepladder. Stacy perched on a sturdy limb that ran parallel to the ground. He held his hand out to assist Jarvis.

In the distance Cooly brought his walnut club down against the thing's spine. The animal flattened, legs straight out, stomach crushed against the ground. The dog's shriek filled the air.

"CLIMB!" Cooly yelled as a pack of twelve dogs burst yelping from the bush.

The boys climbed higher. They got in each other's way as they moved, scrambling like drowning men for a lifeboat.

Ascending, Stacy couldn't take his eyes off Cooly. Dogs clustered around him like mayflies. They jumped, nipped, tore, retreated, charged. All the time their high-pitched yipping and howling ripped at Stacy's nerves.

Two of the bigger dogs, each weighing at least forty-five pounds, bounced as if on springs. They jumped at Cooly's neck. He dodged one in front, but a smaller animal struck him in the back. Cooly lurched forward, used the walking stick to recover his balance.

As the bigger animals led the attack, the females and their young dashed in and out like feeding fish. A reddish pup with a blood-stained belly ripped a piece of flesh from Cooly's thigh. The sight of torn flesh jolted Stacy. He thought he was going to scream. To stop himself he bit down hard on the web between his thumb and forefinger.

Beside him Jarvis was breathing too fast. Hyperventilating.

He moaned, "Oh oh oh oh," and rocked back and forth on the branch.

"Gaaa!" Cooly roared. The descending walnut club took the teeth and lower jaw from one animal. Still it fought, jumping at Cooly, pummeling with its forepaws.

Three dogs lay twitching on the ground. Cooly lifted a kick at the underbelly of another. Vomit blew from its nose and mouth as it retreated on wobbly legs.

Faster than the sting of a cobra, an undersized mutt fastened its teeth into Cooly's arm. Cooly tried to flick it off. It hung on as he whipped it around in the air like a flag in a windstorm.

Another dog hit Cooly's calf, and he was down on one knee. One of the largest flew through the air at the old man's throat. With the reflexes of a street fighter Cooly pushed the heavy end of the stick against the snarling teeth as he struggled to his feet.

The little beast still clung like a snapping turtle to his left arm.

The leader was regrouping for another assault as Cooly raised the stick in his right hand. From out of nowhere an airborne animal hit Cooly's forearm. The stick tumbled to the ground.

Frenzied animals plowed into the backs of the old man's legs. He toppled, tightening into a ball to protect his stomach and genitals.

"We've gotta *do* something," Stacy stammered, looking to his friend for agreement. Jarvis had passed out, propped against the tree trunk. Stacy grabbed Jarvis's belt to keep him from falling from the tree.

Cooly still fought. Half a dozen dogs were down, but those that remained didn't tire. One, moving like a lightning bolt, tore flesh from Cooly's bottom, trotted away proudly with its prize.

Stacy didn't know what to do. Could he sit, cowering, while the old man got torn to pieces?

"Jarvis, wake up!" he whispered, tugging on the belt.

The rest happened very fast.

As Cooly's motions slowed, the five remaining dogs, bouncing and yowling, worked themselves to a frenzy. They leapt, chased their tails in tight little circles, snapped at each other, all the while making bone-shattering noises, and launching quick, efficient, totally unpredictable attacks on the old man.

Then it happened.

A roar, louder than the combined cacophony of the animals, froze them in their bloody tracks.

The beast with the missing lower jaw looked up from his death-like sprawl. When he saw the source of the roar he quivered, partially rose, trying to crawl away on broken legs.

The biggest dog, cringing and whimpering, put its bloody muzzle on the ground between its outstretched paws. It shook, dared not to move.

Through the film of tears and sweat that had formed over his eyes, through the obstruction of the maple leaves where he hid, Stacy saw something move.

About two hundred feet away, from amid the clutter of bushes and branches at the forest's edge, a tall black figure stepped out of the shadows.

The thing was much bigger than Cooly Hawks. It stood in front of the tree line, its arms raised, its hands poised like claws.

Again it roared, then ran with a peculiar squatting lope to the old man's side. It yanked a dog away, snapped the twitching, wriggling spine against a tree. It pulled another off the ground by its tail, swung it like a mace, and slammed its head against an outcropping.

The animal with no lower jaw managed to pull itself about five feet toward safety before the intruder brought a heavy foot down on its back.

The roaring, black, hairy thing knelt down next to Cooly Hawks. It seemed to study Cooly's bleeding face for a moment. Then, as if the old man were a ten-pound bag of flour, the thing scooped him up, and carried him off into the trees.

Stacy waited a long time before he dared to move.

He waited until all the dogs had run—or crawled—away. He waited until the others had stopped their pitiful twitching.

He waited until the intruder was gone for sure, and the noise in the forest was again bluejays and rustling branches.

Then he woke Jarvis and helped him out of the tree.

With no thought of compass or hemlock bough, letting instinct guide them, and allowing nothing to slow them down, the two boys raced for home.

14

Dark Suspicions

EARLY EVENING . . .

It wasn't yet dark. The sun, a red dome on the western peaks, cast shadows sharp as knives across the main street of Eureka.

Elbows out, feet stomping, Harley Spooner charged along the side of the road. His determined progress suggested an undersized bird buffeted by a heavy windstorm.

His baseball cap kept sliding backward on his sweat-slick forehead. From time to time he'd pull it tight with a purposeful tug.

He'd charged right past Laura Drew's trailer. What he had to say most probably would upset the lady. Harley wanted to do his business with Newton.

Owning a telephone would have made the whole thing a lot easier, but Harley wasn't one for modern conveniences; they'd make a man soft.

And he'd never avoided exercise, by God! He attributed his long life and extraordinarily good health to walking, working, and, as a younger man, laboring in the woods during the winter logging season while his wife and daughter managed the farm. Sometimes he thanked the fresh Vermont air as well, but rarely mentioned it anymore, especially around Cooly, who always gave him such a ribbing about breathing through his pipe.

Maybe the old coot has a point, Harley thought. He *was* feeling strangely short of breath. And there was that annoying hitch in his side. But no—that stuff couldn't be from smoking tobacco. More probably it was the beans he'd had for supper. Funny the walk to town hadn't dislodged the gas that kept poking at his gut, paining him something wicked just below the rib cage . . .

The Newsroom came into view. Without breaking stride Harley pried his ancient watch from the pocket of his denims—quarter to seven.

It had been a long walk into town. Harley'd made the distance in forty-five minutes; good thing he'd got that short ride with Gene Bissonnette. Still, he'd walked most of the way. If he paused to think about it, he'd realize that he was tired.

When Harley found the door to The Newsroom locked, he remembered that it was Monday. The place was closed on Mondays. He craned his neck, looking up at Roger Newton's apartment on the floor above.

Roger put down the phone and looked worriedly at David Potter. "That was my girlfriend, Laura. Her son and another boy haven't come home yet. She wondered if they were here."

David looked at him expectantly, obviously not knowing how to respond.

"That worries me a little, Dave. The other boy is the one whose father just died. The suicide. We were all at the funeral this morning."

"Do you think we should go out and look for them?"

"Probably. But I've got no idea where to start. I guess we could drive around." He tried to smile as if he thought it was all some childish prank. "Kids!"

"I'll do anything I can to help. Shall we take two—?"

With the impact of a sudden wind, Harley Spooner burst into the room. Both men looked at him in surprise.

Without pausing for any sort of invitation or go-ahead, Harley began: "I knew that ol' blow-hog shoulda stayed to home and not go *es*-cortin' them youngsters out every which-a-way. Seven o'clock, an' not a one of 'em's back yet." He paused, looked puzzled. "Your boy ain't here, is he?"

Just like that, the explosion of words ended. After asking his question the little old man stood like a delicate bird, round head cocked to one side, squinting at Roger as he waited for an answer. Roger could see concern buried helplessly below Harley's bombast.

"Stacy's not here. His mother just called to say he isn't there either . . ."

"An' what about young Lavigne?"

"I don't know. It might upset his mother to call and ask. She's got plenty to worry about right now as it is."

"Worry her more the boy don't come home."

Roger thought it over. "You're right. We were just on our way out to look for them. We can stop over to the Lavignes'. Why don't you come with us."

"Where you gonna look?"

"I haven't the slightest idea. Your guess is as good as mine."

"No guessin'. I know where they gone. Up the gore. Cooly brung 'em."

"The gore? Why?"

"Lavigne's boy. He wants to know what happened to his daddy."

"Oh, shit," said Roger. Now he realized that he wasn't the only one who'd heard about Claude Lavigne's "vision." And he wasn't the only one who wanted to investigate, either. He shouldn't have waited so long to begin.

"Cooly, he's up there with 'em. Crazy ol' coot. Shoulda knowed better."

"What do you mean? You think they're lost?"

"Well sir, that's what pickles me. They ain't lost if ol' Cooly's with 'em. I can say a lot a things about that scabbidy-assed ol' nigger, but lost he ain't. He'd a never kep' them boys out there this long if everythin' was okay."

"Well, Harley, let's get going. Coming, David?"

"Sure I am . . ."

Having stated his business, Harley Spooner seemed to see David Potter for the first time. Recognition, free of surprise, wrinkled his crusty, whiskered face. "Good t' see ya again, Doc," was all he said.

· · ·

The girl in the passenger's seat kept looking at him. She kept stealing glances from the corner of her eye. It was like she was spying on him. Watching him, sneaky, hidden . . . She'd never turn and look at him directly.

After supper Hank Drew had driven all the way over to Newport, where, he was sure, no one would recognize him. He didn't need anybody plaguing him with questions. He hated their prying, and their phony expressions of sympathy.

Besides—might as well admit it—he'd been lonely. A night out, a night shooting the shit with other people, would be good for him.

He'd put on his new cotton cowboy shirt, shaved, daubed bay rum on his cheeks. He'd worked on his hair before the shaving mirror for a lot longer than he was used to. Then, feeling strangely sad to be getting dressed up for no good reason, he'd driven off in his pickup.

Sad. Alone.

Now, ever since Laura and the boy took off, all he had left was the job. And it was a lonely job. Eight, sometimes twelve hours a day all by himself. Even the extra hundred dollars a month bonus for working in this remote part of the state did little to assuage his feelings of isolation. Sure, the extra money was a help when the family was together. But now it was just . . . just what?

A reminder of better times, perhaps?

She was looking at him again. He could see her eyes glistening in the light from the dashboard.

The silent scrutiny made him uncomfortable in the pickup's darkened cab.

Why is she staring at me?

A midnight fabric of trees and boulders along the roadside pressed in on him, threatening to smother him. Shadows seemed to dance and move, springing to life in the magic beams of his headlights. Things were out there, he knew, dark scheming things, vile creatures in league with the foulest of men, the most treacherous of women . . .

Why doesn't she say something?

When he'd bought her those drinks at the Lion's Share Lounge in Newport she'd been talkative enough. Friendly even.

But after he agreed to give her a ride to St. Johnsbury . . . after they'd gotten into his truck, she'd clammed up.

They'd traveled the last twenty miles without a word. Was she getting some kind of an attitude because he'd asked her to stop at his place for the night?

Naw, she'd been coming on to him; anyone in the bar could see that. Now she was playing hard to get, trying to undermine his confidence with coy behavior.

Maybe she was testing him!

That's it, she's another test!

No doubt sent by . . . whoever . . . , or *whatever* . . . was responsible for all the tests he'd been put through lately.

For many weeks now he'd been convinced that something indefinable . . . some *force* . . . was manipulating him, stopping his luck from improving. It was bent on preventing him from feeling just the way a man of his caliber should feel. It was as if he'd been jinxed, or cursed, or something like that. Something fucked up.

It sounded crazy, even to himself—but he knew it had to be the truth.

Surely the woman beside him was part of the test. She had to be. And Hank knew just how to find out for sure.

"Who are you?" he demanded coldly.

Now she looked at him, her eyes wide.

"Who am I? I told you who I am. Brenda Wiggins. I'm Brenda Wiggins."

He squinted at her. "No. You're somebody else. You're after me for some reason. There's something you want."

She shook her head. She was looking scared now. Good.

"I'm not after you, mister. I don't even know you. I just wanted a ride, that's all. Just a ride. Honest."

He fixed his gaze back on the dark road.

Actually, she wasn't a bad-looking broad. Her hair, though a little dirty, was blonde. It was long and straight. Like Laura's.

Her figure probably wasn't too bad either. Although she dressed like those back-to-the-land Christian hippies in Island Pond, he could still see the swell of large breasts under her too-loose blouse. Big tits. Like Laura's.

"Who was it put you on to me?" he asked through clenched teeth.

The girl edged closer to the passenger-side door. She pushed her cheek against the window.

"You're crazy, mister. Suppose you just stop the truck and let me out right here."

Crazy!

Hank pressed the gas pedal harder. "No way. Not till you tell me what you're up to."

Crazy was a well-chosen word, definitely a word designed to erode his confidence. She'd used it knowingly. As if someone put her up to it. As if she realized that lately he'd been wondering what insanity felt like when it took hold of a man.

Do you simply wake up one morning and discover the whole world looks different? Do people, formerly friends, suddenly appear changed, sinister? Do your loved ones suddenly take on foreign, threatening aspects?

Do demons magically appear?

A tension along Hank's spine made him want to shout. He pounded the seat between them, shaking his head from side to side.

"No . . ." he moaned.

The girl pulled her legs up onto the seat, hugged her knees close to her chest. "Stop the car, mister. Let me out right now!"

Hank hit the brake. The tires squealed in agony as they scraped along the asphalt. The girl pitched forward, gripped the door handle, pumped it, trying to get out.

Hank reached for her.

"Stop!" she screamed. "STOP!"

His hand smashing the side of Laura's face. A red welt rising. Blood dribbling from the corner of her mouth. "Don't you ever tell me what to do!" SLAP! "Don't you ever raise your voice to me!" Laura cowering on the floor in the corner of the trailer, compressed into a tight ball. Crying.

Shaking her head. Tears launching into the air. His black Wellington connecting with her thigh.

The shoulder of the girl's blouse was wadded in his hand as she wrenched the door open. She pulled away. Fabric ripped. Her left breast, braless and kinetic, bounced provocatively in the dome light.

Hank slid across the seat and followed her into the night.

"Come back here! I know what you want! I know what you're trying to do to me!"

The racing figure of the girl disappeared into the trees. Hank bolted after her. The slick leather sole of his boot skidded on the rounded dew-slick surface of a fieldstone. He went down, smashing his knee on another rock.

"Come back here!" he cried at the dark curtain of the forest. "Damn it all! You come back here, I said. God damn you, Laura!"

15

What Harley Saw

NIGHTFALL . . .

A slapping sound.

The soles of sneakers on the concrete sidewalk. Roger stopped, looked up before getting into his station wagon. He saw the boys running toward him.

Stacy cried out from the deepening shadows up the street. "Roger!"

He watched them put on a burst of speed, frightened shades, nearly invisible beneath full, leafy elms.

"Roger!" Terror filled the voice. Stacy's evident fatigue, arms stiff at his sides, alerted Roger that now, perhaps more than ever before, he was needed. Not far behind, Jarvis Lavigne moved awkwardly, running with a faltering limp.

Forgetting Harley and David Potter, Roger moved quickly to them. For the first time since they'd known each other, Stacy Drew threw himself into Roger's arms, hugged him like a parent.

Roger tightened his arms around the shuddering child.

"Cooly!" Stacy cried. "Something got Cooly." Tears and sweat glistened on his dirt-streaked face.

The Lavigne boy came to a halt, wild-eyed, confused, seeming not to know who to approach for comfort. Right arm around Stacy's shoulders, Roger opened his left to Jarvis. Both boys hugged him. He felt them breathing heavily, trembling with fear and exhaustion. "Come on," he said. "Let's get upstairs."

113

Roger made a quick phone call to Laura, requesting she get Mrs. Lavigne's permission for Jarvis to stay overnight. He promised her a full explanation later and hung up. Then the five of them settled into Roger's living room. Stacy and Jarvis huddled together on the couch, each reeling out disconnected accounts of their day's activities. Roger sat on the coffee table, directly in front of the boys. He tried to calm them while struggling to make sense of their story.

Harley fidgeted in the background.

Gulping lungfuls of air, Stacy's chest heaved as he tried to talk. "Some big black thing . . . a monster . . . it came out of the woods and . . . took Cooly! It *was* a monster, Roger! It was big and hairy and grabbed Cooly up like he was a little baby!"

"It's what my father saw. I know it. There *is* something up there."

"Did you see it too, Jarvis?"

Jarvis looked at Stacy. "No, I didn't see it, but Cooly's gone. And I saw the dogs! I did—"

"I believe you, Jarv. I believe both of you." He touched each boy on the arm. "But I have to know what happened."

David Potter approached the boys, looking out of place and miserable. He handed each a large glass of water. They drank greedily. Jarvis choked on his, spat it back into the glass. Water splattered on his jersey and on the couch.

Stacy, wiping his mouth on his wrist, looked up suspiciously at Potter.

"It's okay, fellas," Roger explained. "This is a friend of mine, David Potter. He teaches at UVM in Burlington."

"Hi, guys," said David, sounding timid.

Jarvis and Stacy eyed the professor, nodding uncertainly. When Stacy finished drinking, Roger said, "Okay, Stace, take a deep breath and see if you can talk about it. Slowly now. Step by step. One thing at a time."

Harley Spooner came forward. Roger saw the horrible uncertainty on the old man's face. "So what's happened to Cooly? Where's Cooly?" Harley's voice was quiet with a fragile control. Clearly he was desperate to know about his friend yet he was careful to speak gently to the frightened children.

Stacy's gaze swam from face to face. His shaking had not yet subsided. His teeth chattered; tremors were heavy in his speech. "I thought the dogs were going to get him, and there was nothing I could do. We just hid in the tree, watching. I wanted to help, but I couldn't. I knew it wasn't right to look away . . ."

"And what did you see?" Roger kept his voice quiet, calm as his impatience would permit.

"Cooly was on the ground, curled up but still fighting. Then I heard a roar, like an animal. A big one. A lion or something. And then this thing, like a gorilla or something, came charging out of the woods. It was huge, bigger'n you, lots bigger'n Cooly. And it stomped a couple of the dogs—just *stomped* 'em like they were ants. I thought it was going to stomp Cooly, too, but it didn't. It picked him up and ran off with him. Honest! We gotta go find him, Roger! We gotta help him. Who knows what that thing's doing to him!"

There was no question in Roger's mind—the boys were telling the truth. He'd known Stacy for a couple of years now, he knew what kind of boy he was. Sure, he had an imagination that ran toward the bizarre. He was into magic. He devoured science fiction and horror books as if they were potato chips, but he was bright and honest; he would never tell a story like this to cover up for himself, to mask his own mischief.

When Roger again looked at Harley Spooner, the old man was ashen. He staggered backward to one of the chairs around the dining room table and sat down. His voice was a raspy whisper. "I'd be grateful to you, Mr. Newton, if maybe I could have a shot a somethin'."

David Potter went to the kitchen cabinet and poured each man a double shot of Wild Turkey. Harley downed his with a gulp, exhaled, nearly coughing, and belched. His old eyes, like pellets of buckshot, showed fear. When he spoke his voice sounded far away. "I don't think there's no help for Cooly, boys. Not now." There was a flat, yet confident certainty in his words. They had the finality of a father breaking the news that his child's pet had been killed by a car.

Unformed tears glazed the old man's eyes. They looked like polished glass as he wiped them with his wrinkled blue handkerchief. He stood up. "They's no point in my stayin' here no more. The boys is safe, and I thank the Good Lord for that. Now I'll be on my way."

"Wait a minute, Harley. Not so fast!" Roger held the old man with an insistent glare. "What *really* happened up there? You know, don't you?"

At that moment Harley appeared tiny and lost. His eyes moved helplessly from face to face. Then he looked toward the door, as if he wanted to escape. With resignation he sank back into his chair, clutching his empty glass in a white-knuckled fist. "The ol' fool knew better'n to go up there pokin' around. More'n once I tol' him not to do it. I *tol'* him I didn't like it. But he's an independent old bass-turd, always was, always will be . . ."

All eyes were on the old man, silently coaxing the information from him. Still he searched their faces, as if seeking a conversational detour. It was no use; everyone's silence forced him to continue. "You folks ever heard of the winny-go?" He looked from face to face. "That's what took Cooly. That's why they's no point goin' up there expectin' to find him."

"The winny-go?" Roger prodded gently.

"*Windigo,*" said David Potter. "Isn't that it, Mr. Spooner?" The professor leaned forward. Suddenly he was very interested.

"What's a windigo?" Stacy asked.

"What is it? It's what you seen in the woods. It's what come for Cooly!"

Potter looked at the boy. "It's an old Indian superstition—"

"It *ain't* no superstition." Harley pressed his lips tightly together. Quick twitches of his tiny body revealed he was angry. "I been aroun' these hills longer than you have, Mr. College Perfesser. I don't care what sort of tripe you read in your books, there's them of us who knows. Cooly knew. I know. And any man who wintered in the loggin' camps knows about the winny-go. An' I seen it! That's somethin' you didn't read in none a yer books! I seen it watchin' our camp, standin' way off, hidin' out in the trees up aroun' the East Branch of the Black River, up aroun' Sable Mountain. You go on an' tell me I didn't."

"When was this?" asked Roger.

"Back in the winter of twenty-nine, think 'twas. Cooly seen it too. I figger it was after Herb Smalley, 'cause it weren't long after that that he come up missin'. Jes' like Cooly done now. You boys is lucky it didn't lay its bleedin' eyes on you!"

"What's it look like?" asked Stacy Drew. His eyes were wide, his voice faint as a breeze.

"Same thing you seen. Same thing took Cooly. It was tall an' skinny and dark as the bottom of a tar bucket. I seen it peerin' at the camp, peekin' out from behind the trunk of a tree. It was neked an' hairy, an' its face was an awful gray-black 'cause a frostbite. The skin looked like it was all peelin' away like the bark of a birch tree. An' it looked like its lips was all tore off, like there was nothin' coverin' its long, pointy teeth. That's what I seen, an' that's what I ain't never gonna forget."

Harley pressed his lips so tightly together that his jaw and nose almost met. He sighed heavily, a faraway look in his eyes. "I got a shot off at it, too. Had my huntin' rifle with me, an' squeezed one off in the direction of that horrid face. Didn't s'pect to kill it. Didn't even s'pect to hit the hellish thing. But when I fired it let out one hell of a squall; screeched to high-heaven and disappeared into the woods. I never see it again, but to this day the sound of that screechin' still puts the ice to my soul."

David Potter looked at Roger. The mere turn of the professor's head triggered another round of the old man's anger. "Well, I don't give an owl's fart what your books say or what you think, neither. I know what I know and I seen what I seen. You can waste your time up there searchin' for Cooly, but you're never gonna find him. Never. Not unless he sneaks up on you some dark night and whispers your name. Then you're gonna see a whole lot more of him than you wanna."

Harley Spooner pulled himself up to his full five feet three inches and stomped a path to the door. Before leaving he nodded stiffly but cordially to Roger and the boys. "I thank you for the drink," he said. Then he was gone. The door slammed like the report of a rifle.

For a moment Roger thought he should go after him. Then he thought better of it. The old man's ruse was transparent: He was disguising his grief as anger. It would be best to leave him alone for a while.

"I didn't mean to set him off," said Potter.

"It's probably a good thing you did. He needs to get it out of his system . . ."

"Roger, please," Stacy insisted, "we gotta find Cooly. At least we gotta try. We can't just forget about him. We gotta *help* him."

"You're right, son. But for now we have to figure out the best way to do that."

"I don't want to go back up there," Jarvis's voice cracked, his lower lip quivered. Fat tears slid down his cheeks.

"None of us are going anywhere tonight. Don't worry about that."

"Do you think it was a windigo that we saw?"

"I don't know, boys. I don't know what you saw."

Roger and David drove the exhausted boys to Laura's trailer. The two men stopped in long enough to offer her a simple explanation: Stacy and Jarvis had become separated from Cooly in the woods and were lost for a while. Then they found their way home. They were quite upset, yes, but there was really nothing to worry about. "But I'll stop back in the morning, Laura. I want to be sure everything's okay."

Although Laura was concerned about the youngsters, she knew better than to question them at this late hour. She allowed them to retreat quietly to Stacy's room. When they were gone she felt relieved; she had an agenda of her own.

"Why don't you guys stay for a cup of coffee?" Laura's eyes explored the deep lines around Roger's eyes. "Or how about a drink? You both look like you could use it." She watched as Roger and David exchanged glances.

"We'd like too, but Dave and I have some heavy-duty talking to do."

"Of course," she said, smiling, not wanting to appear disappointed. She knew David must be worried sick about his student. A *coma*—the very word made Laura shudder. The poor guy probably needed a friend at a time like this. "See you fellas in the morning, then?"

She kissed Roger on the lips, her fingers burrowing into his thick brown hair. Then she hugged David, kissed his cheek. As the men left she thought better of blowing them one last kiss. Too childish.

Her agenda, the news she had for Roger, could wait. Now was certainly not the time to announce her decision to move in with him. A more romantic occasion would be better—they'd be able to make the most of it. Celebrate a little. Perhaps a bottle of champagne . . .

Alone now, Laura smiled to herself in the darkness below the oak tree. Glancing skyward she saw the white moon tangled in its branches.

Still, she wished she'd been able to grab just a moment alone with Roger, just long enough to say how much she loved him. She wanted to let him know that Hank, finally, had been relegated to the past.

Perhaps the mind, like the body, can be bruised, made unattractive for a while. Too long she had thought of Hank as simply blemished, refusing to face the truth. Her waiting had been foolish; he'd never be restored. He was on a collision course with himself, and there was no room for anybody else on his wild ride. Hank was exactly where he chose to be, alone.

Inside, Laura sat down in front of the blank television screen, her mind far from the boys in the next room. Thank God, she thought, things are changing. Finally, they're starting to get better.

It was nearly midnight as the two men drove back toward town. The headlights of Roger's station wagon scanned black trees that seemed to crowd too close to the roadside. It was as if the ageless forest were trying to reclaim the town, inching its way nearer, slowly, invisibly, night after night. In spite of himself, Roger experienced a little shudder and eyed the darkness with a certain dread. He searched for motion in its depths, probed for shapes, looked for—

Decisively, he slapped the top of the steering wheel. "We've got to call the police," he said.

"I know, but I hate to do it; they'll think we're a couple psychos. The only evidence we've got is the boys' fantastic chronicle and Spooner's ghost stories."

"And the tape," Roger reminded him. "Don't forget the tape."

"The tape?"

" '*That's no man*,' remember?"

"Of course, but . . ." David Potter's sentence dropped off into a chasm of thought. "You think the two incidents are related?"

Roger shrugged. "It's a possibility."

After another contemplative moment David spoke slowly, each word a precision instrument. "She either said, 'That's-no-man,' or, 'The-snow-man' . . ."

"Exactly. Think about it: She might have seen the same thing the boys saw."

David looked at him. "I see what you mean. Right. And if so, it really was 'no man.'" A glitter of realization sparkled in his voice.

The ambiguity of the injured woman's final words was amazing; regardless of how one interpreted them, they led directly to the same uncomfortable conclusion. Roger was the first to articulate it: "A snowman! Shit! An abominable snowman! Could it be, David? Here in Vermont?"

"The description fits, doesn't it! I wonder if we could be dealing with Bigfoot sightings?" Dr. Potter grasped his chin, looking wide-eyed at Roger. "This is something that has interested me for a while; I don't know how I failed to make the connection. Leslie, Harley, and the two boys could all be describing exactly the same thing! A gigantic, black, hairy manlike creature. Of course! That's just exactly the way Bigfoot is usually described!"

"What do you think, Doc? You're the scientist: Does Bigfoot really exist?"

"I don't know. The conservative side of me wants to shrug it off with a derisive chuckle. But in all fairness, there's some pretty compelling evidence in its favor. You know, there are stories of large man-apes in almost every mountain range in the world. Unconnected cultures continue to report seeing similar phenomena: hairy giants that shun human beings, that leave ten to fourteen-inch footprints, and that cry out at night in high, mournful wails. They've been spotted in almost every state, although reports here in Vermont are pretty uncommon."

"Uncommon maybe, but they occur. We used to get calls about giant hairy beasts all the time when I worked for the paper. We'd run the stories too, now and then, when we were short of copy. There was one, back in—I think it was 1984. I interviewed a guy from Chittenden who said some large, hairy beast had ripped a solid barn door off its hinges."

"Sure, I remember that one. And what about that family from West Rutland who said they'd heard weird noises and went outside to investigate? They said they saw a big gorilla like creature poking curiously at their satellite dish antenna. When it ran away, they said, they could see the light-colored soles of its feet."

"Right. Sure. That was in eighty-five, I think, just before I left the paper."

"But sightings in Vermont go back a lot further. You know the Indians here have been seeing Bigfoots for centuries. Their word for the creature is 'wejuk,' meaning 'wet skins.' Even Samuel de Champlain talked about them in his diaries back in 1609. And you remember Rogers' Rangers? It seems that Major Robert Rogers himself had a run-in with one of the creatures right here in Vermont, somewhere around Missisquoi Bay."

"I hadn't heard about that one."

"Well, a colleague of mine from Castleton State College, Bruce Hallenbeck, keeps me pretty much up-to-date on what he likes to call 'Sasquatchery.' He has personally investigated several highly credible sightings down around Rutland. And several more across the border in New York state. Apparently Bigfoot has been spotted repeatedly near Whitehall and Kinderhook and along the Hudson

Valley. But if the animals are hanging out up here in the Northeast Kingdom, I'm not surprised there aren't many reports. I mean, God, this area's so unpopulated; there's no one around to see them!"

"Or maybe the people who see them are no longer around."

Potter grimaced. "Now, Roger, there's no real call for melodrama. There's very little evidence to suggest that the creature is hostile toward man."

"But there is some . . . ?"

"As far as I know, not around here—"

"David—yes or no—is there some evidence of Bigfoot being hostile toward man?"

"Yes. Some. There is some."

16

The Word of the Descendant

SLEEPTIME . . .

Things should be a lot easier now, the Watcher hoped. Easier, at least for the tribe.

But not easy for the intruders. Not at all. The Watcher felt his spirit fall as he thought of the Northmen, of what was happening to them. And of the things yet to come.

He knew it was not right, and he felt afraid.

In the Watcher's mind there was a great imbalance. Now, in the darkness, in the silence of the forest, it kept sleep away.

Yet, he knew, things would happen as they had to. The Descendant knew the best way; it had always been so.

He waited for sleep to come, paced silently, hoping . . . hoping . . . When at last it was time for rest, he would know. He'd go back to his place and sleep until the new sun called him to a new day.

The Watcher remembered how interested The Descendant had become to learn about the Moonface ritual on the hillside. He remembered how awake The Descendant grew when told the Shadowman was among the intruders.

The Shadowman . . .

At first The Descendant seemed not interested at all, "Ah," (the whisper echoed in his ears) "so there are four who climb upon the hillside . . . ? And they come no further than the water . . . ? It is not wrong."

Not wrong? The stern words echoed and pained. For the first time then the Watcher became frightened—but only for a heartbeat. Then he spoke of the Shadowman and The Descendant was interested, pleased. For bringing these important words, the Watcher was rewarded with passion.

But still sleep would not come.

It was as if The Descendant had known in advance, had planned for this day over many many seasons.

The old ways, the old wisdom, would always direct what was best. And the direction would come through The Descendant. The word of The Descendant was the word of the tribe.

But to the Watcher, letting loose the Stalker seemed very dangerous (with this thought the Watcher felt again the heat of fear). Only in rare seasons was the Stalker released, and always death would follow.

Always.

It should be of no concern to the Watcher; his job was to watch. Only that. The Descendant knew what was right for the tribe. Always. Always.

And it was forever so.

Now the Stalker had found two of the intruders—the white-haired one, and the Shadowman.

Now only two remained.

And for many many seasons the Stalker had eyed the old man who lived alone on the edge of the safeland. Now the Stalker could have his way. Revenge was wrong, the Watcher knew it was wrong.

But perhaps it was just. It wasn't for the Watcher to say.

All he knew was that soon the tribe would be made safe.

Soon each one would sleep easy. And all would be as it was before. Protected. Quiet.

The wolfdogs had done their part. Stalker had hooted when he heard their call, when he saw what prize they held for him. It was just as The Descendant had said: the work of all the forest, the work of all the wild and growing things, is to keep safe and to abide.

And now the Stalker was free.

And now two more invaders were left to the ways of the Stalker.
The Watcher crouched, small as a beaver, at his place amid the
night's thick shadows beneath the tree. The black bear pelt covered
his head and back. He watched the road, the river, and the mountain. He watched the shadows thicken and stretch, watched them
spread and merge like water, until all the world was dark.

PART TWO

In the Kingdom

When you have eliminated the impossible, whatever remains,
however improbable, must be the truth.

SHERLOCK HOLMES

Nothing, but nothing, is impossible.

L. CONNELLY BRONSON

17

Terrors at Daybreak

TUESDAY, AUGUST 30, 1988, 4:10 A.M.

Harley!—The thought jolted Roger Newton from a half sleep. *Harley's in danger!*

Roger shook his head to clear away the fog. His muscles were locked tightly in the tense grip of fear. Sweat dampened his pajamas.

Stupid! I was stupid! Why did I let him go back there alone?

He rose, moved rapidly to the window of his bedroom. On the street below him, dark shapes of parked cars looked like black boulders awash in the river of night. He stared at them, trying to calm his mind, trying to understand his sudden sense of alarm.

Shadows stretched in long tentacles, meshed into intricate, unfathomable patterns of darkness. The lone street lamp in front of Rand's General Store created an island of light in which nothing stirred. Roger blinked, rubbed his eyes, trying to clear away the afterimage of his nightmare.

It was his reporter's instinct again, and it had hit him like a mallet between the eyes!

Last night sleep had come slowly. He had drifted into unconsciousness amid a whirlwind of unsettling thoughts, thoughts of the gore, of Leslie and Cooly, of monsters and sacred stones. They all swirled in his head like vegetables in a food processor. And, like so many times before, his subconscious mind had been working while he slept, weaving nearly overlooked details into a bizarre and frightening tapestry.

He thought hard, focused, tried to put things in order. He wanted to view the events analytically: During the last forty-eight hours two people had apparently been attacked by a large man-like creature that conformed to popular descriptions of Bigfoot. The two victims had been part of the four-person expedition that went into the woods to examine Harley Spooner's "sacred stones."

And suddenly everything was clear!

Unless all this was a magnificent coincidence, the four members of that expedition had been targeted like ducks in a shooting gallery!

Now Roger and Harley were the only targets that hadn't fallen!

I've got to get up there! I should never have let the old man go home alone. He'd be defenseless against something powerful enough to lift Cooly Hawks and carry him away.

Fully awake now, Roger hurried from the window and quickly dressed. He briefly considered waking David Potter, then thought better of it. He could go much faster alone.

He glanced at his watch—4:12. If he allowed a little arguing time he could easily get to the farm and return with Harley before six o'clock. But just in case of a delay he scrawled a quick note for David:

> David—
> Gone to Harley Spooner's place. He may be in danger.
> If you get up before I get back I think you should call the police. We can't put it off any longer after what happened yesterday.
>
> Rog

Roger ran down the stairs and jumped into his station wagon. Not worrying at all about the town's speed limit, he sped off into the morning shadows.

The boys had still not fallen asleep when dawn began to lighten Stacy's bedroom.

All night they had been wrapped up in speculative conversations about the fate of Cooly Hawks. Occasionally one or the other would suggest sleep, and they would dutifully make the attempt—sometimes dozing briefly—until someone suggested a new theory or plan of action.

Stacy sat on the edge of his bed, an oversize paperback book he'd ordered a year ago open on his pajama-covered knees. Eyes wide with nervousness and sore from the lack of sleep, he flipped through the pages of *An Omnibus of Evil Gods* by L. Connelly Bronson.

"I knew I'd have something about the *Windigo* in one of these books. It says right here that . . . Well, I'll read it. Listen to this . . ."

Stacy read aloud from the book . . .

"WINDIGO: Man-eating wilderness god of North American Indian legend. Specific descriptions of this horrifying apparition vary slightly from tribe to tribe.

"Always described as huge, and sometimes as gigantic, the Windigo is thought to be a naked manlike creature horribly disfigured by its unending exposure to the elements.

"Compelled by preternatural forces, the Windigo runs maniacally through the limitless forests, stopping only to feed on tribesmen who have become lost.

"The legend of the Windigo has survived many generations and, surprising though it is, continues until this day. As recently as 1986, many people claim to have heard the Windigo rustling through the bush in the forests of northern Quebec and the Pacific Northwest. The fearsome creatures are said to utter terrifying hissing sounds, whistles, or loud, sinister howls that will strike fear in the hearts of anyone, even the most seasoned woodsmen.

"The Windigo is said to have a limited human vocabulary, usually restricted to the name of its next victim.

"It is commonly believed that the Windigo will, for reasons known only to itself, mark certain individuals for transformation. It will then summon the victim simply by calling his name. When called, the victim is compelled to obey. This 'naming' begins the process by which the Windigo magically transforms humans into its own likeness.

"Some legends hold that the transformation from man to Windigo can also originate through an act of flesh-eating. If, while in the woods, a human being consumes the flesh of another human, the change will begin.

"Many folklorists believe that Windigo legends arose from the American Indian's strong cultural aversion to cannibalism. In the severe northern winters the threat of being visited by, or changing into, a Windigo may have kept many individuals from turning to cannibalism, especially during times of famine."

"Boy, that sure sounds like what you saw," said Jarvis. "But it's really hard to believe, sitting here in the trailer."

"Harley believes it."

"I know." The Lavigne boy pressed his lips tightly together. Stacy thought he was trying not to cry. "Is that all the book says?"

"Yup."

"Any pictures?"

"None of the Windigo."

"Let me see it, okay?"

Stacy handed the book to his friend. Jarvis reread the part about the Windigo, then sat turning pages in silence. Stacy watched him, wondering what was going through his mind. After Jarvis had flipped back to the section on the Windigo, reading it over a third time, he looked up. "I'm just wondering if this really could be what my father saw. I mean, suppose he did see a Windigo, and suppose the Windigo called his name. I mean, he might have did what be did to keep himself from changing into, into . . ."

Jarvis flopped back on his bed and stretched out, turning his back on Stacy. His shoulders trembled. Continuing to flip pages, he ignored his friend, devoting all his attention to the book.

"What do you think we should do?" Stacy spoke softly. Jarvis shook his head. "No one will believe this. No one who can help us, anyway."

"Harley believes it. Roger believes we saw *something*. He promised he'd be back here this morning. He'll know what to do."

"The book doesn't say how to kill a Windigo. It doesn't even say how to protect yourself against it . . ."

It was true. Stacy's eyes wandered around his cluttered room. The horror movie posters, the wax skull, the ten-inch mechanical model of Frankenstein's monster beside the model of Freddy Krueger, the ornate pieces of magical apparatus all faced him but didn't offer a clue.

His library of science fiction and horror books might be a better source of information. He had read of the deaths of many a monster—but not the Windigo. This was the first time he'd ever encountered such a creature. Would it require a wooden stake? A silver bullet? Maybe an ordinary bullet would do the trick. After all, a Windigo was once a human being. Maybe it would be as easy to kill as a man—that is, if you got the drop on it, didn't let it surprise you as it had surprised Cooly Hawks.

The interior of the bedroom was bright now. The new day offered a temporary respite from the frightening thoughts of the night. Soon Roger would arrive. Any minute now. All of them would discuss the situation, maybe make a plan. If they were really dealing with something supernatural—and Stacy was convinced that they were—the authorities would be of no help. They would laugh, make some poorly concealed jokes at the expense of Harley and the boys. Oh, maybe they'd grudgingly do a halfhearted search of the woods. But they wouldn't help. Not really. Stacy had read a hundred horror stories; he knew how the police would react.

Further, for reasons of his own, he really didn't want to talk to the police. Perhaps he could just stick to the story Roger had told Mom: that Cooly had taken them for a hike and they got separated. When they couldn't find the old man, they returned home alone. That would sound believable. It might even get the authorities to search all the way up into the gore.

But what was the point? It would be useless; they'd never find Cooly.

And the Windigo was still loose.

Stacy jumped when he heard the book hit the floor. Jarvis looked at him coldly. "I'm going back up there," he said.

Stacy couldn't believe it. "Are you crazy?"

"Sure. Sure I am. And it's going to get worse if I don't do something. We can take a gun with us. I can get one of Dad's from the house. We can hunt that thing. We can kill it before it does any more harm to people."

"I don't know, Jarv. I mean, what if it gets us instead? You and me aren't fighters. We wouldn't know what to do if it attacked. I'm not saying we shouldn't go, but don't you think we should have some help? If not the police, at least let's talk to Roger or Harley. We can't go up there alone. I mean, you've never even gone hunting, have you?"

"Maybe not hunting, but I've fired a gun. My father showed me. What about you, can you get a gun?"

"I suppose."

"So you gonna come with me?"

"I don't know. I think we should talk to Roger first. Okay?"

Jarvis nodded stiffly. His eyes were dark and hard as stones.

He lay naked and sweaty under the flannel sheet, his pale, twig-thin body tense, full of pains. There would be no possibility of sleep this night.

Now, his anger long passed, he felt a kind of emptiness. His wife, ten years in the grave, weighed heavily on his mind. He missed her. Night after night he conjured the image of her face beaming at him from the next pillow. It was not the face of the wasted old woman who had smiled weakly, even as the cancer tore the pounds away from her once stocky frame. No, at night he saw the young farm girl he'd married, heard again the stammered vows promising she'd stay with him until death. She had been as good as her word; she always was.

Always, but just that once . . .

She had died here at home, in this very bed, after weeks and weeks of suffering. The skin of her back, sallow folds of wrinkled flesh, spotted with red and running sores. At the end she couldn't move enough to take the pressure off them.

"I'll be all right, Harl," she promised. It was said, not with her voice, but with a barely visible quiver of her translucent lips. Her lungs, nearly too damaged to breathe, could no longer drive out words that were loud enough for a man to hear.

Yet Harley knew what she'd said. And he'd believed her.

"I'll be all right." She'd said it over and over. But she'd lied. She went somewhere, leaving her tiny withered corpse in their marriage bed.

Harley had held that lie against her for a long while. He forgave her only when he realized how much he missed her. Wilma had been a good old girl. He was sixty-eight when she left him, too old to consider taking another wife.

Instead, the place took up his time. There was always something here to occupy his mind, to keep it out of the devil's hands. His first project had been to brace up the porch roof, the very job Wilma had been nagging him to do for the last two summers of her life. He did it for her.

Then there was replastering the walls in the parlor. Someday, he figured, he'd hang new paper in there as well. A good bright color would lighten up the room, make it a nice cheery place when friends came to visit.

Friends.

The old grandfather clock in the downstairs hall ticked loudly. It seemed to get louder as it aged, like an old man growing deafer, hollering to hear his own voice. That clock had run for three generations, with never a repair, never a problem. Harley had disconnected the chimes because they'd often wake him up at night. He needed what sleep he could get. As he grew older the sleep he got was as fragile as new ice on a pond. *Funny*, he thought, *won't be long 'fore I get all the sleep I want, and then some.*

Friends.

That Cooly Hawks had been a good old son. Harley would miss the nut-black face appearing at his kitchen window at six-thirty almost every day of the week. He'd miss their morning coffee together. *Why'd he want to go dragging them boys up into the gore for, anyways? He should a known better. Wasn't what happened to Lunker Lavigne warning enough?*

A man of Cooly's years should have known what—at least for

Harley—was a simple truth: Sometimes it's okay to go into the woods, sometimes it ain't.

Harley rolled onto his side, trying to relieve the gas pain that stabbed at his insides just above his stomach. The sharpness faded, but a nagging pressure remained. He pulled his hairless, pasty-white legs up almost to his chest.

Friends.

Thinking of the boys, Jarvis and Stacy, made him smile.

They were pretty good boys, all right. Then his smile collapsed into a stern paternal frown. He just hoped those boys would know better than to go poking around up there a second time. Maybe tomorrow he'd better round them up and give them a talking-to. The winny-go was nothing to mess with, not even for a grown man as woods-smart as Cooly'd been.

Two little fellas like that, why, they'd be nothing more than dessert for the hungry creature.

The thought of dessert evoked a loathsome image of Cooly being devoured, his front side split open like the carcass of a deer. Standing over him, slavering hungrily, a red-eyed horror tore the stringy flesh from his old brittle bones.

Harley imagined what must have occurred, what the little boys must have seen:

Screeching, the frost-black monster swoops down from the treetops, eyes stretched wide, bleeding from the tremendous velocity. It runs on burn-scarred limbs, deformed by its unending race through the wilderness. Jagged spikes of bone protrude from the stumpy ends of its legs where, over the years, the flesh has worn away. Its fang-filled face, only human by suggestion, splits open into a savage, lipless grin.

Roaring, it grabs the black man, runs with him—screaming—into the woods. Then, with Cooly limp and powerless, it begins to feed . . .

"Jumpin' Jonah, I gotta cut this out," said Harley to the empty bedroom. He flopped onto his back again, tight muscles tugging angrily within his chest.

Eyes wide open, he surveyed the room. The August moon turned the drawn window shade into an opaque rectangle the size of a door. Its bottom rose into the room with even the tiniest rustling of a breeze, then fell back, flapping into place with an irritating click.

Outside the window, the porch roof groaned and creaked.

Across the room he could see his collection of framed photographs, like dark little tombstones, on top of his chest of drawers. Although he couldn't make out the details, Harley knew those pictures as well as he knew his own face in the bathroom mirror: there were his father and mother seated in wooden lawn chairs, a half-circle of sons and daughters, Harley's brothers and sisters, standing behind; beside that one was Harley and Wilma on their wedding day, her gap-toothed grin, shy, but with just a dash of the devil's mischief in it. And there was a picture of the old dog, Sampson, who had once saved Harley's life by turning a charging bull, losing its own in the effort.

Friends.

Harley decided to count the ticks of the grandfather clock in an effort to get to sleep.

One, two . . .

The tapping window shade occasionally intruded (snap, snap . . .), but Harley tried not to let it bother him.

. . . eighteen, nineteen . . .

While he counted, his imagination, as undisciplined as a new puppy, tried to pull him back into the gore, back to the battle between Cooly and the winny-go.

Harley fought the pull of his imagination.

. . . thirty-three, thirty-four . . .

A breeze puckered the window shade again, scraped its thin, plastic edge along the wooden frame. Its weighted bottom clattered against the sill.

"That's 'bout enough a *that*," Harley blurted. Throwing his spindly legs out of bed he stomped across the pegged pine floor to the window.

For a moment he thought the dark silhouette on the window shade was his own shadow.

He grasped the shade, released it, letting it snap up and flutter its tension away at the top.

Frozen, Harley stared out the window. A massive hulking form loomed before him, framed in the dirty glass.

Harley stood face-to-face with a creature so alien, so grotesque, that all the details of its appearance failed to register at once. The only thing the old man sensed was his own primitive dread, a fear that pushed him backward one, two stumbling steps, his eyes never leaving the eyes that watched him.

"Har-ley." The ghastly whisper seemed to fill the bedroom.

Harley stared, dumbstruck, his own heartbeat thundering in his ears.

"Har-ley. Come. With me . . ."

Harley backed another step. "C . . . Cooly? Is that—"

But no! This thing couldn't be Cooly, it was too massive, too hideous.

Before Harley could take a fourth reflexive step backward, the thing was on him. With an agile bend and leap it vaulted through the open window and grabbed Harley by the hair.

It pulled the old man's face forward, so close that Harley could smell its fetid breath.

"Har-ley . . ." it whispered again. Then, with a downward flex of the thing's elbow, Harley dropped to his knees. Strands of thin white hair ripped painfully from their follicles.

"Aahh," Harley screamed. It felt as if the thing had pounded him in the chest, slammed him with a fist like a sledgehammer.

His mind flashed to the revolver in the drawer beside the bed. He'd put it there during that rash of break-ins during the sixties. Could Wilma have moved it? Was it loaded? Could twenty-year-old bullets still be good?

It *must* be there. It *had* to be.

Unbearable pain in his chest. Had the ungodly thing stabbed him with something? He tried to wriggle away from the powerful paw that clenched his hair. Struggling, he felt more hairs tearing free.

He realized that his only chance for freedom was to let the thing rip away his scalp. Bracing himself for another jolt of pain he yanked his head to the right. Still the thing held on. Harley felt the bones of his knees grinding against the pine flooring, folds of loose skin pinched and split in the cracks between the boards. He could smell the foul odor that now filled the room; it was sweet, like the smell of decaying leaves; at the same time it was fetid like carrion.

If this was the whiny-go, then he'd fight, although he knew it was pointless. But Harley was a man; he refused to go easily.

His chest hammered; cold sweat flowed from his open pores. The profusion of glassy beads made his skin as slick as grease . . .

Ah! There! The thing's hand slipped off Harley's neck!

He made three faltering steps toward the bedside table, his chest pounding like an ax on a chopping block. As be reached for the drawer powerful hands seized him by the shoulders.

Harley felt weightless in the arms that forced his face to the floorboards. His nose flattened against the dark pine. He could feel the sickening grind of cartilage, the sharp shattering of bone. He didn't wonder, what the thing was doing to him—he knew. He just wondered why it was doing it in this way?

When he remembered what the boys had said about the wild dogs, he understood: The thing was going to stomp him. Before the blow occurred, Harley Spooner imagined the big foot descending with tremendous force toward the back of his neck . . .

When the impact came it was as if his ribs snapped closed like a fist, crushing his lungs and heart like eggshells in their bony grip. The name of the Lord stuck in his throat. It came out neither as a prayer nor a curse.

Harley's house looked faded, old, and oddly still in the clear morning light. A mist rose from the tall grass surrounding the place as last night's dew transformed into vapor. The swirling vapor-ghosts vanished quickly as they drifted up to meet warmer air.

The sagging porch roof, braced by new-looking two-by-fours, had the gentle sloping contours of a smiling mouth. Above it two upstairs windows stared like vacant eyes at the sunrise. The house's faded paint peeled like sunburned skin.

Roger rushed across the lawn. In two noisy steps he clattered across the porch and pounded loudly on the closed door.

He listened for a stirring within.

Nothing.

Still no response when he knocked again.

He looked through the porch window on the left, then its twin on the right. No movement in the dark interior. The upright shapes of Harley's ancient furniture looked like the shadowy forms of crouching attackers waiting for the order to spring.

Roger felt a moment of self-doubt. He wasn't sure why. Perhaps morning light and clarity of thought had made his nightmare-fears vanish like the vapor-ghosts.

What if all this is a false alarm?

What if he was making a 14-karat fool of himself?

He waited, looked around, listened. Still Harley didn't answer his knock. The old boy was certainly a sound sleeper.

Roger tried the door; it was unlocked. Pushing it open a crack, he called, "Harley!"

No answer.

Warm musty air from inside wafted across Roger's nostrils. He detected the pungent blend of wood and tobacco smoke. Many years had made these odors a permanent part of the house's atmosphere. Mixed among those scents was the trace of something else, something sharp, unpleasant, a sweet-sickly odor. Roger figured cleanliness was not a high priority for the old man.

After knocking again Roger entered the house. He grappled around near the door frame, searching for a light switch. Then he remembered—Harley had never seen the need for electricity. Fortunately, the morning sun burning through the dirty windows provided enough light for Roger to move around without knocking things over.

Something clanged.

Metal on metal.

Roger's breath locked in his lungs. Someone was in the kitchen!

He stuck his head through the kitchen door, looking for the source of the sound, calling out for Harley. The room was a mess— dirty plates, crusted pots and pans strewn everywhere. Empty cans littered the tabletop and counter: beans, hash, chili. Old Ballantine

Ale bottles, containers for Harley's home brew, stood like green-uniformed soldiers in random formation.

A field mouse darted across the countertop, rattling a pot's lid in its frantic flight.

Roger exhaled. Heart still pounding from surprise, he checked the parlor, the back room, and the tiny pantry. When he found the door to the cellar he pulled it open.

"Harley!"

Nope. Not down there . . .

That's it, thought Roger, he's gotta be sleeping. He headed back toward the front door where the stairway led to the second floor.

For a moment his attention arrested on the tall grandfather clock in the hail. It was seventeen minutes after five.

I can't believe all this noise hasn't wakened him.

Then, full force, uneasiness returned.

Roger thundered up the stairs. From the small foyer at the top two doors opened into tiny peaked rooms. The first was used for storage. Boxes, trunks, canning jars, tied bundles of books, magazines, and yellowing newspapers were scattered haphazardly around the linoleum floor. It looked like a treasure house for a junk collector. Roger smiled and chuckled—apparently the old man never threw anything away.

The second door led to Harley's bedroom. Roger tapped a few times, then stuck his head through the slightly opened door. The scent of urine was most noticeable. Probably keeps a chamber pot, Roger guessed.

As he pushed the door all the way open and entered the room, he noticed another odor: the same one he had smelled downstairs. But here it was stronger. It was a rotting smell, sweet enough to turn his stomach. Questions about Harley's cleanliness again intruded. Perhaps the old man didn't bathe regularly. Perhaps he didn't bathe at all . . .

The old brass bed was a panic of tangled sheets and coverless pillows. The sheets—gray from age and stained from things Roger chose not to consider—were twisted in knots, pulled from under the mattress at two opposing corners.

It appeared that the old man had had a restless night. Roger wasn't surprised.

Taking a final look around, he satisfied himself that the bedroom was as empty as the rest of the house. More important—and he concluded this with a sense of relief—nothing looked out of place; nothing seemed wrong.

The obvious assumption was that Harley, like many old Vermonters, was an early riser. Perhaps earlier than most. Up before the sun, down after twilight.

But if Harley was up, where could he be?

Roger tried to imagine: maybe Harley'd decided to go out looking for Cooly after all. Sure, that was it. Roger knew how close those old codgers were. They'd been friends for years, decades, ever since they were lumberjacks together long before Roger was born. Now, in their old age, each was all the other had. They were like kin, if not joined by blood then joined by the years.

"Shit!" Roger said aloud. "The gore. That's just where he is . . ."

And if he's really in danger I'd better find him fast. He probably wouldn't have headed up there in the dark. And it's only been light for a half hour or so; he can't have gone too far.

Roger hurriedly left the house, stopping at his station wagon just long enough to get his 12-gauge. Then he headed up into the woods, following the same trail he had recently walked with Leslie Winthrop and Cooly Hawks and Harley Spooner.

18

Inside the Walls

8:00 A.M.

At eight o'clock David Potter found Roger's note. He went directly to the telephone, determined to call the police as Roger had requested. With the receiver to his ear, his index finger dialed the first number. He watched as the anachronistic telephone dial spun back to its original position.

He dialed the next number, then he stopped.

This simple phone call could derail his entire life. First, he would have to tell about the tape containing Leslie Winthrop's mysterious final words. That alone would be trouble; his relationship with Leslie would come out in the open. The impact on his academic career might be disastrous, but worse and more important, his marriage would suffer, possibly end. God, he didn't want to hurt his wife, not like that; he loved her too much.

Things had been so crazy lately; the days were zipping by way too fast. Somehow he had to get hold of things, slow them down, return them to a more manageable perspective.

He dialed another number.

In his forty-fifth year the increasing awareness of his vanishing youth had led to an indiscretion. Okay. So what? It was normal.

Maybe.

In any event, there was no reason to torture Gwen with his lapse

143

of faithfulness. In truth, he had intended to put a stop to the whole thing at that Sunday morning brunch—the brunch that never happened.

Roger was right, God *was* throwing some real sucker punches lately.

He dialed an eight. The dial rotated back in maddening slow motion.

And suppose he were to skirt the whole issue of Leslie with the police. Suppose he simply reported the disappearance of Cooly Hawks? He would still be made to look like a fool. Could he honestly tell the Vermont State Police that a Bigfoot came out of the woods and ran off with an elderly black man? Jesus, how would that look in the papers?

Of course the whole business about Bigfoot had come from the boy. And boys tend to have colorful imaginations. Okay, so how would it look for a respected Vermont archaeologist to be spreading rumors started by a thirteen-year-old kid?

Christ! Who cares? he thought, trying to be cavalier; then more conservatively: *I better think about it. I'd better plan.*

Potter put the phone down, sagged into the chair beside it. God, how could this be happening? How?

What should he do?

David stared at the telephone.

Sure, the police would eventually have to be notified; there was no way around it. But perhaps he could delay just a bit. Maybe Roger would agree to omit the stuff about Leslie. Why not? Telling wouldn't change things, it wouldn't improve her condition. And the police had already decided it was an accident. Now the business with the old man's—Cooly's—disappearance was far more pressing. That's all the police needed to concentrate on.

Why not wait for Roger to come back before phoning? Sure. Together they could decide exactly what to say. Since the boy, Stacy, was the only real witness, Potter could remain pretty much in the background. He wouldn't have to jeopardize either his profession or his marriage. He wouldn't need to be embarrassed. No one would. All he needed was Roger's cooperation.

And Roger should be back at any time. A short delay of the phone call wouldn't matter. No, not at all. How could it?

The best thing he could do now was call the hospital, see how Leslie's doing.

It was a little after noon when the boys finally woke up. Laura had looked in on them at eight, and again a little after ten. She had heard them talking on and off throughout the night, and she understood their need to do so. Now, mercifully, they had both managed to catch a little sleep. She didn't disturb them until it was almost lunchtime, when she had to start preparing to go to work.

While the kids were getting dressed she made a follow-up phone call to Peggy Lavigne. In calm, friendly tones she assured Peggy that the boys were fine. Peggy seemed happy, maybe even relieved, to hear from her.

The women had known each other for many years. They had met in the first grade of Eureka's one-room schoolhouse. *Almost thirty years ago; is it possible?* Of course, back then Laura's friend had been Peggy Jarvis.

God, how the marriages have changed things.

Laura and Peggy still got together occasionally, usually by accident. They'd run into each other at the general store, then go to the drugstore for coffee. Or they'd meet at the PTA, or sit together at a dance at the legion.

Yet this friendship, formed in their early years, remained solid as Vermont granite.

In a quiet voice, Peggy thanked Laura for her help with Jarvis. "Now don't you be worrying about me," Peggy said, "I'm just fine. The relatives and in-laws are making about as much fuss over me as I can stand. I'm just thankful Jarvis has a friend to be with during all this . . ."

"Yes," Laura agreed, "I know it's tough on him. And don't you worry about anything, either; I'll have Jarvis home by suppertime."

"Do you think you could find a few minutes to stop by?" Peggy asked, her voice faint on the other end of the phone. She sniffed, cleared her throat. She was crying, but trying not to sound like it.

"You bet I can. I just wanted to phone you first. I'll stop in on my way to work."

"Please do, Laura . . ."

"I promise." Laura wished Peggy Lavigne the best, and hung up.

When Stacy stumbled sleepy-eyed out of the bedroom, his first question was, "Where's Roger?"

Laura looked up from her *Redbook*. She smiled at her son. She wanted to hug him but waited. "I s'pect he's home. And good morning to you, too."

"Mornin'. He said he'd come back today, first thing."

"You know Roger. If he said he'll come, he will. But give him a break. Maybe he needs some sleep, too. And don't forget, he has a guest to take care of."

"Why don't you call him?"

"Call him yourself. What are you, shy all of a sudden?"

"Okay." Stacy walked to the phone as Jarvis came out of the bedroom rubbing his eyes.

"Morning, Mrs. Drew."

"Good *afternoon*, Mr. Lavigne. Which do you prefer, breakfast or lunch?"

Jarvis looked puzzled. "I'm not really very hungry. Can I have a glass of juice, if you have it?"

"I think we do. Have a seat at the table, I'll get it for you. How 'bout some toast?"

"No thanks."

Jarvis sat at the table as Stacy dialed Roger's number.

David Potter rushed to the phone, picked it up on the second ring. Was it Leslie's doctor calling back?

The caller's youthful voice was very direct.

"Hello, Roger there?"

"I'm afraid he stepped out for a little while."

"Is he coming up here?"

"Well, I don't know. Who's calling, please?"

"Stacy."

"Oh, hi, Stacy. This is Dave Potter. Actually, Roger's gone up to Harley Spooner's house. I expected him back before this. How are you doing today, sport?"

"Okay."

"Did you get a good night's sleep?"

"Pretty good."

"How's your friend?"

"He's okay."

David laughed to himself. *They're getting more nonverbal every year*. He hoped he'd be out of the teaching profession by the time the thirteen-year-olds hit college. "Would you like me to have him call you, or what?"

"Have him come up. He said he would."

"Okay, pal. Just as soon as he comes in I'll tell him." As he hung up David Potter heard a noise behind him. *Shit*, he thought, *that must be him now*. He quickly retrieved the receiver in hopes that the boy was still there. All he heard was the dial tone.

It had sounded like someone walking up the steps. David went over to the entranceway and opened the door. The closed-in hall, the straight stairway, the landing below, all were empty.

Strange, he thought.

Maybe someone was making noise in the bar downstairs? It was probably Laura coming in to get the place ready for opening. Sounds could bounce around, distort, echo unpredictably in these old houses.

He listened again, but now he could hear nothing. Restless, he walked to the bookshelf, scanned the titles. Perhaps he could occupy his mind with research. He wanted to read up on Bigfoot, review those rare cases where the alleged creature did harm to human beings.

There were tales he recalled from some of the shoddily researched "speculative science books" he occasionally picked up for vacation reading—his "guilty pleasures," as he liked to call them. But his memories of specific references were scrambled.

One case involved a logger from the Pacific Northwest who was captured at night by a Bigfoot, stuffed into his own sleeping bag, and carried off into the mountains like a sack full of groceries.

And there was another tale involving thirteen boys from someplace in Oregon who were attacked by a Bigfoot—or did they attack it? David couldn't remember.

Then there was something about a Texas oil man who sponsored a monster hunt after the beasts had allegedly attacked a village, killing at least five people. But maybe they were Yetis, not Bigfoots —and maybe the story took place in Nepal, not the USA.

The absence of reference materials in Roger's library was frustrating, infuriating. Forget it! He'd call his office. Someone there could do the research and get back to him.

Or he could call Hallenbeck at Castleton State College.

He wished he could call Leslie.

David sat down, trying to exorcise the painful image of his lover. *I do miss her*, he thought. *I should be there with her now. God, I hope she'll pull out of this—*

No, by God, I'll call my wife.

As he stood up a board creaked somewhere nearby.

Turning, he faced the empty, sun-bright apartment. Listening intently, his eyes explored the corners of the room. Again he noticed Roger's note on the table.

Gone to Harley Spooner's place. He may be in danger . . .

Danger?

Why should Harley be in danger? How could Roger have come to such a conclusion? And why in the middle of the night? Is he psychic all of a sudden?

It didn't make sense.

Another noise in the apartment wrenched Potter's mind from speculation. It sounded as if something were moving around inside the walls. Occasional creaks and groans like boards straining under pressure held his attention. He found himself sweating. Perspiration along his spine chilled him, made him cringe. An atavistic response identical to the one that freezes wild animals sensing danger rooted Potter to the spot. His heartbeat was loud in his ears.

Holy Moses, what the hell am I so nervous about? he wondered. *Why am I so jumpy?*

Then he knew: Something was definitely moving around *inside* the wall!

The hidden passageway! He and Roger had examined it more than two years ago. A cleverly concealed part of Vermont's Underground Railroad system, the passage was designed to let fugitives move from floor to floor without being seen. David remembered the one hundred-foot tunnel extending from the house's basement. It would permit escape from the building and into what, a hundred and fifty years ago, must have been a thickness of vast nearby woodland.

Could Roger, for some reason, be reentering by way of the hidden passage?

Somewhere on the wide pine wainscoting, Potter remembered, there was a release bolt. Senses alert, he inched toward the wall, ran his hand along the underside of the molding. He could feel his fingernails clicking against the gaps between the vertical boards.

Touching the white-painted wood jogged his memory. All he had to do was lift a piece of top molding as if it were a lever. Four hinged strips of wainscoting would be released; they'd open like a door.

He paused, his hand on the lever. *Suppose it isn't Roger?* Maybe the two boys had lost patience, come back to find Roger, opting to enter in a manner preferred by any youngster.

Could they have come all this way so quickly?

He grinned. Maybe he should give them a scare?

Stupid, he thought, *stupid! Scare a kid whose father just shot himself. Good, Potter. You're as clearheaded and sensitive as ever.*

Besides, it was probably just a rat, possibly a squirrel. Or more likely (noting the silence now), nothing at all . . .

He put his ear against the sixteen-inch-by-four-foot doorway. There was a faint scratching on the other side, like fingers searching for a catch. The noises, soft and persistent, were identical to the ones he'd made while feeling for the release bolt.

"Roger?" he said to the closed door.

The scratching stopped. Since no one answered, Potter concluded that it must be an animal.

After carefully releasing the lock he pulled the door open, just a crack, just enough to look inside.

At first he saw nothing. Then be recoiled from a horrible stench that scraped at his nostrils. It smelled like something had died in there! Squinting into the narrow crack of darkness, an image registered consciously and unconsciously at the same time.

Reflexively he pushed the door closed before he had a moment to doubt what he had seen.

Wide, glaring eyes. Long, fanglike teeth.

But the door wouldn't close! Something held it, pushed back from the other side. Guttural breathing, punctuated with sharp primitive grunts, erupted from the darkness. Potter's nerves turned to icicles.

Christ, something's trying to get in!

David quickly realized his awkward crouching position would not allow him the purchase necessary to force the door closed. He flopped over, sat on the floor, wedged his back against the door. His rubber-soled shoes pressed firmly against the floor like brake pads against a disk.

Panic seized him. Yet part of his mind was clear enough to realize his mistake: With his back against the door his hands were useless, they had no role in the struggle. He moved them from his lap, pushed hard against the floor for additional braking power.

But when his left hand hit the floor it was too near the opening.

Something shot toward it with the speed of a rattler's attack.

It seized his wrist.

A black hairy paw. A hand!

Fingers like a coil of steel cables surrounded his wrist. They pulled his hand, his arm, backward through the opening. His own weight closed the door against his bicep, crushing it, charging it with tremendous pain.

My shoulder's dislocating!

Trying to ease the pressure, David leaned forward, moving his back away from the door. A powerful tug yanked his arm farther into the darkness. Something tore within his throbbing shoulder. For a moment the entire world filled with white searing agony. Without knowing how it happened he found himself flipped over, stretched out, lying facedown on the floor.

Nearly unconscious now, he felt himself sliding helplessly along the floor. The thing was hauling him through the open door and into—

A new panic brought alertness. He struggled to free himself, but the torture of his ruined shoulder was too great. Waves of nausea blurred his thoughts. He cried out, groped frantically at the door-jamb with his good hand.

Now something had him by the hair, pulling, pulling.

Large, coarse fingers locked around his neck, used his rigid jaw-line to secure their grip. Feet kicking, body wriggling like a landed trout, David Potter could not prevent himself from being pulled through the opening.

19

Taking Arms

Laura Drew kissed Stacy good-bye. She gave Jarvis a quick hug, got in her car, and drove away.

The boys had passed up her offer of a ride to the Lavigne house, saying they wanted to watch "Star Trek," then do some fishing. As soon as Laura's vw was out of sight they started walking aimlessly in the direction of town.

Stacy had some vague notion about confronting Roger. In his mind he rehearsed what he might say: You *told* me you'd come. You *promised*!

The stubby shadows at their feet reminded him of the hour. Jarvis didn't have to be home until supper; they had plenty of time for planning.

Stacy had a half dollar in his hand with which he nervously practiced his magical moves: palming it, then making fake passes from one hand to the other. It was easy for him to entertain himself in this way. Especially at times when he didn't feel like talking. Like now.

Roger hadn't showed up. And he had *promised*. The awful thing that happened to Cooly was *important*; didn't Roger realize that? How could he take serious things so lightly?

Maybe he had even lied to them. Maybe he really didn't believe a monster had come out of the woods at all. Maybe he had been humoring them, just the way Dad used to.

Damn, Stacy thought, there's no one you can rely on. He knew he was angry. And with that anger came a fierce determination and an independence. "You know Jarv, we just might have to take things into our own hands."

Jarvis slowed his pace, watched the coin in Stacy's hand tumbling from knuckle to knuckle, left to right, then somersaulting back again. "That's pretty good!" he said.

"Yeah, thanks." Pocketing the coin, Stacy asked, "What do you think?"

Jarvis looked at him blankly, his head jutting forward, seeming to float in front of his body. "Well, I'm not so sure. I know I said I wanted to go back up there, but now I don't know. I ain't too anxious to do it. But I guess we might have to."

"What if we go get Harley? He believes us." Stacy stared levelly into his friend's eyes.

"But what if he won't go? Then what?"

"Then we go alone. Let's go back to the trailer and get a camera."

"How about a gun?"

The word chilled Stacy, but he knew Jarvis was right. There was a High Standard .22 target pistol that had belonged to his father. Dad had left it at the trailer for Mom's protection. And that's just what they needed now—protection.

Stacy was a good shot with it, but he'd never used it against anything other than cans and bull's-eyes. "Yup," he said. "Good idea."

"Don't forget, I gotta be home for supper. Think we got time?"

Stacy thought about it. "No. We better tell your ma something. Wanna call her from my house? Say you're staying here for supper?"

"It's gonna piss her off. I haven't been home since after the funeral."

"Yeah, you're right. Maybe we should stop in there for a while. I can ride you over on my bicycle . . ."

"Naw. It'll waste too much time. Let's just call. I'll think of something to tell her."

They about-faced and walked quickly back to the trailer.

Jarvis stood watch as Stacy took the holstered pistol from the hook in his mother's closet. He strapped it high on his waist, buckling the belt tightly, concealing it beneath the tail of his overlong T-shirt.

"Aren't you gonna phone your ma?"

Stacy watched as courage and resolve seemed to collect behind Jarvis's eyes. Then Jarvis pressed his lips together. "Forget about calling," he said. "If we hurry we can be up there and back by suppertime. If we're late, I'll call when we get back."

They looked around to make sure the coast was clear, left the trailer, and headed up the road toward Harley Spooner's house.

At a quarter to three Laura parked her vw in the space beside The Newsroom. She felt drained after her visit with Peggy Lavigne. Peggy had seemed so fragile, so desperate for her company. Laura felt like a traitor when she broke off their conversation to go to work.

She sighed, got out of the car, and went to the door that opened onto the stairway leading up to Roger's apartment. She found the door unlocked, opened it, called, "Roger!"

There was no answer.

After seeing Peggy she was more eager than ever to get a few minutes alone with Roger. She actually needed to see him and the need felt good.

Although generally she felt nearly as at home here as in her own trailer, today she was a bit uneasy about barging in on Roger and his friend.

She called again, "Hello! Roger! You up there?"

Silence.

As she started to climb the stairs she noticed that the door at the top was slightly ajar. *That's funny,* she thought. She had often kidded Roger about the way he locked everything up, a big city habit he'd brought with him from Burlington. It was out of character for him to leave the door unlocked, much less open.

Cautiously, she continued to climb, listening carefully for the men. When she reached the top she pushed the door open all the way. A peculiar smell permeated the apartment. Had one of the men been sick during the night?

Laura entered the kitchen, looking around expectantly. There was no sign of breakfast dishes on the table or counter. Nothing in the sink. Could they still be asleep?

"Roger!"

Maybe they weren't here at all. She should have thought to notice if Roger's car was in the garage.

"Roger, you here?"

Moving into the living room she saw that the small table was overturned. The decanter and ceramic lamp it had supported were smashed on the wooden floor. A chill seized her, held her immobile.

The secret panel! The slave door—as Roger referred to it—was open! Its invisible hinges groaned slightly as a current of foul air passed through the opening.

She wanted to make light of it, to persuade herself that the guys were playing in the passageway, just like a couple of kids. But she knew better. All her fine-tuned senses told her that something was wrong.

Heels tapping on the pine floor, she walked over to the secret door, pulled it open all the way.

"Rog . . ." Her fingers touched something wet. Bringing her hand to her face, she saw blood. Wet red smudges stained her white fingertips.

There was blood on the wainscot door, more on the pine floorboards. It was streaked, smeared, as if something had been pulled through it and into the opening.

She wiped her hand on her denim skirt, then, noting the dark stain, felt stupid for having done so. What happened here? she asked herself. She called again, "Roger! David!" knowing it was useless.

Keeping a safe distance from the door, she peered into the dark opening. The inside was too black to see anything, and that made her more nervous. Someone could be hiding in there! Someone she'd just as soon not meet.

She closed the door quickly, replacing the molding that served
as a latch.

Walking rapidly from room to room, she took a quick but thorough look around the apartment. She saw that nothing else was
out of order. All the time she assured herself that she was alone.
Satisfied that there were no more signs of bloodshed, she went
to the phone and dialed the state police. She knew the number
by heart.

It was a simple conclusion: Since no one was home at Harley's,
and since Roger's station wagon was in the dooryard, the two men
must have gone into the woods without them.

Stacy kicked the gravel drive with the toe of his sneaker. *Damn!*
Not only had Roger failed to come back as promised, but also he'd
driven right past the trailer on his way to Harley's house! It wasn't
fair. Roger and Harley were treating him like a kid. Without him
and Jarvis, the two men wouldn't even know where to start looking
for Cooly. Not to be included in the search party was . . . Well, it
just wasn't fair.

From the sagging porch the two boys looked off into the green
distance. Which way could the men have gone? There were hundreds of acres of woodland. Thousands! Where should they begin
to look?

Never mentioning his hurt feelings to his friend, Stacy, stiff-
jawed and determined, stepped off the porch. Forging ahead, he
led Jarvis through the parted grass toward the trail that ran through
Harley's neglected apple orchard. "Come on," he said, the holstered pistol weighing heavily on his hip.

In single file the two boys made their way to the forests of
the gore.

20

The Skin of the Bear

AFTERNOON CONTINUES . . .

The Watcher sat alone, eating dry fish and drinking water.

He kept looking at the entrance, trying to hear what The Descendant and the Stalker were saying.

The Stalker had made a mistake.

He had taken the wrong one.

And if The Descendant could not forgive him, if The Descendant could not plan a way to make things right, there would have to be a new Stalker. Such was the law. But no one in the tribe was as big or as strong. No one else had been grown for the job.

The Watcher feared that he might be called the new Stalker. He *did* know the trees and the ways of the forest better than any other, and it had been his work to go nearly to the otherland.

No. It could not happen, not with his weakened leg, not with the limp that slowed his pace at dangerous times.

No, it was never to be.

He was happy to be the Watcher. It had always been his place.

To be Stalker would be more difficult. It could require more than strength. It could require the hurting, or the killing, of others.

Killing was not the way of the Watcher. Killing was the hard way.

In moments it would be decided. Then it would be law forever until death.

He looked again at the entrance. The voices were like the sound of a river; he could hear them, but he could not understand.

But if he *had* to become the Stalker, then most of his work was done. Three of the intruders were down. And there was a fourth, the one who was a mistake.

Only that one—the one with ice upon his eyes—remained.

And that other man, though younger than two, and stronger than one, would still be easy.

Easy to find.

Easy to take.

Then the Stalker came from The Descendant's entrance. He would meet no one's eyes.

He had been shamed.

Yet still he wore the skin of the bear.

He was still the Stalker. The largest. The strongest.

And he had one more man to take.

He must do it well.

The Descendant had given him a chance. The Descendant had been kind. Such was The Descendant's way.

Now, with this chance, the Stalker must make everything new, everything right.

The Watcher looked on as the Stalker, anger in his face, vanished like smoke among the black, black trees.

21

A Gathering of Forces

He had been walking compulsively for a long time. Hours. Much longer than he'd planned. Changing direction, running, trotting, backtracking, and still no sign of Harley.

Too often he had yielded to the temptation of the next rise, the next bend in the nearly invisible trail. He was sure that any minute he'd overtake the old man, hear him rustling through the trees not far ahead, probably sputtering to himself.

Roger had forgotten his watch. From the truncated shadows of the trees he judged that it was early afternoon.

Still he pushed onward. He was experiencing the same mindless, driving curiosity that had forced him to research story after story while he'd worked at the newspaper. Now, as then, he was ignoring his obligations to other people, caught helplessly in this seemingly futile quest. He had promised to meet with the boys first thing this morning, and he hadn't. Soon Laura would be expecting him to help her open the bar. There was no way to tell her he'd be late.

And surely David Potter would have expected him back long before this.

Conscious of his abandoned obligations, Roger still hoped to locate the old man. Harley was a stubborn old coot. If he got it into his head to find Cooly, he'd spend all day canvassing the woodland, oblivious to, or disregarding altogether, any danger to himself.

Roger didn't worry about Harley's encountering the windigo, the whole idea was just too fanciful. Probably Bigfoot was not a problem either, but somehow Roger gave that notion a bit more credence. If Bigfoot existed, at least it was natural, an animal vulnerable to the twelve gauge.

Still, fear lent an unpleasant dimension to Roger's speculation. One fact was inescapable: Leslie Winthrop and Cooly Hawks had encountered a person or thing unknown. They, along with Harley Spooner and Roger himself, were linked to that late afternoon expedition, their fatal trek to the Indian campsite.

And now something was after them.

Although Roger was aware of the possibility of personal danger, it hadn't weighed heavily on his mind. He was too preoccupied with warning Harley. Now, in the lush sultry greens and harsh browns of the forest, he began to realize how alone, how potentially vulnerable he was. And he was tired. His legs were stiff, aching from the long uphill climb. The twelve gauge took on additional weight with every step.

Roger knew he would have to impose some limit on himself. Sooner or later he'd have to call off his search and go back for help. Of course, help might already be on the way. Hopefully, David Potter had phoned the police as Roger had requested. With luck his delayed return would add urgency to the request.

Looking ahead, the trace of a path reached a summit some two hundred yards above. Roger told himself he'd walk to that rise, see what he could see, and if the new panorama revealed nothing promising, he would turn back. This time for sure.

He had never been this far into the woods before. Twin ruts, barely visible, told him this path hadn't been used for a long time. This must be the remains of a logging road, he thought, or quite possibly the road that led to the old hotel in the gore.

By now his upward hike was as much an effort of will as of strength. Occasionally he'd push his palms down against his throbbing knees, adding the strength of his arms to that of his legs.

Silently he reaffirmed his decision: When he got to the top of the rise he'd turn back. But first he'd stop to rest. He needed to sit down, take a few minutes to recharge.

The heat was uncomfortable. He was soaked with sweat; it made his skin slippery, caused his glasses to slide repeatedly down his nose.

His stomach growled like a hungry beast. He should have had something to eat before leaving the house. No wonder he was so tired.

Pausing, breathing deeply, he switched the shotgun from one hand to the other. He listened for sounds that might be out of place. A crow called from somewhere above. Leaves and branches moved softly in a wind that Roger could not feel. Taking his damp handkerchief from his back pocket he rubbed at the perspiration from his face. A glass of cold water would taste pretty good right now, he thought. There must be a stream around here someplace. Perhaps over the next rise . . .

Again forcing his heavy legs into reluctant motion, he made for the rise. Two hundred yards changed to one hundred, and soon he was there, viewing a scene he had long been curious to see.

The remains of the hotel were nothing like he'd expected. Ever since he'd heard about it, he'd imagined the fire-blackened ruins of one of those vast sprawling resorts that were so popular before the proliferation of private automobiles. He'd expected something like the Overlook in that Stanley Kubrick film of Stephen King's *The Shining*: at least four stories tall with acres of roof pitted with gaping, black-rimmed holes, and pointed gables, their windows smashed, high above endless manicured grounds.

He hadn't expected this.

This place couldn't have been any larger than the biggest house in the town of Eureka, more the size of a rooming house than a grand hotel. It was impossible to imagine how it had appeared during its heyday; extensive fire damage made guesswork impossible. However, the place had not burned to the ground.

The structure had been built of wood and stone. Now, what wood remained was in thick, angled support beams, their black-charred ends, like lead in dull pencils, pointed at the clouds.

The stonework, stained but undamaged by fire or the elements, gave the whole place an unworldly, ruined look, as if it were some long-forgotten castle in a fantastic fairy-tale kingdom. Granite walls framed glassless windows; two semicircular stairways rose from the dirty marble floor, winding gracefully toward the sky, leading nowhere. Interior partitions, once topped with fancy woodwork, divided the floor space like the walls of a maze. The highest walls, with their second-story windows of various sizes, looked like the battlements of a medieval fortress—a strange anachronism within the anachronism of Eureka itself.

As he stared at the structure Roger felt a sense of awe. The sight tugged playfully at that part of him that had never grown up, the part that was still a small boy with an active imagination. He wanted to share his discovery with Stacy and Jarvis.

A stillness hung about the place. Green grasses, progeny of a well-kept lawn, swayed hypnotically against the foundation. There was something restful about the scene, something tranquil. The grasses silently stroking the stones were like calm waves lapping gently at wind-whipped granite bluffs. Tiny islands of color—Queen Anne's lace, black-eyed Susans, and goldenrod—floated on the green tide. Roger searched for words to describe what he saw, how it made him feel. Was the hotel like the tip of an iceberg, adrift in an endless green sea?

A shadow rippled over the structure. Roger looked up, saw a dark form circling overhead. A crow. It swooped and banked, finally perching at the top of the tallest stone wall, black against the blue of the sky.

In his excitement Roger forgot how tired he was. Indeed, he forgot why he was tired. His legs ached only to make the short walk to the structure. He wanted to walk upon those floors, climb those stairways to nowhere, poke around in dark holes, and explore darker passageways.

The shadow of the wall was a straight black ribbon hugging the building's foundation. It reminded him how late it was. Responsibility warred with his sense of adventure. His small-boy curiosity grew to that of a seasoned reporter. He wanted to know everything about this place, wanted to research it, wanted to write its history, its life story. There must be one hell of an article here, he thought. If only he had brought his camera instead of the shotgun.

Stepping for the first time onto the marble slabs of the floor, he was surprised not to find the scattering of beer or soda cans, the empty potato chip bags and other litter, predictable signs of the human transients, hunters, and teenage lovers who usually discovered, used, and abandoned places such as this.

This spot was too remote to suffer such unappreciative traffic. Roger felt that the hotel was his secret, his discovery. The story it was inspiring would be his story.

He wondered when the fire had occurred, and when the place had last been in use. He wondered what stories the stone walls, like the covers of a book, might enclose.

The first thing he did was climb the winding stone stairway. From the top he'd be able to survey not only the ruin itself, but also the surrounding land. Fourteen steps brought him to a stone platform that had once joined the boards of a wooden floor. Thick stumps of hand-hewn beams embedded in the stonework extended outward for about a foot. Their black, fire-gnawed ends looked like bones protruding from a cauterized wound.

After studying the maze of partitions below, he raised his eyes to the surrounding woods. Behind him the hills of the gore rose for several thousand feet. Here and there a scattering of early fall colors began the autumn transformation. To the east, the surface of a small pond glittered in the sun.

He sat down where the stone floor ended, letting his feet dangle in space. He was in a perfect spot from which to watch for movement in the woods.

He was about to call Harley's name when directly in front of him something moved. Just one hundred yards uphill, where a stone wall bordered the massive forest, a deer stepped onto the once-cleared lawn.

Smiling, Roger watched the elegant animal move in its precise slow motion. Then it froze, assumed its scenting-listening pose.

Its ears perked up, its white tail stood erect, motionless; its head was as still as a photograph.

Soft brown eyes looked directly at Roger.

He watched it, hypnotized by its beauty and immobility. Perhaps it was wondering about him, too. Evidently the animal's keen senses had alerted it to the nearby stranger. It had heard him, or smelled him, and now, quite possibly, was studying him just as he studied it.

As he watched, the animal's head snapped forward like a boxer's fist. Its knees buckled and it collapsed soundlessly into the swaying grass. Roger saw it kick convulsively a couple of times. Then it was still.

My God, what happened?

There had been no shot. At least none that he'd heard. The thing just . . . fell.

Roger stood up at once, a clammy, cold feeling replacing his moment of relaxation. By God, he would have a look at that animal!

As be turned to descend the stone steps he saw someone standing at the bottom. Someone with a pistol. Its barrel pointed directly at Roger's head.

Trooper First Class Dalton "Hank" Drew was not a big man. He stood five-foot-six in his shiny black Wellington boots. The too-long pants of his green and brown Vermont State Police uniform did what they could to disguise the boots' elevated heels.

Although it would have given the illusion of extra height, the day was far too hot for the Stetson that regulations required. Because he knew the caller—intimately—he was confident that she would overlook this small breech of protocol.

Hank's sideburns, tightly cropped and descending to his earlobes, framed wide, dark, penetrating eyes that were never free of suspicion, that never smiled with genuine mirth. Their cold, unrelenting stare had intimidated many lawbreakers into timid submission long before it became necessary to unholster the Smith and Wesson .357 magnum that he carried on his belt.

When he arrived at The Newsroom he parked the cruiser directly in front of the entrance. Hank noted an awkwardly scrawled sign on the door; it read: Closed for the Day.

He wrote something on his clipboard and got out. Hiking up his pants, he looked around. When he saw Laura's car at the side of the building, he made for the entrance to the upstairs apartment.

Laura met him on the stairs. At first neither spoke.

"Thanks for coming," she finally said. Her tone was not as cold as it might have been; it wasn't warm, either.

She turned and led him up into the kitchen of Newton's apartment.

All along Hank had known that she would call him sooner or later. It was just a matter of time. It didn't surprise him that she had disguised the contact as police business. He'd play along, see where it all was heading.

Laura sat in one of the kitchen chairs. Hank sat opposite, never taking his cold eyes from hers. He saw that she had trouble meeting his gaze; that was a good sign.

"So what's up?" he said, careful to betray no emotion in his monotone.

"Something's happening here, Hank. I don't know what." She quickly explained about the blood, the signs of a struggle, the strange events of the night before. Then she showed him the note she'd found: Roger telling David Potter to call the police.

Hank shrugged noncommittally.

"He never called," Hank said, thinking maybe he should have brought his notebook in with him. He might need it after all. Perhaps there was more going on than he'd expected, more than just Laura's feminine play to win him back.

"So where's Stacy?"

This time she met his eyes, then looked away. "He's okay, Hank. He's gone fishing with Jarvis Lavigne."

Hank tapped the tabletop with his pen. "Christ, Laura, you shoulda called me last night! If the boy was as shook up as you say, I shoulda been with him."

Nope, by God, she hadn't changed at all; not one bit. With tight lips he blew air disgustedly through his nostrils. "Come on, show me this blood."

The blood on the floor and on the frame of the secret panel had dried to a waxy brown paste. Hank examined it carefully without touching it. He had to decide whether to take a sample or leave it for the lab boys. "Maybe he was working in here, cut himself, and his buddy drove him down to Island Pond to the doctor."

"Come on, Hank, there's no tools. And what about the broken table? And the lamp? What about the note?"

She looked him square in the face now. God, she's beautiful, he thought. Why does she have to be so dumb? If she hadn't got mixed up with that pissant from Burlington, none of this would be happening.

He looked around the room without saying anything more. Silently he allowed the possibility that maybe there was something for him to investigate after all. And he would if he had to; it was his duty. But more likely all this was some shrewd feminine trick leading . . . where? He wasn't sure. And if not a trick, it's a false alarm. Either way it was something that would eventually backfire and embarrass him.

"Well, Christ, Laura. You haven't got nothin' here. A bit of blood on the floor. Maybe he cut himself shaving, maybe he knocked over the lamp when he done it. Maybe—"

"And the note?"

"Okay, your buddy Roger was going to report something. I admit it. But with him and his friend off somewhere, we don't know what that is, now do we? And it couldn't've been too damn important, if they run off like this."

She glared at him. She was angry now. It made him feel powerful, completely in control.

"Yeah, we do know what, Hank. We got a little boy, your son, who says Cooly Hawks got lost in the woods yesterday. The poor kid was up all night, scared, worried sick. Maybe the old man's still out there. And now David and Roger are missing, too. That's what we got."

"I told you, you should've called me."

"I did call you, God damn it. You're here, aren't you? Now what are you going to do about it? Stand around and argue?"

She had always been an expert at making him think he was wrong even when he wasn't. She seemed to enjoy making him feel like a heel. There had never been any point in discussing things with her. She saw discussions not as attempts at communication, but as competitions—competitions she wanted to win. But he wouldn't rise to the bait—not this time. Instead, just to be on the safe side, he'd humor her. "Your friend's note says he went up to Harley Spooner's. Suppose I take a ride up there and have a talk with them, see what all this is about. You want to ride up with me?"

"Maybe you should go have a talk with your son. Let him tell you the story himself. Maybe it would be good for him to see his father right now. You ever think of that?"

"I guess prob'ly. We'll pick him up on the way to Spooner's, how's that suit you?"

Laura walked toward the door. When Hank tried to put his arm around her waist, she turned quickly, pulling away.

He followed her single file down the stairs.

"Jesus, Stacy, what are you doing? Put the gun down!"

"Roger!" The boy, shielding his eyes against the sun, lowered the High Standard as Roger walked down the stairs to meet him.

Stacy was shaking, nearly in tears. "I didn't know it was you, honest, Roger. I couldn't see clear with the sun in my eyes.

Jarvis Lavigne stood behind Stacy, looking uncomfortable, eyes toward the stone floor.

"What are you guys doing up here? And what's with the gun?"

"You were supposed to come back for us this morning. You didn't show up so we went to find Harley. I'm sorry about the gun, Roger. I thought maybe you were . . ."

"It's okay." Roger patted the boy's shoulder. "I'm looking for Harley, too."

"He's not with you?"

Roger shook his head. "I figure he came up here. Probably went out looking for Cooly, or maybe this 'winny-go' of his."

Jarvis spoke up, his voice crackling like paper. "Do you believe that stuff about the windigo?"

Roger sat down on the stone step. It felt warm. "I don't think I do, Jarvis. But I believe there's something out here. And I believe what you guys told me yesterday." He tossed his head in the direction of the forest. "Did you guys see the deer?"

The boys shook their heads.

"Then follow me. I was about to have a look at it."

As he led the two boys toward the fallen animal, Roger tried to decide whether he should lecture Stacy about the pistol. No, maybe now was not the time, especially while he himself carried the twelve gauge. "Your mothers know where you guys are?"

Their silence answered the question. Roger was equally guilty of thoughtlessness; again he chose not to lecture.

Crossing the knee-high grass, Stacy and Jarvis followed Roger to the edge of the forest. With the stone wall as a point of orientation, Roger quickly located the body of the deer.

It lay on its side, motionless in its matted bed of grass. The green tips of timothy, like miniature cattails, waved over the brown, seemingly unscarred corpse. Roger could tell immediately that the animal had not been shot.

So what had killed it?

The creature was small; it could have weighed no more than one hundred pounds. It was young, well-nourished, sleek, and brown, with a patch of pure white below its jaw. Its long tongue protruded like a pink snake; its one visible eye was open and lifeless. Already flies were collecting.

Roger handed the shotgun to Jarvis. The boy hesitated, then clutched it with both hands as Roger knelt beside the young buck. He ran his hand over the wiry coat, looking for wounds, finding none. He seized the ear, lifted the head, and examined its underside. Here was the problem. Its skull was crushed. A bloodless depression showed that something hard and heavy had fatally struck it, apparently killing it instantly.

"Look at this," Stacy said, holding up a strange object. Two fist-sized stones tied together with a twenty-inch rawhide cord dangled from the boy's hand.

"Jesus," said Roger. As he stood up to take the odd weapon from the boy, he stopped, froze. On top of the knoll, their backs to the sun, four hazy, humanlike forms stoodsilhouetted against the blue sky. Two of them carried similar stone weapons; they hung from outstretched arms, swaying like accelerated pendulums. The other two carried long thin shafts pointing skyward. As Roger's eyes cut to the neighboring trees, he saw other forms moving among them.

"Don't move, boys," he said softly. "Stay perfectly still."

His voice was too calm to betray the crippling fear that clenched his stomach in its icy fist.

22

Survival Instincts

1:30 P.M.

Jarvis bolted.

Before Roger could analyze what he saw, before he could make any sense of the odd assortment of humanoid forms surrounding them, Jarvis Lavigne had dropped the shotgun and was running down the mountainside. The boy's misshapen back caused him to run with a lurching, painful-looking lope. With every stride he seemed in danger of falling.

In response, one of the dark shapes on the horizon became animated. Squinting into the painful sunlight, Roger watched it lunge after the boy, quickly gaining on him. As the distance closed from fifty to thirty feet, it began to twirl the belted stone sling.

Nearly within launching distance, the creature passed Roger and Stacy.

"NO!" Roger cried. He dove at the passing form, tackling it around the legs. On impact his glasses flew away from his head, landing unseen in the moving grasses.

As they rolled together in the tail grass, guttural grunting filled Roger's ears. A disgusting smell, horrifying yet somehow familiar, sickened him as he fought to overpower the arm that controlled the deadly sling.

The thing was powerful. In less than a second Roger found himself on his back, strong arms pinning his hands to the earth. The pungent animal stench made him wince, turn his head away from the cruel eyes staring down at him. A thick, hairy arm obscured his blurry view of the circle of shapes rapidly tightening around him. They were coming to assist their peer.

If only he could see clearly!

With a sudden motion coarse hands were on his throat.

He flipped his head from side to aide, pounded at the steel-solid forearms that held him. In the background, like a movie out of focus, Stacy approached, the High Standard outstretched in both hands.

Stacy's pistol pointed at the creature's head. "Watch out, Roger," he called.

Roger fought for breath; he needed it to cry out. He had to warn Stacy that another fleet black blur was rushing him from behind.

The approaching form leapt at the boy, collided with his lower back. Stacy toppled forward. He smashed into the struggling bodies, knocking the beast off Roger.

Released from the terrible grip, Roger tried to get up. "The gun!" he cried, but the pistol was lost among thrashing bodies and tall grass.

Now, with four individuals on the ground, Roger and Stacy were quickly subdued. Tipping his bead backward, Roger briefly glimpsed another indistinct form, trudging uphill, carrying the limp body of Jarvis Lavigne under its right arm.

Roger's mind struggled with several notions at once: Is Jarvis dead? What are these strange, violent creatures? Are they Bigfoot? Some lost tribe of renegade Indians? If only he could see them clearly! If only—

But he couldn't follow his thoughts to a logical conclusion; powerful survival instincts overrode his rational mind.

Instantly he knew that violence, not rational thought, was the only thing that might save him and the boys.

With new energy spurred by panic Roger bucked and thrashed, trying to release himself from the crushing hands of his attacker. It was no use. He was overpowered, outnumbered. Perhaps the most rational decision was simply to lie still, to submit.

He looked up weakly as six hazy forms crowded around him, their heads cocked to the side. One of them carried Jarvis over its shoulder. The boy wasn't moving.

Roger turned his head; Stacy was lying still, a black form sitting on his chest, pinning his arms to the ground with its hands and knees. It looked gigantic compared with the helpless boy.

"Stacy," Roger said. Terror stretched his vocal cords to high frequency.

"Hhhmmm."

"Don't fight 'em. Don't—"

As he spoke the biggest form approached him from the left, shaking its broad, flat head. It bent over him, gradually coming into focus, bringing its face closer and closer to his own. For a moment everything was as still as the silence between heartbeats. Roger saw the eyes, night-black islands floating on round white ponds. The hair was long, matted with some thick greasy substance at the sides of the head where it blended into an unkempt beard. The body, too, was hairy, but not as much as it had first appeared: the creature wore a vest of animal skin.

The blurry black face, less than two feet away, studied Roger with great interest. From behind, one of the others grunted something that Roger couldn't understand. It almost sounded like language.

"Stogger. Tay ghimm . . ."

In response, the thing moved its face even closer. It almost seemed to smile before pursing its dark lips as if it were going to kiss him. Instead, it blew a stream of hot fetid breath into Roger's face. Reflexively, Roger turned away to avoid the stink. Then, quicker than a diving hawk, a black hand smashed alongside Roger's head. The blow jarred him at first. Just as he began to think he hadn't been hurt, everything seemed to jump as if in an earthquake, and he slipped helplessly into an inky blackness that quickly flooded the whole world.

When he awoke he could see nothing at all.

His head throbbed as if a piston were inside, pounding against the back of his skull. He tried to move, couldn't. A scratching, burning pressure around his wrists told him he was tied up, his arms outstretched to the sides.

The air felt strange. It was uncomfortably hot, uncomfortably humid even for late August. And it smelled bad, like earth and mildew and rot.

Where was he? He couldn't see anything. Was it nighttime?

For a moment the pain in his head and the menacing blackness forced a horrible conclusion—*they've blinded me!*

In this explosion of panic, he lurched forward reflexively, then fell back choking. Another rope bound his neck to the hard floor.

Forcing himself to be calm, he blinked his eyes. There was no pain in them, just a tickling sensation as his lashes flicked against some sort of fabric. They'd put something over his head; he was blindfolded.

He squirmed a bit, explored the ground beneath him with his shoulder blades and his bottom. It was unyielding, not like earth or grass. It was hard, lumpy, probably stone.

As he became more conscious, a new panic began to corrupt his reasoning process. He fought waves of terror, knowing that if he yielded to them the fight was lost; escape would be impossible.

He took a deep breath. Moist air filled his lungs, expanded his chest against still another set of restraints. Dull pain throbbed below his ribs, probably a souvenir of his struggle with the strange attackers.

He held very still, his mind as calm as possible. "Stacy! Jarvis!" he called. The nauseating taste of mildewed fabric bit at his tongue.

Not moving, holding his breath, he listened.

There was no response.

He called a little louder. Again nothing. Was he alone? Had they locked him away, left him someplace to die?

He strained his ears to detect any sound that might help identify his location. Somewhere, not too far away, he could hear water running, gurgling, like tiny rapids in a miniature stream. That was all.

I'm in a cave, he thought. *I'm on the stone floor of a cave.*

He tried to confirm that theory by sniffing the air, but all he could smell was the earthy, mildewy odor of the mask that enclosed his head.

He couldn't see, he couldn't move, he couldn't smell, and there was nothing to hear but the steady flow of water. He was trapped, utterly, in a hot, sweaty prison. He was as helpless as a chicken before a beheading.

And the boys, what of them?

And what of Laura?

His senses useless, Roger closed his eyes. Inhaling slowly, he tried to breathe in some more calmness.

When Stacy Drew finally wriggled out of the cords that bound his wrists, he immediately pulled the burlap sack off his head. The first thing he saw was the body of Harley Spooner.

It was directly in front of him, tied by the feet, laid out on a plank supported by two wooden barrels. The old man's tiny frame, naked and blue-tinged, did not move at all.

He's dead, thought Stacy, eyes widening in terror and disbelief.

The old man's face was pale and waxy, his backside discolored where blood and blended bodily fluids had settled and stained. He looked bruised and ugly.

The body was stiff with rigor mortis. Stacy knew the old man had been dead for some time.

The awful sight caused Stacy to stiffen too. It felt as if his lungs had suddenly deflated, flattened against his rigid backbone. He was out of breath, nauseated. A horrible taste formed at the base of his tongue.

He wanted to speak to Harley, knowing it would be pointless. Maybe he should pray for him.

No. He had to stay alert, couldn't drop his guard for a moment.

What frightened him most was the position of the body. Laid out flat, naked, like the carcass of a deer on a butcher block. Before it's carved up. Before it's eaten.

Eaten!

Mindless panic seized Stacy as he pulled the cloth cords from his ankles. His fingers wouldn't work at the speed he was trying to drive them. Yet somehow, within moments, all the cords were off and lying like a tangle of snakes on the floor.

He massaged his wrists and forearms. If those knots had been any tighter even his magic training wouldn't have helped. He briefly wondered if Houdini or the Amazing Randi could have escaped from tighter bonds.

Jarvis Lavigne lay motionless beside him, wrapped in long brown strips of material torn from burlap sacks. Stacy reached over and pushed at him.

"Jarvis, wake up. You okay, Jarvis?"

The other boy groaned, moved sluggishly. Stacy pulled the mask off and quickly placed a hand over his friend's mouth. "Ssshh!"

Jarvis opened his eyes. Blinked. "Stace!"

Stacy watched fear contort the boy's face as memory returned.

"Wh . . . where are we? Where's Roger?"

Stacy shook his head; he didn't know. He worked hurriedly to untie Jarvis's hands and feet. When he noticed Harley, Jarvis jumped, cried out.

"He's dead," Stacy said. "Come on, we gotta get out of here."

Rising to their feet was a chore for both boys. With the circulation in their legs impaired for so long, they staggered clumsily. Painful cramps knotted Stacy's muscles as blood returned to his extremities.

Looking around the darkness for an exit, Stacy realized they were in some kind of windowless stone building.

Possibly a cellar. The cellar of the old hotel!

Yet there was some light. Why?

Near the ceiling Stacy could see slivers of sunlight shining through pencil-thin slits between the stones.

The boys moved among tumbled rocks looking for a way out. All the time they tried to ignore the conspicuous corpse of the old man. Soon, behind rotting wood shelves, they found stairs leading upward. The opening at the top was closed off with a row of thick logs. The size of the barrier told Stacy the logs would be too heavy to move.

Directly across from the platform on which they'd awakened, a small open gutter contained a tiny stream of water. It ran the entire length of the wall, hugging its base. Beside it, like fishermen on the side of a stream, stood an assortment of green, cobweb-shrouded bottles and dusty carboys in gray wooden crates.

Stacy carefully studied the mysterious tiny canal. He saw that it entered through a duct at the bottom of the left wall, flowed all the way across the room, and exited through a hole in the wall to the right. At no place was the white marble trough more than six inches deep.

What was it for? Its purpose was a puzzle.

Stacy led Jarvis to the opening at the right through which the water flowed out.

"Let's crawl through," he said. "We'll just follow the stream right out of here."

Jarvis looked at him, skepticism distorting his eyes, "I don't know . . ."

"Come on. It's gotta flow out somewhere. And we can't stay here. Look what they did to Harley."

On his knees now, Stacy peered into the opening. The interior was black; it was like looking down the barrel of a cannon. The tunnel might lead to an adjacent room, or it could travel under the rock walls for a long distance. Worse yet, this might be an underground brook; it might flow through the earth forever.

Stacy made up his mind; he'd have to chance it. It was lucky that he was so small. If he were a grown man he'd never be able to fit through the tiny channel.

Bracing himself, he knelt in the water. "Hey! This is warm!" Tasting it he found it bitter. "Maybe its poison or something. Try not to swallow any."

Water about half filled the stone conduit. Stacy realized that he would have to travel on his back; it was the only way he could keep his nose and mouth above water level.

Settling back into the mineral stream, his clothes quickly became saturated. Because the water was warm the sensation of submerging was nowhere near as uncomfortable as he'd anticipated.

He moved through the opening, head first, face up, propelling himself with his elbows, heels, and the soles of his sneakers. Before he was completely enclosed he whispered, "It's okay. It's not so bad. Come on."

He fought the feeling that he was being swallowed. It was as if he were being squeezed down the earth's tight esophagus, with rock muscles tightening around him. He shuddered, chilled in the tepid stream.

When he had traveled about six feet he was able to crane his neck enough to see faint light ahead—an opening!

Every movement caused a splash of water. Some burned as it found his eyes, stung as it flowed into his mouth and nose. He spat disgustedly, pushing inches closer to the distant circle of light.

Just when he thought he was home free, a painful ridge of rock caused him to arch his back and wriggle as the tunnel became tighter around him.

Lifting his head with great difficulty, he could see Jarvis settling down into the bitter bath. The position of his neck made watching painful, so he squirmed onward.

When Stacy's face was less than two feet from the opening he was able to flip over onto his stomach, crossing his arms under his chest for support. Now it was easy to avoid inhaling water. As the opening widened the water level decreased.

"Just a few feet more," he whispered to Jarvis. Then he heard a frantic splashing behind him.

"Stacy!" called Jarvis, a tremor of panic echoed in his hushed cry. "Stacy, I'm *stuck*!"

The whispered words echoed in the tunnel, splashed around Stacy's ears like water. Stuck, oh, shit!

Stacy flopped onto his back again and reversed direction, inching feet first toward his friend.

"Help me!" Jarvis whispered urgently. "I can't move. I'm stuck."

"Can you back up?"

"I don't know. There's a rock, or something, under me." It was the same protrusion of stone that Stacy had crawled over just moments before. Because of its position, that stone ridge decreased the interior diameter of the tunnel to the point that Jarvis, with his bulging, twisted spine, could not proceed.

"Okay," Stacy whispered as calmly as he could. "See if you can back up. Can you?"

Jarvis grunted, spit out water. "No! I can't move at all! I'm really stuck!"

"Here, I'll try to push you with my feet." He placed his soggy sneakers as gently as he could on Jarvis's shoulders. Pushing steadily, he asked, "How's that? You off?"

Stacy winced as Jarvis cried out in pain. Then, "Hey! Okay, I'm free now."

"Great! You'll have to wait here, though. There's an opening right up ahead. I'll get out and run for help."

"No! Wait a minute! I can't stay here. Harley's in here!"

"You've got to, Jarv! It's our only chance. We can't waste time arguing about it."

"But what if they come for me?"

"Hide. Play along with 'em. Stall 'em. I'll be back as fast as I can. I'll bring help."

"But Stace—" The tears were audible, but invisible in the wet, black enclosure. "Stace, wait up. Please! Don't leave me here!"

"SSsshh. I've got to. I'll hurry. You'll be okay, but you've got to stay quiet."

"Stacyyyyy . . ."

Deliberately closing his mind to Jarvis's pleas, Stacy turned over onto his stomach. He began working his way toward the opening. Before daring to leave the tunnel he peeked cautiously out. The watery passage opened on a large room, much like the one he had just left. The rushing stream spread out into a brick basin, like an undersized swimming pool, or an oversize bathtub.

For a moment the boy dared progress no farther. As he peered into the room he saw that it was dimly lit with half a dozen candles. Amid the candles, and all facing a slightly elevated platform, some twelve or fifteen black, hairy monsters listened to a seated speaker.

The speaker, obscured by a vertical beam and the density of shadows, addressed the crowd in a raspy forced whisper. Although he could understand nothing, Stacy listened attentively. He dared not move, he dared not breathe.

23

With the Flow

MOMENTS LATER . . .

It looks like some kind of meeting, Stacy thought. He stared, blinking his eyes, not believing.

Squinting into the subterranean gloom, he studied the dark forms assembled in the vast shadow-crowded chamber. It was eerie the way the creatures seemed to speak, talking in hoarse, urgent whispers. He listened hard, trying to make out what they were saying, but the words were never loud enough to compete with the sound of water lapping at his ears. One of the creatures, the one closest to Stacy, squatted on the lid of an old wooden barrel. Black, hairy legs, thick with muscles, supported its weight as it hunkered, pygmy-style. Its bare feet looked as large and knotted as wooden clubs. The thing wore a vest of animal hide with a leather wrap around its waist. Nearly motionless, it scratched absently at its sides and scalp.

Stacy was convinced that the things were animals. He was sure he'd been taken prisoner by a Bigfoot tribe, just like the ones he had read about. Apparently they lived here in the basement of the ruined hotel.

But why? What did they want with him?

Whatever their motives, Stacy knew that unless he could escape and bring help, he and Jarvis would meet the same fate as Harley

Spooner; they'd be murdered, laid out on a block like sides of beef. And then—

It was too horrible to think about.

A sensation like seasickness pumped bile into Stacy's throat. He wanted someone to help him. What had become of Roger? Was he dead, too?

And what could he, a twelve-year-old boy, do on his own?

Certainly he couldn't follow the stream into the crowded room. Perhaps he should go back by crawling upstream, try to escape through the other hole in the wall of the room that had been his prison.

He looked behind him. The tunnel was clear. Apparently Jarvis had worked his way back into the neighboring chamber. He pictured his friend alone in the half-light with the naked corpse of the old man.

As he began to reverse direction be heard a faint scream echoing through the tunnel.

Jarvis!

He watched the opening behind him darken as Jarvis tried to crawl in again.

"Stacy! Help!" Jarvis cried, grappling with the jagged stones around the tunnel's mouth. Stacy watched helplessly as Jarvis plunged headfirst into the opening, blotting out most of the light, his humped back an asymmetrical shadow in the water-slick confinement.

The irregular halo of light surrounding Jarvis's silhouette was abruptly cut off, throwing the tunnel into utter blackness. As this happened Jarvis screamed hysterically. "Help! Get off! Help! Stacyyyyy!"

It was chillingly clear that one of the monsters had grabbed his friend, was pulling him out, feet first.

Stacy's first impulse was to help—but what could he do? If he moved he'd give away his own location, ending the possibility of help for any of them.

Terrified, Stacy flattened himself into the warm stream just as the creature on the barrel turned, reacting to Jarvis's muffled cries. It seemed not to notice Stacy, and didn't even get up to investigate.

Now the only direction was forward. The wide brick basin into which the stream flowed was nearly four feet deep. It swirled around like a hot tub, then emptied to the left, through a water-level opening in the wall. Perhaps this was a drain! Perhaps it led outside!

Stacy had always been a good swimmer. If he could crawl lizard-like over the threshold, and if he could hold his breath long enough, maybe—without being noticed—he could pass under-water through the brick pool and out the drain hole. It was worth a try. It had to be; it was his only option. It was Jarvis's only chance.

As he inhaled and exhaled several times, preparing to take his sustaining breath, he studied the churning pool. There seemed to be no obstructions under the surface, nothing that would get in his way. Hopefully, there were no bars or wire mesh over the drain. He couldn't tell, he'd just have to chance it.

Filling his lungs with air he wriggled like a snake over the stone hump and slipped noiselessly into the swirling basin.

Roger Newton was surprised to find that he was praying. It was something he hadn't done for a good long time. Yet, the words came easily to mind. They were a return to the familiar language patterns of his youth; they were comfortable, like Sunday school and bedtime prayers.

When he realized what he was doing, he felt hypocritical; he hadn't even prayed at his father's funeral. Now, in this hopeless sit-uation, his life on the line, prayer seemed his only source of appeal.

His arms, spread-eagled and tightly bound, ached dully. There was no way he could move to relieve the strain on them. His back pressed uncomfortably against the stone floor.

Moments ago, he had pulled and thrashed in a fit of desperate activity. He learned, painfully, that the binding material was much stronger than he was. Now, tired and afraid, he resigned himself to whatever Fate held in store for him.

Roger let his cramping muscles relax as best he could. The painful pounding in his head eased a little as he closed his eyes beneath the blinding hood.

In the distance water gurgled and splattered. It was the only noise he could hear. In other circumstances it might have been a restful sound.

A moist, foggy sensation further blunted his diminished perceptions. It was the inevitable relaxation brought about by utter defeat. It was giving up.

The humid air seemed to crowd him, reinforcing his sense of exhaustion. An escape mechanism, never before experienced, began to make him sleepy. *I can't fall asleep,* he thought. *It doesn't make any sense. How can I be sleepy at a time like this?*

Yet, sleep might be his only comfort, the only escape available to him. In his present situation, he could as well be paralyzed; he couldn't see, he couldn't move, he was totally at the mercy of those horrible black creatures. Whenever they got around to coming for him, he'd be there.

As Roger started to slip into unconsciousness, he detected a new motion in the muggy air. He heard the metallic scrape and thunk of a bolt moving in a latch. The screech of creaking hinges followed as a door opened, then closed with a resounding slam.

Alert now, listening with great concentration, he heard the choking sounds of a familiar laugh.

Warm water closed around him like a shroud. Even with his eyes open and stinging in the brick pool, Stacy could see nothing. He had to rely totally on his sense of direction as be held his breath, feeling his way along the coarse bottom toward the sound of the rushing drain.

He discovered that if he allowed himself to be limp the current would pull him in the desired direction. He spidered his fingers across the bottom to maintain balance.

Already his lungs were beginning to ache. The more he thought about it, the worse they felt. He pictured them as red balloons, their rubber walls becoming more and more transparent as they expanded, straining, about to burst.

It was difficult to fight the panic that threatened his progress. The growl of rushing current harmonized in his ears with the amplified drumming of his accelerated heartbeat.

Again he fought the strong urge to burst to the surface, to glut himself with fresh air.

Surely you can hold your breath for three minutes, he encouraged himself. Just three minutes. That should be more than enough time to work his way into the outlet tunnel.

His own buoyancy worked against him, pushing him upward, floating him to the surface. He exhaled a little to relieve the pressure on his lungs. Bubbles tickled his face as they drifted toward the air.

He felt lost, hopelessly disoriented. A quick inhalation, a lungful of water, and he'd never have to face those monsters who waited above.

At last, groping frantically ahead, his fingers discovered the circular opening in the foundation. He swam through, pulling and navigating with his hands and forearms. When he was confident that he was completely concealed within the drain, he turned onto his back and lifted his head.

There was a space between the water's surface and the top of the tunnel. Greedily, gratefully, Stacy slurped the air.

He experienced tremendous relief with each inhalation. He was safe, at least for awhile.

Now all he had to do was follow this tunnel to the outside. With any luck it would pass through a few feet of stone wall, draining directly into an outdoor pool. But it might not be that simple. He feared the drain might be long and winding, emptying at some great distance from the hotel's foundation.

When he had traveled what felt to be six to ten feet, still on his back, he came to an air shaft above his head. Although the stream continued underground, the vertical shaft led upward, directly to a round metal grate, like a perforated manhole cover.

It was a welcome sight, but Stacy knew better than to become too eager.

Slowly, he struggled into a sitting position. Sunlight shone from above, casting dark, weblike shadows throughout the pit.

He stood up. His waterlogged clothing made him heavy and sluggish. He stretched, reaching upward for the grate.

It couldn't have been more than five feet above his head. Bracing his sneakers on tiny ledges of uneven stonework, he found it surprisingly easy to climb.

Before he knew it his hand was on the round metal door!

First he made sure that his footing was stable, then he gave the grate a tentative push.

It moved, grinding heavily against its rock seat.

Biting his lower lip, Stacy gave a massive heave. The grate moved enough for him to lock his hands around its rim.

As he pushed he lost his footing. A stone tore away, splashed into the water below. Stacy clung to the metal door as if it were the bar of a trapeze, his feet pedaling frantically in the open air.

The cavity from which the rock had fallen provided better purchase for his soggy sneaker. He braced both feet in the recession, planted his back against the opposite side of the well, and pushed mightily. The grate ground partially away, leaving half the opening for escape.

I can't blow it now, he said to himself. *I've got to be real careful.* With great strength and precision he reaffirmed his two-handed grip on the side of the grate. Then he did a chin-up.

He nearly cried out in ecstasy as his head moved into the open air. The sky, the trees, everything was visible again. The world looked bright and beautiful.

He was free!

With a tremendous effort he pulled himself out of the hole. Without pausing at all, without looking back, he made a frenzied dash toward the woods.

24

Death of a Reporter

LATE AFTERNOON . . .

"David!" cried Roger Newton as the fetid sack was pulled from over his head. "David, what are you doing here?" He blinked, shook his head, trying to get his eyes to focus. The world was a myopic blur, everything was shadowy and dull.

"How'd you find me, David? Are the police with you?"

David Potter laughed again. But there was no mirth in the sound, no amusement in his hollow eyes. Instead of answering he began to tug at the cord around Roger's left wrist.

Roger saw that David's arm was in a sling.

"I think they're going to let us go. They . . . they made a mistake. It's all a mistake, can you believe it? But I think they're going to let us go . . ." David's voice was a monotone; he spoke as if in a trance.

"What are you talking about? *Who* made a mistake?"

"They took me and they wanted you. That's how I got here." Potter assumed a phony-sounding Vermont accent, it was totally out of place. "Clumsy, ain't they?" And again the dry, mirthless laugh.

There was something strangely mechanical about David's behavior, something uncomfortable. But it wasn't the right time to question him; in fact, Roger didn't even want to think about it.

Left wrist free now, he rubbed his eyes and looked around. The room was made of stone: floor, walls, and ceiling. It appeared to be a prison and felt like a dungeon. Everywhere the out-of-focus shapes of wrecked furniture, collapsing shelving, and broken barrels littered the humid, foul-smelling chamber. At the base of the far wall, deep in the shadows, a tiny stream splattered and splashed in its shallow trough.

When both of Roger's hands were free, he massaged his wrists and flexed his fingers. "Where the hell are we?"

"A hotel. Don't you like your accommodations?" The laugh.

"David, look at me." Roger grabbed the other man by he upper arm, pulled him face-to-face. Squinting, he studied the bruises and cuts on David's chin, the smudges of grime on his cheeks. A crust of dried blood surrounded David's nostrils.

"Oh God, David, what's happened to you?"

Roger looked deeply into his friend's eyes, but there was no depth there; they were like vacant glass spheres, with no sparkle, no luster. Roger knew these lifeless eyes warned that the man was in shock.

He shook David's shoulders a bit roughly, hoping for a flash of anger, of something. "What it is, David? What's wrong with you?"

"Nothing. I've just made a million-dollar discovery, that's all. And it's not worth a cent . . ." He pulled away, lurched to his feet, and paced nervously in a tight circle. "I could be written up in every academic journal in the country. Maybe even make *Time* and *Newsweek*. What could be wrong with that?"

"What the hell are you talking about?"

"Our hosts. Don't you realize what they are?"

Roger shook his head. His feet were free now. He stood up with difficulty, almost toppled. "No. I don't know, and I really don't give much of a shit at the moment. I just want to find the boys and get the hell out of here. Where are they, David? Are they all right?"

"Sure, sure. Everybody's okay. I think they're going to let us go soon."

David plopped down, sitting cross-legged on the stone floor. His white pants were foul with muddy stains. From the shadowy distance he glared vapidly at Roger. "The whole thing is amazing, the whole set-up. I simply can't believe any of it . . ."

Roger crawled across the stone floor and squatted directly in front of David, eye to eye, hands on his shoulders. Roger was shaken, in a near panic himself; he had no time for David's mysteries. Yet he wanted to be calm and gentle with his friend; he had to help David pull himself together.

Then he had to find the boys

He willed himself to speak slowly, quietly. "David, I think you know what's happening here. I think you know what those creatures are, and what they want. You've got to tell me, David. The boys' lives might depend on it. Do you know where the boys are?"

"Oh yes. They're right here. They're tied up, too."

"Why not you? How come you're not tied up?"

"Me? Oh, I just came back from my audience with The Descendant. They're going to let me go. They're going to let all of us go. Pretty soon."

"Who are *they*?"

"They're slaves."

"They're wha—They're slaves?" Roger drew back. "What are you talking about?"

David's eyes grew wide. He was looking at Roger but seemed to see nothing. When he began to talk it was like blood spurting from an artery—there was no way to stop it, and the more he talked, the sicker he seemed to become. "They're escaped slaves, only they escaped well over a hundred years ago. Probably around 1850, maybe even earlier. They were traveling through Vermont on their way to Canada—on the Underground Railroad. Thousands of slaves did it in the last century, thousands. But this bunch. They were on the eastern trunk: you know, Montpelier to Hardwick, to Barton, and up to the border . . . ? The way I put it together they must have run off into the woods, lost, panicky, not knowing where they were going.

"Imagine that! Imagine what the woods must have been like a hundred, two hundred years ago! God, talk about the forest primeval . . . Eventually they settled in somewhere, hid out, avoided *all* white people. They kept to the densest parts of the forest, like animals trying to avoid capture. But for them the hiding never ended.

"Think of it. Year after year, decade after decade, keeping to themselves, living furtively off the land. They never knew who was their enemy and who wasn't. So they avoided everyone.

"It would have been easy for them to lose themselves up here. And it was probably easy for the owner of the safe house to give them up as dead. But they didn't die, and that's what amazes me. Maybe they reverted to certain of their tribal ways, maybe they just acted like anybody else would act in the same situation: They stuck together, took care of each other, did what they had to to survive.

"Luck certainly played a role in it; somehow they found these hot springs. But later had to give them up when the hotel was built. So they kept burning it down, and scaring people off until they got their springs back.

"Now they've got this place, the basement of this hotel. This is where they live, Roger. They've got the hot springs to keep them warm, and to heat their food. I guess they never make fires; they're afraid the smoke will give them away." David laughed again, that hoarse, dry laugh. "And I get a kick out of the way they always talk in whispers, you ever notice that? It's a thoroughly inbred tribal custom at this point . . ."

"David, come on. How can they still be alive after more than a hundred years?"

"It's not the same ones. My guess is they've had enough of a breeding pool to keep going generation after generation. I think maybe there's been some cross-culturalization with the Indians of the region, the Abenaki. And maybe they even recruited a white person once or twice along the way. I hear it in their speech. But now—"

"They speak English?"

"Oh yes, it's English all right. English of a sort. I didn't recognize it at first, but it's English, the English that would evolve from original speakers who weren't particularly fluent to begin with." He laughed dryly.

"This is amazing! Incredible!" Involuntarily, a reflex caused Roger to add, silently, *This'll make a hell of a story!*

Roger moved closer to David, who was shaking his head from

side to side as he continued to speak. "I know what you're thinking. The same thing I'm thinking. But that's just it, Roger—they
don't want us to tell their story. They don't want word to get out at
all. Don't you see, that's what this is all about. They might let us go
if they think their secret will be safe. But they might keep us here. I
just don't know what's going to happen."

"Can't we just . . . leave?"

"No!" David tensed. "They're right outside the door. They sent
me in to talk to you."

"We could—"

"Forget it, Roger. They've got the boys."

The realization struck like a blow to the solar plexus. Roger
squinted at David. "So how'd you learn all this?"

A certain clarity was returning to David's speech. His eyes were
starting to show a glimmer of life. The verbal bloodletting had
been good for him. "Like I said, one of them brought me here,
thinking I was you. They were after you, my friend. Believe it or
not, they were apologetic about the mistake. Not enough to let me
go, though. Not just yet."

"What about Harley?"

"Harley's dead. I guess the old boy didn't survive his run-in with
the Stalker."

"Dead?" Roger looked away and shook his head sadly. Then,
"And the Stalker? What's the Stalker . . . ?"

" 'Stogger' is what they call him. It took me a few minutes to
understand what they meant. Evidently each member of the tribe
has specific responsibilities. It's fascinating, a perfect little society.
They get their names, indeed their whole identity, by the role they
play in the settlement. There's Watchers, Gatherers, Feeders, there
used to be Birthers. And there's the Stalker. Only one. He's kind of
the policeman, a one-man army, responsible only to the tribal
leader. He keeps order, doles out punishment, deals with invaders."

"Invaders?"

"Yes. Like you, and the rest of the people who went to the Indian site. I gather rights to this land were given to the tribe by
Abenaki Indians—as if they had any right to it themselves. That's

what the stones mean to them—property markers. You and Harley and Leslie were messing with their boundaries. It got them upset. And look where it got us."

"Jesus. Why didn't you just assure them we have no interest in the stones?"

"I did. But that's not the problem now. Their secret is out; we know about them. They don't want to kill us, but they can't trust our silence."

"So they rounded us up, is that it? And now we're going to be put on trial?"

"That's pretty much the long and the short of it, my friend." Again the dry, choking laugh. David buried his face in his hand, rocking back and forth, his legs still crossed on the floor.

"What are we going to do, David?"

David continued to rock. Now he was humming softly to himself, a tedious, tuneless dirge that filled Roger Newton with an entirely new sense of dread.

Perhaps David wasn't in shock. Perhaps he had gone beyond that. It looked as if he was experiencing the first symptoms of a breakdown. Roger couldn't blame him; the events of the last couple of days were like a nightmare. Roger focused all his concentration on his friend.

"David, how do you know all this? And how come you're untied and walking around?"

David looked up, his eyes slick with tears. "Because, I've been talking to one of them. One who wants to help us. You might say he's our defense attorney. He'll be here soon, I think. He's—"

Before David could finish, the wooden door burst open with an explosive crash. Two tribesmen entered, their faces contorted with anger. One pointed at Roger.

"Chyle man, he go, leef stayhouse. Comenow, you."

Roger tried not to flinch with fear at the whispered bombast, though with his diminished vision he felt helpless, vulnerable.

He looked to David for a translation of the odd syllables, but David had collapsed against a support timber. Hugging it tightly, he cringed among the shadows as loud sobs jogged the muscles of his back. Apparently the professor had retreated to some faraway and private place. There was nothing Roger could do for him now.

The two black men moved quickly to David, stood menacingly above him. His tear-glazed eyes were wide with terror. He screamed at Roger, "The kids have run off! That's it for us. We're done!"

The bigger man yanked David to his feet, then pushed him forward. David stumbled, bumped the door frame, cried out shrilly in pain. Clutching his wounded shoulder he stumbled out the door.

The other man turned on Roger. Seizing his arm, he pulled Roger after the others.

Roger wanted to push the man away, make a run for it, but he didn't know where to run. In this underground settlement he could as easily stumble into the thick of the tribe as find his way to freedom.

The black men shoved and jostled David and Roger toward the neighboring room, then herded them through the doorway. There Jarvis Lavigne sat cowering against the wall. His face lit up when he saw Roger, then darkened quickly at the appearance of the tribesmen. Harley Spooner's pale body stretched lifelessly beside the boy.

The heavy door slammed behind them.

Jarvis raced to Roger, hugged him like a father. Behind them David Potter sat dejectedly on a raised stone platform.

"When will they let us go home, Roger?" the boy asked.

"Pretty soon, Jarvis. Pretty soon they will." He hugged the trembling child, speaking softly. "Can you tell me what happened to Stacy? Where's Stacy, son?"

"He escaped. He swam out through the water." The boy pointed to the flowing stream. "He got out just in time. I'd've gone too, but I got stuck in the hole, and they caught me."

Now Roger was keenly aware of their problem, with all its subtleties. Immediate rescue was unlikely unless Stacy somehow returned with a professional SWAT team instead of a small band of untrained villagers. Either way, any rescue attempt would start a chain of events that would quickly get out of hand, possibly leading to the deaths of many people.

And an escape attempt? The odds of failure were too great to risk injuring Jarvis, David, or Roger himself. Even if they weren't executed outright, they'd never be turned loose. And their credibility would be destroyed, making further negotiations impossible.

Roger had no doubt that these people would kill to protect their privacy. Indeed, killing might be easy for them after several generations of pent-up fear and more than a century of growing hatred for anyone white.

"Damn that kid!" David slammed a fist against his knee.

When the black men returned they supported a third individual who moved with great difficulty between them. This one was tiny, shriveled, shrouded in a long black cape—the hide of a bear. The biggest of the three spoke in a harsh whisper. "Oldwun wantok. You tok."

With a surprising gentleness the blacks assisted the sunken figure to a seat beside David on the platform. Potter inched away, crablike.

Their gentleness gone, the two big men grabbed Roger, forced him to kneel in front of the dark-clothed form. When he was in position the infirm one nodded and the black men left the room.

Lifting gnarled, crippled-looking hands, she pulled the shroud back from her delicate, toothless face. Her every movement suggested great effort and concentration, as if some nerve disease were fighting for control of her limbs.

Roger looked at her in awe, rubbed his eyes to bring her into focus. He was unable to guess how old she might be. She looked impossibly ancient; her face a knot of ebony wrinkles. Distended earlobes hid among sparse wisps of silky white hair, as delicate as spiderwebs. Cataracts sealed her eyes behind a milky film.

She reached out, her fingers convulsing minutely, and touched Roger's face. She smelled like earth. The aged hands explored his features: They tugged on his ears, pushed at the corners of his mouth, stroked the breadth of his forehead. They paused, as if with curiosity, when they discovered the little depression on the bridge of his nose, a hollow left by many years of wearing eyeglasses. Her caress was like the scratching of dry leaves against his skin.

When she had seen enough she spoke, her voice an unnatural

whisper, like wind in a pipe, barely audible. "I speeg you now. Your tongue, my tongue, the same. Your trouble, my trouble, the same. I am boss this place. I am Descendant. I come from first people. Now my people live here. This stayhouse. We live safe, free, because ol' white catcher never know we here. All change. Now he know. Now your boy go tell. Stayhouse no good. Woods no good. No place safe now for us. For safe, we must keep in dark. We must keep small voice, must stay from eyes of white catcher. Now boy bring othermen. Our trouble, your trouble."

Roger was surprised how easily he understood what the old woman was saying. Not only did he understand, in spite of his predicament, he sympathized. She was right, her problem was his problem. If he were to cooperate, it could benefit both groups. A balance could be preserved, lives could be spared.

"Maybe I could stop him before he reaches town. I could bring him back. Would that prove that I wish you no harm?"

"You go, stop boy?" Her face, her voice, were kind, imploring, a fading diplomat negotiating for the survival of her dying country.

Roger fell silent, thinking. He took a deep breath, momentarily unsure of the offer he had made—an offer built on trust without guarantees. Yet he was certain of one thing: there was no reason to betray these people, no reason to splash their story all over every tabloid in the country. Their secret need not be told. Not now, not ever. "I would do that, yes."

"And you take boy to stayhouse? To here?"

His journalistic past was unimportant in this situation. He was dealing with real issues of survival and safety. Leslie Winthrop's words about the Indian site came to mind: *It has been in the earth for hundreds of years. And that's the safest place for it.* Wasn't the same thing true of the tribe? "Yes, I'll bring him here. And when I do, you and I can make an agreement: we will keep your secret; you will let us go. That way no one would have to be hurt."

At that moment the newspaper reporter died in Roger Newton. And from its ghost a new certainty was born: It was not his professional duty to expose these people. Rather, it was his responsibility as a human being not to.

The old woman thought in silence, her tiny body trembling slightly. In time she squinted her cloudy eyes. "Now say how this boss know you come back stayhouse?" The old woman's whisper was hoarse and unpleasant—full of suspicion. Yet somehow Roger knew she wished them no harm. If harm had to be done though, he sensed she would be capable of ordering it.

"I can only promise—"

"Promise, yes. But more. You leave this boy, this man at stayhouse?"

Jarvis looked up at Roger pleadingly, his thick glasses magnifying his terrified eyes. Shaking his head, he implored silently, *No.*

Roger patted the boy's arm. With the contact, intended to reassure, he could almost feel the child's terror pulsing in his hand. He squinted at David Potter; the professor had withdrawn almost completely. He sat with his eyes closed, rocking, ever so slightly, back and forth.

Trembling inside, Roger gave Jarvis's arm a squeeze. "Yes," he said to the old woman, "these two will stay here. If I catch Stacy before he reaches town, I'll bring him back at once. If he reaches town before me, I'll do what I can to keep your secret. I'll say it's all in the boy's imagination."

"Him-magination?"

"A boy's tale. A story."

The old woman nodded. "A story. Yes." Her voice trailed off and she became silent again, remaining that way for a long while.

Roger watched her milky eyes, trying to anticipate her decision. He was surprised to find himself praying again, this time that the solution to their shared problem would include no more violence. He was hopeful; evidently violence was not her way. But it could be, the tribe had already demonstrated that; and he'd be a fool to lose sight of it. In a moment, after her meditation, he'd find out for certain.

Again she extended a palsied hand. "This boss very old. Know many men, many years. I think you good man. You go."

The hand rested gently on his shoulder.

She leaned unsteadily forward, her face almost touching his.

"But know this one thing: Stogger go too. Go before now. An' Stogger is . . . is wild, like wolfdog. I say, 'Bring boy here,' but maybe Stogger not bring. Maybe kill. Stogger wild. But not bad. Stogger 'fraid. We all 'fraid. You see?"

Roger nodded, he understood.

The old woman sat back and reached under her hairy cloak, brought something out. She clutched the shiny object in her twisted fingers. Then she handed the thing to Roger: his glasses.

"Now," she whispered, "you go fast."

25

Somewhere in the Forest

TWILIGHT . . .

As Roger Newton stepped from the darkness of the hotel's basement into the fading twilight, he realized just how weak he was. His legs were like saplings bending beneath his weight and he ached as if he'd suffered a brutal beating. Tired and hungry, he knew there would be no time for rest or refreshment. He had only one thing to do: Find Stacy and bring him back before he could tell anyone about the gore's inhabitants.

Roger knew that somewhere in the endless acres of forest the Stalker was also searching for the boy.

And the Stalker was dangerous.

That the Stalker didn't know about Roger's release, that it might be dealt with as an escape, made him additionally wary, especially now, because he was completely unarmed and too weak to defend himself.

Communication with the black people had been difficult, even in the comparatively unthreatening atmosphere of the stone rooms. In the wilds it would be impossible. If he encountered the Stalker, negotiation would be out of the question.

He *had* to find Stacy before anything happened.

The metal grate at his feet was the first clue. He noted how it had been pushed away from the circular opening in the ground. If this had been Stacy's exit, he would have taken the most direct path to the safety of the trees.

So that was the path Roger chose.

Roger knew nothing of tracking. When he stepped under the cover of the pines he was as good as lost; Stacy could have headed in any of a thousand directions. He reasoned that the boy, too, would have been nearly exhausted. It was likely then that he'd head straight downhill: Progress would be easier and a downhill course would lead most directly back to town. On the other hand it was possible Stacy was in such panic and confusion that he'd charged aimlessly into the woods, running horizontally, or even up the steep mountainside and deeper into the gore.

No matter. If Roger headed downward, he might be lucky and overtake Stacy, or, quite possibly, arrive at the trailer first and be there waiting when the boy showed up.

After traveling about five hundred yards, his downhill course was blocked by a stream that ran northwest. If Stacy had not crossed the stream—and probably he hadn't; it was twelve feet wide, even more in places—he would have followed its route, walking along the riverbank as it wound through spruce trees, past outcroppings and steep sandy banks, until (if Roger wasn't mistaken) it came out somewhere near Harley Spooner's land, probably right behind the cabin where Cooly Hawks had lived.

Although he was tired, and his legs felt heavy as stone columns, Roger knew that speed was essential. Nighttime was coming on fast. He quickened his pace, stumbled over serpentine roots, and fell headlong when he tripped on a rabbit hole.

He wasn't sure if be should call out to Stacy. His voice might frighten the boy. Worse yet, it might attract the Stalker.

Roger was surprised at how quickly darkness fell. It was light one moment, nearly dark the next. The thick ceiling of leaves kept out much of the light, making it appear later than it really was. Surely he still had an hour or more of this half-light. Enough time, he hoped, to find Stacy and get safely out of the woods.

So far he had avoided one important question: What would happen if Stacy eluded him? Would he dare return to the hotel empty-handed? Would failure inspire a quick kill of the hostages and the tribe's retreat farther into the wilderness of the gore?

And what if the old woman went back on her word? Perhaps they'd be held as prisoners for the rest of their lives, possibly treated as slaves themselves.

The ethics of the situation were confusing: Could he in good conscience break his agreement with the old woman? Certainly the easiest thing to do was to get directly out of the woods and phone the police.

But that just wasn't right. After all, what crimes had the tribes-people committed? They took over a hotel that nobody owned, on land that was part of no town. They avoided white men who had sold them like cattle. On rare occasions they had apprehended people who threatened to expose their whereabouts. What real harm had they done? If he could excuse the kidnappings, then their greatest offense was causing discomfort and inconvenience. Apparently they had not killed Harley Spooner, as Roger had first believed . . .

Then there was Leslie Winthrop. What had actually happened in that car?

And what about Cooly? What had become of him?

The stream narrowed into a miniature waterfall that fed a piano-shaped pool, banked on the far side by a steep ledge. A dark opening in the rock two feet above water level gaped at Roger like a mouth. This split-rock cave held his attention.

Staring into the dark fissure he spoke for the first time since leaving the hotel. His voice sounded weak, timid. "Stacy!"

A muffled groan came from the opening; something was in that cave!

His mind raced to evaluate the situation. The cave might have appealed to the boy as a hiding place. Certainly it offered the illusion of safety; one would have to cross the pool to get to it. Once inside an occupant would be out of sight, protected by stone walls on three sides.

"Stace, it's Rog. You in there?"

"Ummmh mmmmmh."

As he waded into the chill mountain water, he felt a tickle of pride. The boy had been easy to find. But mixed with pride was a sense of alarm; Stacy sounded funny. What if he were hurt?

What if it weren't Stacy at all?

Roger stumbled and slid on slick, submerged rocks. Nearly losing his balance, he plunged his arms into the numbing water all the way to his shoulder to keep from falling in.

As he carefully regained his balance and straightened up, the mouth of the cave darkened as a black roaring form shot forth as if from a cannon.

"Well, I'm ready to pack it in," said Trooper Hank Drew, feeling winded and perspiring profusely. He turned, looking downhill at Laura. Behind her, far in the distance, Harley Spooner's place seemed as tiny as a plastic house on a Monopoly board. "I bet those boys will be waiting for us back at the trailer. You wait and see what I tell you."

Laura's eyes were dry now, but blemished with long black stains of mascara. She looked so tired and helpless. He wanted to go to her, comfort her with a hug, or an arm around the shoulders. In his mind he heard her saying sweet soft things to him, telling him how proud she was of his bravery, how safe she felt in his company.

In the dimming light she looked like a small child, one he would be happy to care for. He was fascinated by the way her chest rose and fell, the way her nipples pushed hard and erect against her tight-fitting jersey. He remembered them so clearly he could almost see them through the fabric.

"Stacy!" she called into the breeze, her voice hoarse from repeated shouting. The trees surrounded them like a regiment of faceless soldiers, each with a terrible secret to protect.

"Stacy! Jarvis!"

One secret, Hank believed, was that the boys were not in the woods at all. Most certainly they were watching TV, or playing, or perhaps waiting at their homes, wondering when supper would be ready.

Just because they had found the fish poles at the trailer didn't mean the boys had run off into the woods. All it meant was that they had decided not to go fishing. Jeez, wasn't it just like a woman to jump to a conclusion like that?

"Come on, girl, let's go get us a bite to eat."

Laura didn't look at him, only at the trees and the lengthening shadows that bled from their thick roots. When she turned, the tears that Hank expected were not there. Her eyes were cold, determined.

"He's our son Hank, yours and mine. How can you think of eating?"

"Look, you don't have to remind me of nothin'. But Christ, Laura, life's gotta go on. And I know that boy. Betcha when we get home he'll be there. You wait an' see."

He saw that she didn't take exception to the word "home." It pleased him. In his imagination they were already at the trailer, preparing to comfort each other in her bed—their bed. A supposed tragedy like this is all it would take to bring the family back together.

"Maybe, but I think we should look a while longer. It's not just Stacy, you know. It's Jarvis and Roger, too."

Hank bristled at the name *Roger*. Maybe that newcomer had not caused their separation, but his arrival drove a wedge into their relationship, kept husband and wife from getting back together as they should.

"Okay, if that's what you want. But it ain't good police work."

"Fuck good police work!"

Hank felt something seize up in his gut. "Don't you talk like that, girl. You've turned into a real gutter-tongue since you took up with that Newton fella."

"Oh, shit!" Laura stomped her foot, turned away from him, her arms folded tightly on her breasts. It was a familiar gesture; she used it to emphasize her impatience with him and he hated it.

"You sound just like all the sluts I haul in for drunk and disorderly. You was never like that before."

She spoke into the distance. "That's right, Hank, because it's not like it was before. And one difference is that now it's none of your goddamn business. You don't seem to understand that."

"What ya mean?"

"I mean I didn't phone you this morning because you're my husband and Stacy's father. I called you because you're the only law around here." She turned to face him. "Now I can see I'd have been better off not calling at all."

That stung. He turned and started off down the hill by himself.

"Where you going, Hank?"

"Back, like I told you. There's no point standing out here."

Laura started down the slope after him. She'd soon learn that he was right. He had to be fair though, she was under stress, not acting like herself. She'd understand the wisdom of his decision soon enough.

It surprised him when she grabbed him by the shirtsleeve.

"You can go back if you want. I'm staying here. I'm going to look some more. I'll find that kid if it takes me all night. You just go on back, Hank. Walk right on off, just like you always did."

"I ain't lettin' you stay here—"

"Not letting me? Just what do you presume you have to say about it?"

"—'Cause I'm your husband—"

"Were, Hank, *were* . . ."

"—and I'm the law, and I'm tellin' you to come with me."

"A whole lot of good 'the law's' doing! We may not be married anymore, Hank, but Stacy's still your son. He doesn't have any choice about that and neither do you!"

It happened without his even knowing it. His right hand came up as if to salute, then cracked down across the side of Laura's face. With eyes wide she backed away, her hand on her reddening cheek.

He wanted to hit her again, and he wanted to apologize at the same time. It was just like the old days; she got his head so twisted-up that he didn't know what was right and what wasn't.

"I'm going down. If the boys ain't there I'll call Derby and see about organizin' a search."

Their shadows stretched long in front of him like burned patches on the green meadow grass. As his shadow started to move, hers remained motionless.

"HEY!" the piping cry came from far behind him. "HEYYYYY!"

As Hank turned he saw the boy thrashing through the woods above where Laura stood. Laura hurried in the direction of the running figure. Hank easily passed her, his Sam Browne belt bouncing heavily up and down. He put his hand on his .357 to steady it.

The small figure hollered and waved, running, falling, picking himself up, and continuing toward Hank and Laura.

"Stacy!" Laura called, moving faster now. The boy tumbled again, started to get up just as Laura reached him. He fell sobbing into her arms.

Hank moved up, stood beside them. He watched as they embraced. Stacy's hair was matted to his head, he seemed to be dripping with perspiration. He was scratched and bleeding, his face and arms covered with raw, painful-looking lesions. The boy's wrists were discolored as if burned. Hank had seen those marks before—his son had been tied up.

Good Christ, maybe this was serious after all.

He reached for the embracing couple, put a firm hand on Stacy's shoulder. "It's okay now, son. You're safe. Come on, we'll take you home."

It was as if Stacy hadn't seen or recognized him. "Dad!" The boy looked up in surprise. He moved from his mother, giving his father a hug. "We *can't* go home. They got Roger and Jarvis. They killed Harley Spooner and . . . and . . . We've got to *help* them!"

"Now slow down, boy. *Who's* got Jarvis?"

"I don't know . . . The Bigfoots! The ones that got Cooly. They're up there in the old hotel!"

"Bigfoots? Now wait a minute, son. Take it easy. What are you talkin' about?"

The boy looked to his mother for help. She looked back at him, her puzzled expression turning to a look of horror. "I told you, Hank," she said, stammering. "Cooly and the boys got separated in the woods—"

"But Bigfoot? What's this about Bigfoot . . . ?" Hank stood up. Laura's arm found the boy's shoulder.

"Come on," Stacy whined. "We gotta go. We gotta help them." He pulled away from his mother, took several wavering steps uphill, and collapsed.

Laura ran to him, knelt beside him. She looked up, glaring at Hank. "See. If we'd left when you wanted to we'd have missed him." She cradled Stacy's head against her breast. "We've got to get him to a doctor."

Stacy's eyelids fluttered. "Roger . . . ?" he said weakly. Then his eyes closed.

Hank wasn't sure what to do. He could carry Stacy back to the cruiser—it would take less than an hour—then radio for help. However, that would mean more than a two-hour wait, maybe three, before help could reach whoever was at the hotel.

Or, he could go on to the hotel by himself, leaving Laura to take care of Stacy. If she could walk the boy back to the cruiser then she could call for a backup.

But Hank wanted more information before going on alone. Something was wrong with the boy's story, something didn't quite fit. He knelt beside his son. "Stacy? Stace, boy, can you hear me?"

Stacy groaned, his head rolled to the side. He opened his eyes part way. "Are they all right? Roger and Jarvis . . . ?"

"You're all right, son. But I need to know, who's holdin' Roger and Jarvis?"

"It's Bigfoot, Dad. I saw 'em. A whole room full of 'em."

Hank eyed Laura, feeling discouraged. He didn't want to push the boy, yet he needed the facts. If Stacy had seen anything at all, it was probably little more than a bunch of squatters, or maybe some religious nuts dressed in black. The backwoods of Vermont had a history of way-out goings-on, including strange religious cults; it had always been that way.

"Okay, son. Now try to think. Do these 'Bigfoots' have weapons? Are they armed?"

Stacy seemed more awake now. "No. I didn't see any guns or

anything. They had clubs, and spears, and some kind of sling. They killed a deer . . ."

Eyebrows raised, Hank's gaze flicked to Laura again. She shook her head furiously. "He's not making it up, Hank. Look at him. Can't you tell?"

"It's *true*, Dad. I saw 'em."

"How many'd you see, son?"

"Maybe a dozen. They were all together in a room at the hotel."

Hank glanced at Laura, then back at Stacy. He'd found the hole in the boy's story. "Son, the hotel's burned down. It's been that way for—"

"I know, Dad. They're in the *basement*. That's where they live. In the basement. That's where they've got Jarvis. Roger too, I think."

Hank stood up. He looked down the hill, then up into the dense forest beyond. "Okay. Laura, you take Stacy back to the vehicle. When you get there, before you do anything else, you radio for help. Don't say nothin' about no Bigfoots. Just say . . . just say 'some crazy mountain men,' or something like that. But whatever you say, say it so you get 'em here. There's water and first aid in the cruiser. You wait there for the other units. It might take a while, but sit tight. I'm going on ahead."

For once the woman didn't argue. She helped Stacy to his feet and they slowly walked off, arms around each other. Hank loosened the retaining strap on the .357. He started up the hill.

"Hank," Laura called from behind him.

He turned.

"Be careful, Hank."

The Stalker was on him!

Both men hit the pond with a tremendous splash. Roger, struggling to get his head above water, beat wildly at the muscle-knotted arms that held him. Hands like lead weights tightened around his throat, forcing his head to the bottom.

Knowing that he was battling a man rather than a monster gave little comfort. He tried to roll free, grinding his back on the rocky river bottom.

With more reflex than thought he kicked with his right leg, the one the Stalker was straddling. His shin connected solidly with the Stalker's genitals. The black man howled like a demon and toppled to the side, loosening the grip of one hand.

Roger slammed his wrist against the remaining arm; the hand snapped away. He was free!

His head shot to the surface. Scrambling toward the bank, he gulped greedily at the air.

The Stalker, still howling—now more from ferocity than pain—dove after him.

Roger managed to turn over and right himself. He quickly assumed a crouching position, like a runner before a race. He was about to make a dash for the trees when his sprint was stopped abruptly. An iron hand gripped his ankle, yanked his leg out from under him. His face smashed into the wet gravel on the shore. Closing his eyes to protect them, he spat gritty particles through torn lips.

A heavy knee landed against the small of his back, flattening him, nearly knocking him senseless.

"Stop!" he choked, the side of his mouth scraping on the wet gravel. "Listen to me—"

Now the Stalker held him by both ankles. With a mighty heave he flipped Roger onto his back. Then the Stalker began dragging him back into the water.

He's going to drown me, Roger realized in a white-hot flash.

Cold water splashed over his chest, began lapping at his chin. Painfully, he craned his head back, trying to elevate his nose and mouth.

It was then that he saw the man.

Although he couldn't tell who it was, he recognized the uniform of either a game warden or state policeman.

"Help!" Roger cried. Water cascaded freely into his open mouth. He gagged, choked, and spat.

The Stalker, too, had seen the intruder. He froze for a moment, then waved his black arm, growling fiercely, warning the new-comer away.

The man held a revolver in his outstretched hands.

Why doesn't he fire? Roger wondered. He's got a clear shot. Why doesn't he fire?

Yet the man didn't fire, he just watched. The Stalker—apparently not seeing the stranger as a threat, or perhaps too driven or confused to leave his job incomplete—grabbed Roger's legs again, lifted them high, forcing Roger's head and shoulders under water.

"Hey!" screamed Roger, his voice bubbling through six inches of water.

Although his vision was distorted by ripples and splashes, Roger saw the uniformed man raise his weapon toward the sky. There was no mistaking the noise. The man fired once . . .

Twice . . .

The Stalker roared and dropped Roger's legs, then backed toward the stone cliff, his arms raised to protect his face. Teeth exposed, hands flexed like claws, he hissed like a frenzied mountain cat.

Roger sat up. He sighed with relief as he watched Hank Drew level the .357 at the snarling giant.

Then the muzzle shifted toward Roger.

"Don't neither of you move," the policeman commanded.

26

Fireworks

DARKNESS . . .

When they heard the shots Stacy looked at his mother, an expression of great fear in his eyes.

"Shots! Two of 'em," he whispered.

Laura grabbed the microphone and tried the radio again. She still couldn't summon help from Derby or the outpost in Island Pond. Perhaps it was the particular position of the cruiser in front of Harley Spooner's house that made radio contact impossible—the nearby hills surrounding the house and the high distant mountains could easily deflect radio waves. They were in a dead spot.

And Harley didn't have a telephone.

Of course Roger's car was nearby, but—as Laura knew too well—he was always compulsive about taking the keys, and leaving the vehicle locked and secure.

Damn! she thought. *How could Hank have forgotten to give me the keys to the cruiser? Now we're stuck here until he comes down.*

On some level she knew Hank had done it deliberately. She tried to ignore her rising anger; it wouldn't help the situation.

Unable to raise anyone on the radio, and unable to phone or drive to get help, Laura felt she'd have to go back into the woods. She couldn't just sit there doing nothing!

There was a 12-gauge shotgun fastened below the dashboard. As she opened the glove compartment looking for shells, she found a snub-nosed .38. She recognized it immediately: Hank's backup weapon. She quickly grabbed the pistol.

"Stacy," said Laura, "I'm going back and help your father."

"I'm coming too."

"I don't think you should. You're exhausted. It's better you stay here and rest. Just lock the doors and stay in the car."

He would have no part of it. "I can't stay here. Not alone. I'm afraid."

She couldn't argue with him. And she knew she couldn't leave him alone, either. "Okay, then. But stay close to me and be careful."

Laura made sure the handgun's safety was on. She hadn't handled a weapon for a long time, but her deft fingers remembered what to do. Somehow she felt better when the gun was loaded and ready.

Mother and son got out of the cruiser, headed in the direction from which the shots had come.

What a day this has been! Laura thought. Just when she'd figured things were starting to get better, everything began to fall apart. *Like Roger says, God's throwing us a sucker punch again.*

As she climbed she could still feel the psychic fatigue from her afternoon visit with Peggy Lavigne.

"Claude had a tumor," Peggy had told her. "In his head. Doctor told me so after the funeral. But Claude never said nothing to me about it. He never said nothing . . ."

Peggy had collapsed into Laura's arms, vibrating with stifled sobs. "Doctor said he woulda got worse an' worse. Said it woulda killed him if he hadn't done the job himself. An' Claude never said nothin' about it, Laura. That man never said so much as a word . . ."

Laura had been eager to tell Roger. It might relieve him to learn that Lunker Lavigne had worries about things far greater than whatever it was he had seen that day in the gore.

And now this . . .

She took a deep breath, walking as rapidly as she could.

The sun had settled behind the blunted peaks to the west. Darkness was very close.

. . .

With his Smith and Wesson trained on the dripping men, Trooper Hank Drew looked on in confusion. Sweat poured from his forehead, his nerves were electric, a prickly sensation tingled in his forearms.

No one spoke. Hank could think of nothing to say. As he cold-eyed Roger Newton, he realized that the man had been through a tremendous ordeal. He looked haggard, exhausted. He was shivering and his lips were blue. Yet it was impossible to summon any compassion. Newton deserved all that and more. Hank realized how easily he could drop both men where they stood. It would certainly solve more problems than it would create. He could simply hide the bodies and report finding no one at all.

—*Be careful, Hank*—

He would never be questioned, especially if he reported that he'd been out searching for Bigfoot. Corporal Kinney in the Derby office would just roll his eyes and chuckle. Even so, it would be easy to retain the corporal's respect if Hank laughed too and made a big deal out of *not* finding Bigfoot. *Couldn't've had very big feet. Tracks were so small I couldn't even see 'em!* Then he'd follow up with properly disparaging remarks about those imaginative boys who'd phoned in the sighting.

Hank felt his tight lips curling into a smile.

The wild-eyed black man pressed his spine against the rock ledge. He sure didn't look like much of a monster. Though abnormally hairy, and dressed in furs even in the heat of August, the "monster" looked crazy as hell, but definitely human. Through clenched teeth the man-beast snarled menacingly at the policeman.

Still smiling, Hank pointed his jaw at the eccentric. "You speak English, do you?"

The black man looked furtively from side to side.

Hank tried again. *"Vous parlez anglais?"*

In response to the silence Hank redirected his inquiry to Roger. "Okay, Newton, what's going on here? Who is this guy? And what kinda costume party is he dressed up for?"

Roger started to lower his hands. Hank jerked the weapon, commanding Roger to stand as he was.

"He's some kind of a hermit. He thought I was after him or something. Why don't you put the gun down, Hank?"

"Not just yet. You been telling my boy Bigfoot stories?" Roger's face lit up. "Did you find Stacy? Is he all right?"

"He's safe. He's with my wife. But that's none of your concern. Now suppose you walk outta there, real careful. And keep your hands up high where I can see 'em."

—Hank, be careful . . . —

Roger waded out of the pool. Water dripped from his clothes and hair, splattering heavily onto the moist sand.

"What the hell are you doing, Drew? Are you going to arrest me or something? Why don't you quit playing John Wayne for a second and let me explain this to you."

John Wayne! An anger months in the making exploded inside him. With a motion faster than the eye could measure, Hank smashed the barrel of the Smith and Wesson against Roger's skull. Roger collapsed like a bag of grain suddenly emptied.

Again Hank leveled the revolver at the black man.

"Another shot," Stacy said, looking in the direction of the sharp report. Its echo bounced from hill to hill.

"I don't think it was too far from here," Laura answered, her voice hushed, frightened.

They changed their course, following the sound of the gunfire. Laura's hand was on her weapon's safety switch. She was ready to flick it off at a moment's notice.

Stacy lagged slightly behind her. Laura could sense that the boy's fear rivaled her own. She was proud of him; he was showing great strength while making not the slightest appeal to turn back.

If Stacy were not with her, Laura thought, she probably would never have dared to climb this hill. She'd still be waiting for Hank in the safety of the cruiser, dependent, helpless, just the way he wanted her. It was strange how people could pull courage from one another . . .

She looked around, noting how dark it had become. Individual trees blended with their shadows into a solid, sinister wall of night. She wished she'd looked for a flashlight in the car.

Consciousness returned with sudden and unexpected clarity; he was being dragged across the stony ground. He knew better than to resist; he didn't even open his eyes. All he could safely do was wait and try to figure out what was going on.

He could still hear the water; apparently he hadn't been moved too far.

Hands released Roger's legs; they slammed limply to the ground. A moment later he heard splashing.

Now he dared to open his eyes, but no more than a slit. His glasses were long gone, lost, forgotten during the struggle. Still, he was able to see Hank, six feet away, rinsing his muddy hands in the pond. The .357 was back in its holster; that relieved Roger a little.

It was difficult for Roger to believe what he suspected Hank Drew was doing. Even in his vulnerable state, Roger's capacity for denial was great. But when he looked beyond Hank's stooping form, saw the hazy shape of a body floating limply on the surface of the red swirling pool, his suspicions were confirmed, his denial evaporated. He could hear Hank's official report very clearly in his imagination: *When I arrived on the scene the black man was in the process of strangling (or beating, or drowning) the victim. I fired a couple of warning shots and instructed him to desist. When he continued I had no choice but to fire . . .*

Roger didn't think he had enough strength left to fight any more. Yet he knew that somehow he had to get the jump on Hank before he made his fatal move.

A weapon would help. Slowly, cautiously, he extended his right hand trying to locate a stone. He didn't dare move too much, Hank would surely notice. The tiny circle available to his spidering fingers offered no suitable rocks—they were all too big to clutch effectively, or too small to do any harm.

Another strategy might be to attempt reasoning with Hank, appeal to his police ethics, his humanity. If he could be made to understand that even with Roger out of the way Laura and Stacy would never return to him . . .

No, he'd never buy it. Hank was desperate, driven, and probably insane. He didn't want to hear his family was lost to him forever. In fact, he was exhibiting the very behaviors that had driven Laura away. But this was worse, far crazier than anything Laura had ever described.

Roger was forced to admit he had only one choice—prepare himself for a fight, a fight that would leave another man dead.

As Hank rose, shaking his hands to dry them, Roger closed his eyes again. Soon he felt Hank grab him by the shirtfront, lift him off the sand, and drag him headfirst into the water.

Roger fought the panic rising inside him; he struggled to remain limp, feigning unconsciousness.

So it *was* to be drowning!

. . . with the assailant subdued I attempted to assist the victim, but I was too late—he had been drowned . . .

Roger cursed himself for not reacting sooner. Now, dragged into the pool, his legs submerged below his buoyant torso, any motion he made would be slowed by the water, rendered ineffective.

The tug on Roger's shirtfront turned abruptly to a steady downward push against his chest. Head below the water, Roger tried not to move. If he were passive, hopefully Hank would not become more forceful, or more cautious.

Then Roger remembered something! Something he had learned from the Stalker. Slowly, he filled his mouth with water. Then with all possible speed he jerked his hands to the surface, clutched Hank by the sleeves. He yanked himself up. Face-to-face now, he spat the water into Hank's eyes.

Hank gasped, turned his head, spitting. Roger smashed the startled man's hands away.

Hank cried out, more in surprise than pain. It allowed Roger the second he needed to grab the holstered revolver. Hank swatted at his hand, knocking the gun into the water. Roger knew it was lost somewhere below the splashing surface.

He tried to turn and run, but the policeman immobilized him with a hatchet-fist to the kidney. Roger flopped back into the pond. He heard himself moaning in agony.

The pain was incredible. He felt as if he were going to faint. Coughs, dry heaves, racked his stomach and chest. He realized he had swallowed water.

He had no more strength to fight.

Ominously, Hank Drew advanced, wading deeper into the pool. The policeman's hands were flat like hatchet blades, his eyes were steady and dangerous. He smiled a deadly smile.

Roger was outmatched, helpless. He was sure he was going to die.

"Hank," he gasped, "let's talk about it, for God's sake. You don't want to kill me . . ?"

"You're a thief, you bastard. And if I could arrest you for what you done, it'd be too good for you."

Kneeling on the pond's rocky bottom, Roger raised his arms in a feeble defense. Again Hank lunged at him. Bony fingers dug into Roger's neck. Locked in splattering combat, the two men rolled and splashed, a human squall in the shallow pool.

Roger's blows were ineffectual, dulled by fatigue and the cushion of water. He dug his nails into Hank's hands and wrists, trying to pull them away from his throat. Although his head was underwater, he could hear Hank scream, "Breathe, damn you! Breathe!"

Roger held his breath until he thought his lungs would explode. A savage energy coursed through his body, but it was useless, Hank had a deadly advantage. The policeman was in total control.

Kicking and clawing, Roger felt his surge of strength waning. His arms collapsed at his sides, useless as fallen birds.

Lightheaded and beaten, he realized that all he had to do was inhale, just once, and this agony would end.

Then Hank fell on top of him.

And Roger was able to sit up, the roar of a gunshot reverberating in his ears.

The policeman tumbled weightlessly to the side, buoyant as a beach ball in the stream's current. Blood, like swirling liquid rust, colored the water around Hank's head.

Confused, Roger looked up. Laura stood above him, staring in horror at the smoking weapon in her hands. She dropped the gun and screamed. From a few steps behind her Stacy ran forward, pushing her aside and high-stepping into the water, moving toward his father.

The boy tugged at Hank's pant leg, trying to pull him closer to shore. Laura waded in beside him as Roger watched immobile. Her hands trembling, she lifted Hank's head from the water, cradled it against her breast.

"Hank, wake up." She looked entreatingly at Roger. "Oh, God! I think I've killed him . . ."

Somehow Roger staggered to his feet, stood knee-deep in the pool. He saw Hank open his eyes and look up into Laura's face. "Laura . . . Stacy . . ." The eyelids fluttered and closed, the body sagged.

Moving as rapidly as he could, Roger helped Laura drag Hank to the shore. He bent over the other man, listening for breath, feeling for a heartbeat.

Roger looked into Laura's dark, expectant eyes. "Hank's gone," he whispered.

Laura stood up, took a few steps backward, as if trying to escape the damage she had caused. Stacy looked from one adult to the other. Though his eyes were furious with activity, he appeared ready to collapse.

"Stacy . . ." said Roger, reaching out a hand to the boy. But it was too late. Stacy turned and started to run into the woods. Roger wanted to go after him, but he staggered from weakness with his first step.

"Stacy, wait!"

Laura and Roger stood paralyzed as the boy raced into the darkness.

Before he was completely out of sight a brilliant flash exploded from a knoll less than a hundred yards in front of him. Stacy stopped, looking up. Laura and Roger froze behind him.

All three stood transfixed as a fountain of flame gushed upward from the ground, transforming into dazzling woven tentacles of fire that rent the black sky. It was like lightning in reverse, tearing a jagged blazing pattern in the fabric of night.

Tiny twisting streamers of white flame curled and drifted to the ground like a fiery snowstorm.

At first the sight made no sense to Roger at all. His mind as weary as his body, he struggled to understand what he witnessed.

Roger watched as the pillar of flame took the shape of a tree, a tree of fire, growing before his eyes!

Silhouetted before the fiery apparition, lurching shapes appeared and moved forward in the darkness. They approached unsteadily from the knoll. Stacy saw them too, and began to back away, his face red and terrified in the hot crimson light. Side by side Laura and Roger walked tentatively uphill to join the boy.

They stared with new horror as three shadows lurched toward them, solid and frightfully distinct. The burning tree faded like a display of fireworks, and once again everything darkened into night.

27

Before the Sun Can Shine

THE FINAL HOUR . . .

"Cooly!" Stacy cried, his face exploding into a smile of recognition and delight.

The old man, flanked by Jarvis Lavigne and David Potter, walked unsteadily out of the darkness, the fading red embers of the burning tree dying in the background.

To their right, in the briefly illuminated distance, another figure, unrecognizable and dark, limped off into the black, shadow-filled forest. Roger saw it in the flash, then it was gone.

As Cooly approached, his haggard expression twisted into an exhausted rendering of his engaging smile. Showing no caution, Stacy ran to him, embraced him, smiled up at him happily.

The old man hugged the boy.

"Now that there's a little trick I was gonna show you boys, an' I jest never got 'round to it," Cooly said with a chuckle, squeezing Stacy's shoulder. "I had to do *somethin'*; I couldn't have you runnin' off, gettin' lost in the woods again—I don't think I got the energy to track you down a second time."

He flicked his head in the direction of the smoldering tree. Now its trunk was covered with tiny strips of bark, glowing crimson, like red tinsel on a Christmas tree. "What you see there's called a yellow birch tree," Cooly said. "They ain't too many of 'em around no more, but when you find one, it can make one heck of a signal fire. Won't hurt the tree none, though, jest burns the old skin off'n 'er. See, all them old yellow birches is covered with a bunch a long curly stringers of old bark. They's highly flammable—more'n paper. I touched a match to 'er an' you seen what happened. Why heck, we used to have some fun with 'em back in the old days at the lumber camp. 'Course if I'd a known you folks was so nearby I wouldn't a bothered to touch 'er off."

Cooly chuckled, speaking with one hand on each boy's shoulder. Laura and Roger walked over to join them.

"Cooly," said Stacy, "I thought they'd killed you. I thought—"

"Saved me from them wild dogs is more like it. I don't look like no ghost, do I? I guess they didn't know you boys was watchin' when they snatched me up. An' you can bet your boots I didn't tell 'em . . ."

Cooly looked in the direction of the pool. On the water's edge Hank Drew's lifeless form glistened wetly in the moonlight. "Looks like they saved you, too, Mr. Newton." The old man moved toward the corpse, bent stiffly to examine it.

Laura remained where she stood. Roger sensed her pulling toward Hank and Cooly, then drawing back. Instead she took Jarvis Lavigne gently by the arm. "Are you okay, Jarvis?"

"Yes, Mrs. Drew. But I'm awful tired." The boy's eyes were half-closed, his body looked limp with fatigue.

"We'd better all be gettin' home," said Cooly as he rejoined them. "Missis Lavigne's surely gonna be wonderin' what's become of this boy of hers."

"How'd you get out of there?" Roger asked.

"Well sir, Mister Newton, me an' the old woman come to an understandin'. Trouble is, what we agreed to involves more'n jest me an' her. It's gonna have to involve all of us here, every single one of us. I was jest actin' as spokesman for our side, same as she acts as spokesman for hers."

"What do you mean?"

"Well sir, I'll tell you everythin' you wanna know, an' prob'ly a good deal more, once I get rollin'. I'll be tellin' ya stuff I ain't never breathed a word about to nobody, not even Mister Spooner, for one heck of a lotta years. But for now, what say we get down outta these woods? I've jest about had my fill of 'em for a while. We can go to my cabin, or, better yet, we can go to your place, Missis Drew. It ain't a whole lot further. That way we can call Mister Jarvis's ma, an' maybe we can get us a bite to eat. I for one have worked up one powerful hunger."

"That's fine, Cooly. Let's go," Roger said.

Laura nodded her agreement.

Cooly led the weary procession, one boy on each side of him. Roger and Laura followed. David Potter stumbled along behind, quiet and looking confused.

Laura made sandwiches and coffee. Before they could eat anything, both boys had fallen asleep on the sofa. Roger carried them into Stacy's bedroom.

Now, sitting around the kitchen table, David, Roger, and Cooly discussed the events of the day. As Roger explained about Hank Drew and the Stalker, the old black man's face clouded.

"Well sir," Cooly said, "I was afraid somethin' like that was gonna happen." As he sipped his coffee, wisps of steam curled lazily in front of his tired eyes. He sniffed, ran the back of his hand over his mouth, and spoke quietly. "After you folks've heard what I got to say, we're all gonna have to decide what to do about them bodies. Once that's done we can get on to our grievin'. It looks as if we ain't none of us gonna get no sleep tonight."

David Potter buried his face in his hands. "I can't believe any of this, it's all . . . it's all crazy."

Cooly smiled, spoke in a soothing voice. "It is that, Mister Potter. It most certainly is that."

Laura returned from phoning Peggy Lavigne. At Cooly's request she had told a protective lie to Jarvis's mother, attempting to stall for time. She'd said that the boys had become lost in the woods, but it was nothing to worry about, Roger had quickly found them. After he gave them a thorough bawling out, both boys had fallen asleep, exhausted.

The black man rubbed his swollen eyes and blinked at his wearied audience. "The story I got to tell you folks is an old story. I think by now Mister Potter here has pieced it together in pretty good shape on his own. An' I don't blame him for thinkin' it's all crazy. It is. It never shoulda happened—not none of it. An' I suppose I'm the craziest one, 'cause I'm right smack-dab in the middle of the whole darn mess."

Roger chewed his sandwich, listening intently as the old man went on.

"It started a good long time ago. Way before Mister Lavigne seen that 'shape-shifter' of his in the woods. Matter of fact, it was way back around 1830, mebbe even a little earlier. An' my part in it started, not with me, but with my old gran'daddy, an awful lotta years ago . . .

"You prob'ly know the Hawks family weren't the first black folks to pass through Vermont on their way up north to Canady. Most folks kept right on goin', but not my gran'dad. No sir. When he see Eureka he liked what he seen. 'This here's far enough,' he says, an' he digs his heels in real deep an' stays put.

"But that ain't where it started, neither. We gotta back up a little bit further for the real beginnin' of things. Back then a bunch of slaves was gettin' assisted on their way up to Troy, Vermont, travelin' from Barton on whatcha call that Underground Railroad. Only trouble was, this bunch had one of them southern slave catchers right tight on their tails. Real no-good sorta fella, he was, bully and a murderer. Meaner'n Satan with a sunburn, or so the story goes . . .

"Way I hear it, they was four, maybe six of 'em, all tol'. An' they was real young 'uns, too, prob'ly not much more'n kids. They was scared stiff, all alone, an' hundreds of miles from home.

"Well sir, when they got wind of that catcher bein' so close, they musta panicked. Lit out into the woods on their own, runnin' scared, headin' east, plowin' deeper and deeper into the wilderness. Finally made it all the way up into the gore. Now maybe the gore was worthless land to the white folks, but to them it prob'ly looked like a little piece of heaven.

"So there they stayed.

"They took to buildin' a home for themselves in hidin', always careful to steer clear of anybody white, not knowin' who they could trust or who was likely to shoot 'em, or run 'em in for the hundred dollars reward money. See, they didn't know how hospitable Vermonters really was to runaway slaves back in them days. Hospitable? Why cripes; I 'member hearin' about that judge down to Middlebury—Harrington, I think his name was—who wouldn't give no slave back to his owner without a bill of sale from God Aw'mighty."

Cooly forced a chuckle, then took a big bite of his ham sandwich and chewed for a while. "Their legends say they struck up a friendship with some of the Abenaki Indians that the white folks had drove offa their land. So the both of 'em, the black men an' the red men, had enough in common to make 'em friends of a sort, though they never married up with one another far as I know. I guess the Indians taught them people a good deal, least enough to keep outta sight an' to stay alive.

"They learned pretty quick that they could get what they needed to eat an' to wear from wild plants an' animals. Cattail an' sugar pine was somethin' they had all year round. In spring they had milkweed, an' dandelions, an' wild onion. Summer an' fall brung all sorts a berries an' nuts an' even wild apples. The woods is full of food, if you know what to eat an' what to leave alone. Point is, they was no reason for 'em to go hungry."

Cooly sipped his coffee. "Yes sir, Vermont mighta been a hospitable state back then, but them folks hidin' out in the wilderness didn't know that. An' I s'pect my own gran'daddy forgot, 'cause a the terrible thing that he done to 'em."

Roger leaned forward, listening in fascination, resisting the persistent urge to take notes.

"Fair amount a time passed before the leader of the slaves—fella by the name of Benj Hattin—somehow got wind that they was another black man, once a slave himself, livin' right up here in Eureka! Well sir, one night ol' Benj, he sneaks out a the woods an' comes a-tappin' on my gran'daddy's door in the middle of the night.

" 'Course you unnerstan' this was quite a spell 'fore I come into the world—an' my own daddy was jest a babe in arms at the time— so I can't say I know none of this firsthand. I'm jest goin' on what my daddy tol' me later on."

Roger nodded, encouraging Cooly to continue as Laura refilled the coffee mugs. Cooly smiled a thank you to her.

"Anyways, ol' Benj shows up in the middle of the night, rappin' on the cabin door. Bet he give my gran'parents quite a start! Reckon he musta looked a sight after all them years o' living in the woods. So Benj, he ups an' asks gran'pa to help 'em. I ain't really clear on what was said, or jest exactly what they wanted from Gramp. All I know for sure is that Gramp turned 'em away. I guess that's the long an' the short of it. He jest shut the door on 'em, an' that was that.

"So ol' Benj goes back into the woods figgerin' there ain't never gonna be no help for 'em. So, by jeepers, they're gonna have to keep right on makin' it on their own."

Cooly pressed his lips tightly together, then took a sip of coffee. Looking down at the tabletop, he spoke a bit more softly. "I reckon they held it against Gran'pa, though, an' I s'pect they had every right to. Oh, they didn't try to get back at him or nothin'; they never was a vengeful lot. What happened was they ended up be-lievin' Gran'pa wasn't really like them, even though he was jest as black. So they started callin' him *the Shadowman*. A whole kind of legend growed up around my ol' gran'daddy. He even played kind of a part in their religion; for them the Shadowman was evil, like a devil, or a Judas, or somethin' like that. Somethin' not to be trusted.

"Well sir, there's always been a good strong streak a somethin' runnin' through the Hawks family. My gran'pa had it. My pa and me got a pretty good dose of it, too. Reckon it makes all of us jest alike in one way: Every one of us can be troubled somethin' wicked by conscience.

"My gran'pa, he got to feelin' real bad about what he done to them people, real shamed. He tol' my pa—gosh, I guess it musta been when he was a boy in his teens—that he felt guilty as a soul in Hell.

"But at the time it happened I guess Gran'pa didn't feel too much a part of the white community hisself. Sure, he was accepted up to a point; he was makin' a livin' an' raisin' a family. But he was still a colored man in a white state, an' I guess he just wasn't ready to stick his neck out too far for no runaway slaves. Who knows? Maybe he was afraid he'd get captured right along with 'em an' sent back down South. Maybe he was scared he'd get sold right back into slavery. I know for sure that back in them days the federal gover'ment overrode the Vermont constitution, sayin' anybody helpin' a runaway slave could be fined or sent off to prison.

"So afterwards Gramp tried to make amends. He took to leavin' things out in the woods for 'em: food, clothes, old boots, stuff he figured they could use. He even cooked up a bunch of stories about scary goin's-on up in the gore. Guess he figgered to scare folks off, get 'em to leave the slaves alone.

"Things got pretty well patched up after awhile. Then, when Gran'daddy passed on, my pa took over the job of Shadowman. Him and their leader used to meet from time to time in secret. Pa become somethin' of a link with the outside world. So now the idea of the Shadowman started to change; now he was somebody who could be both good an' bad, do you see?"

Laura and Roger nodded solemnly. David stared at his hands on the tabletop.

"Then," Cooly said, "after Pa was gone, I took over that job myself."

He polished off the rest of his ham sandwich and licked a spot of mustard off his thumb. Then he wiped his mouth on a paper towel. "An' it's still goin' on. Right up until this day me an' the old woman meets all alone, off by ourselves, one, mebbe two times a year. She used to be called Sister Betsy. Born right up there in the woods to Benj Hattin's boy an' the daughter of another couple of slaves out there with 'em. Since she's descended direct from Benj, by-an'-by she become their leader. Now they calls her The Descendant.

"For her, our meetin's is kind of a religious thing, kind of a pilgrimage I guess you'd say. As for me, I still bring 'em things, I advise 'em if they's somethin' they should be watchin' out for, like back when that powerline come down through from Quebec . . .

"See, I like to do what I can for 'em. I wanna do everythin' I can so's they'll keep seein' the Shadowman as a friend. 'Cause that's what I am, whether they know it or not. An' lately, mister, they's had their doubts."

"I don't understand," said Laura. "Doubts? What do you mean?"

"See, ma'am, I guess when they seen me up there on that Indian site, diggin' at Mister Spooner's sacred stones, they figured ol' Shadowman had turned on 'em again. For them, you gotta unnerstan', them old stones is boundary lines, property markers. Took me an' Sister Betsy a whole pile a talkin' to get things ironed out."

Cooly rubbed his eyes with the pink palms of his hands. Then he massaged his temples. The skin of his scalp slid around like loose rubber.

"Me an' Sister Betsy knows it's way too late for 'em to come out an' join the white folks. Oh, there might've been a time—way long ago—when it might've been possible. But not no more. It jest ain't safe. Why, they're jest too different, too strange; they got their own way of life, an' I s'pect they ain't got too much longer to live it. I figger they got a few more years, mebbe another decade or so, then they'll be all gone. An' they's no young 'uns up there now, you know.

"But I respect 'em. I wish 'em well. An' I think we oughtta leave 'em be. So that's what I'm askin' ya—to leave 'em be. I know how bad things got out of hand, but now we got a chance to set 'em right again."

Cooly looked from face to face. He'd said his piece. For a long time everyone exchanged glances in silence. Laura sipped coffee. David Potter poked at his untouched sandwich.

Soon Roger found that all eyes had come to rest on him. Suddenly he felt the responsibility of leadership; he knew whatever he decided was likely to sway the opinions of Laura and David.

After taking a swig of coffee, he cleared his throat. "I can imagine what would happen to those people if the state police went up there to flush them out . . ."

"Where would they go?" Laura asked, her voice softened with concern.

Roger had been wondering the same thing. "Beats me. Welfare rooming houses, maybe? To the homes of do-gooder sponsors like those who took in the Cambodian refugees or the people from Nicaragua? If not that, quite possibly into an asylum. Who knows? Maybe, after being poked and prodded and questioned and tested and observed, they might be granted a reservation where they could do their bit to advance Vermont's tourist industry. Sounds pretty bleak, doesn't it?"

"Umm-hmm." Cooly nodded.

"But we've got to think about what they can contribute to historical research," said David, blinking rapidly. He seemed to be coming out of his daze. "We also would have the rare opportunity to study the evolution of a tiny isolated pocket of civilization. It would be fantastic to look at how their religion has evolved, to study how the English language has changed over more than a hundred and fifty years. God, Roger, from a sociological viewpoint it would mean—"

"It would mean destroying people that we already set adrift to fend for themselves," said Laura. "I vote that we forget all about them."

"But the murders . . ." said David.

"Murders?" Roger looked the other man directly in the eyes.

"Harley Spooner, remember? And what about the policeman? And . . . and . . ." his voice cracked. His blinking eyes shone with unformed moisture. Laura put her hand on David's.

Roger spoke softly. "I think that a balance has occurred here— and without the help of the American judicial system. Don't forget, in the early eighteen hundreds Vermonters willingly broke unjust laws in order to protect the runaway slaves. Now, in retrospect, the whole country is proud of it. We've got the opportunity to do it again today, simply by keeping quiet. Besides, considering the circumstances, I don't think they have done anything to hurt anyone, not willfully."

"Claude Lavigne's death was his own doing . . . ," said Laura. "He was sick. Dying. It had nothing to do with these people."

Roger looked at her, surprised. This was news to him. Before he could question her David blurted, "But what about Leslie?"

Cooly's deep, earnest eyes fastened on David. "That was ol' Stogger's work. An' he admits it, too. He panicked when he couldn't figger how to get her out of them darned seat belts! He shouldn't a done it, he didn't plan to do it, but right or wrong he had the protection of his own people to worry about. He was jest doin' what his law told him was the right thing. That's all anyone can do. Stogger made a bad choice, and look where it got him." Cooly nodded once, emphatically.

When no one spoke, he continued, "Then o'course there's Mister Spooner. An' that's a whole 'nother kettle of fish."

"What do you mean?" Roger asked.

"I mean that no one on this earth thought more of Mister Harley Spooner than I did. And, same's before, ol' Stogger was right there when the old man died. But Stogger didn't kill him, he just tried to round him up, jest like he done with me. Fact is, Mister Spooner died of a bad heart. That ol' ticker of his had been actin' up for a while now. But never once would he admit it! By *golly* that man was a stubborn ol' cuss, wouldn't see no doctor no matter how much I nagged him. I guess a run-in with Stogger just finished him off. Likely scairt ol' Mister Spooner to death. I ain't so sure Stogger's to blame, though . . .

"But in all fairness I gotta tell ya, they *was* some bad feelin's between the two of them. Years ago Mister Spooner seen one of them people just a lookin' at him from behind a tree up at loggin' camp. A female it was, one a the only two or three women left. Guess her curiosity got the best of her in the end. Too bad. Mebbe they coulda kept the group goin' if she'd've had female kids of her own . . ."

Cooly shook his head sadly, his eyes on some far-off scene way in the distant past.

"But no matter. This girl, Runna, was promised to Stogger, an' he was courtin' her at the time. But he had no business bringin' her out an' showin' her no white folks. He was dead wrong to do that.

"When Mister Spooner see her peekin' around a tree it scairt the b'jesus out of him; he thought it was that winny-go thing of his. 'Course I knew what he'd seen all along, but I jest couldn't tell him, not then, not never.

"Anyways, he gets off a shot that took her in the belly. Two days later she died."

Cooly took a deep breath and looked down at the dark pool of coffee in his cup. "Like I says, they was never a vengeful lot. But Stogger didn't forget. Mebbe when he come for Mister Spooner he was a little rougher'n he needed to be. Mebbe not. Only the good Lord knows for sure. Reckon He'll have the say-so in the end. But from what you tell me, the law's already settled with Stogger, right or wrong . . ."

"And I settled with the law," said Laura, her eyes filmed with tears.

Roger reached out and took her hand. "You saved my life when you did it, Laura. There was nothing else you could have done. Hank had—"

"I know. He'd gone crazy. I'd seen it coming for a long time. But I didn't mean to kill—"

"Kill him?" said Cooly, his voice rising in astonishment. "Why, you didn't kill nobody, Missis Drew . . ."

"No . . . I did. I shot him. I shot him when he was trying to drown Roger . . ."

"Oh no, Missis. It was Watcher done that. I looked at Mister Drew's body myself. They wasn't no bullet hole, jest the smash of ol' Watcher's sling. An' I even seen Watcher, limpin' off, tryin' to get out of the fireworks from that burnin' tree . . ."

"But I shot—"

"Mebbe you did ma'am, but I reckon you missed." Cooly smiled wanly. "Worst thing I can say about you is you're a bad shot; you sure ain't no murderer. Crazy thing is, all this commotion, the whole kit an' caboodle happened 'cause a nothin' more'n some stones . . . jest some dirty stinkin' pieces of earth . . ."

Laura and Roger looked at each other. An understanding passed silently between them.

The old black man looked thoughtfully from face to face. "Yup, things was out of balance for a while—now they's balanced again. We can leave 'em that way, or . . ."

"My vote's to keep the secret," said Roger.

"Mine too," Laura agreed. "And I know Stacy will feel the same way."

Cooly nodded. "My bet is young Lavigne will go right along with your boy. They's both smart, fair-minded boys. Gonna be fine young men. They'll do the right thing, you bet."

Now all eyes were on David Potter. It was a moment of truth; Roger could feel the tension growing in the kitchen. He tried to understand what David might be thinking. He could sense David's scientific curiosity wrestling with his humanity. At the same time he knew the man was under a tremendous strain, nearly at a breaking point.

There was the issue of Leslie and David's affair. The need for keeping it secret might be enough to tip the scales one way or the other. Either way, David Potter, like the rest of them, would have more than one secret to keep when all this was over.

David's gaze, full of confusion, drifted across the waiting faces, then up to the hanging light over the table. His attention remained there; he seemed to be in a trance.

The trailer was as silent as a confessional. Roger could hear the boys breathing heavily in the far bedroom.

David looked at him, held Roger's stare. Then he spoke in a whisper. "If Leslie wakes up . . . If she pulls out of this, she could tell everything . . ."

Roger glanced at the suspense-filled faces of the others. When he spoke it was directly to David. "We all pray that she pulls out of it, David. But you know her better than any of us. If she recovers, what would her decision be?"

After a moment of tight-lipped concentration, David Potter nodded affirmatively.

"Let's not forget," said the old man, "we still got some cleanin' up to do. First, we gotta hike back up there an' take care of them two men in the pool. An' we'll need us a good cover story about Officer Drew; somebody's sure to be checkin' up on him pretty quick. Then we gotta explain things out for them two boys; this's gotta be their secret, too, jest like it's ours. A real big responsibility for a couple of little fellas.

"An' we can't forget ol' Mister Spooner; we gotta do somethin' with his body—it's only fittin'. He deserves a funeral an' a good Christian burial.

"An' prob'ly—jest to be on the safe side—we oughtta get most a this done by mornin'. It'll be my job to tell Sister Betsy that she an' her folks is safe. At least for now."

"Yes," agreed Roger, "at least for now."

Epilogue

From his place atop the wind-beaten granite cliff, the Watcher followed the progress of the two boys who made their way along the frozen, snow-covered riverbed.

Their colorful parkas, visible through the curtain of falling snow, stood out like bright flowers against the white landscape. It was easy to follow them amid the dark skeletons of leafless trees along the icy banks.

The boy with the twisted spine walked slightly behind. The one carrying the backpack—the leader—paused, waited for his companion to catch up. Then they continued together, walking side by side.

They were following the ritual that the Shadowman had taught them two, maybe three, summers ago.

This time, like most times, the two boys made the journey together. Sometimes the straight-backed one came alone. Two times, in the very beginning, the tall woman—the one the Watcher had long ago mistaken for a silver-haired man—made the journey with the Shadowman. Both had carried much food, and sweet summer fruits the tribe had never before tasted.

Now, the Shadowman came no more.

The Watcher had been the one to find his old lifeless body deep in the woodland, lying peacefully on the banks of a river, his fishing stick quivering in his hand. The Watcher had removed the trout from the metal hook and had let it go. It was the right thing.

At last the boys stopped walking. They stood on the surface of the frozen pond, the black mouth of the split-rock cave above their shoulders.

One boy took the pack from his back. He removed a burlap sack and handed it to his friend who held it open. Then he began to fill it with other objects from the pack: cans, small boxes, tiny bags, and something wrapped in silver paper.

When the sack was full the boy tied it with a length of rope.

With a swing and a heave, he tossed the bulging parcel up into the opening of the cave. The two boys stood for a moment, exchanging words that the Watcher could not hear.

Soon they turned and walked back the way they had come.

The Watcher knew that the fat, weightless flakes drifting from the gray sky would quickly cover all evidence that the boys had been there.

As soon as they were out of sight he would take the sack from the cave and bring it to the safehouse.

The Watcher moved with difficulty as he made his way down the granite cliff. The fire in his stiffening legs slowed him down, the coughing sickness made him light-headed and weak; but he had to do this thing—there was no one to take his place.

It saddened him to think that one day the boys would return and find that their gifts had not been taken. It would tell them that the tribe was gone.

And their memories would be the only record of its ever having been.

DIANE FOULDS

AUTHOR'S NOTE

The moment I stumbled upon the notion of Vermont "gores" this book took root and almost grew itself.

I was working on a historical script for ETV when I discovered that gores are unorganized parcels of land that lie outside the borders of official townships. Since they are in no town, they are quite literally "no-man's-lands." And gores do not exist by design. They came about because of blunders made by colonial surveyors while measuring the land. Further, most Vermont gores remained uninhabited because they were comprised of some of the state's most inhospitable terrain.

I thought, What a perfect place to set a book: an uninhabited no-man's-land created by mistake!

Even the book's elegantly ambiguous title was essentially handed to me: *The Gore*. Alas, when Warner Books originally published it in 1990, they—for reasons that will never be clear to me—called it *The Unseen*. I feared that title might predict the book's fate.

Now, thanks to the University Press of New England, this novel will be seen again.

Since I was studying stage magic at the time I wrote it, I conceived *The Gore* as kind of a sleight-of-hand book; nothing is as it appears. At first glance it may look like a good old fashioned horror story, but it is as much a mystery. Essentially, it is about ambiguity, about appearance and reality. It's built upon misunderstandings and misperceptions and the real-life horror they can lead to.

As with my other novels, the background elements of history and folklore are legitimate.